PRAISE F

Sinkhole, and Other Inexplicable Voids

"Leyna Krow's *Sinkhole, and Other Inexplicable Voids* is a stunning collection that transforms the mundane into the magical. Each story brims with wonder and the surreal, pushing the boundaries of reality while plunging the reader deep into human emotions. Krow, a masterful storyteller, captures the bizarre and beautiful in equal measure, making this collection both riveting and unforgettable. *Sinkhole, and Other Inexplicable Voids* is a dazzling testament to Krow's talent, offering readers not just a captivating journey into the unknown, but a brilliant return to our everyday lives forever marked by what we had witnessed."

—Morgan Talty, national bestselling author of *Night of the Living Rez* and *Fire Exit*

"A gorgeous book that also serves as a series of unanswerable, probing questions: How did we get here? How will we move forward? Can we still love, despite the wreckage? This is devastating work, and I mean that as a compliment. Very rarely have I come across a set of stories so genuinely moving. A searing collection that attempts to place the world delicately in our fumbling, undeserving hands."

—Kristen Arnett, *New York Times* bestselling author of *Mostly Dead Things* and *With Teeth*

"This book doesn't just entertain—it explodes. *Sinkhole, and Other Inexplicable Voids* balances unearthly happenings with those concretely upon us. Krow deftly pulls readers into her tilted universe through the veneer of domesticity. Once there, we are haunted by something far more absurd than babies who become men in nine weeks and supplements that turn women into werewolves—a natural world that cries for our attention and goes unheard. Krow writes with both a masterful weirdness and the wise compassion of a human who loves our beautiful Earth."

—Emily Habeck, national bestselling author of *Shark Heart: A Love Story*

"Leyna Krow's *Sinkhole, and Other Inexplicable Voids* is beguiling and beautiful, funny and poignant, and mesmerizing at every turn. These strange stories have a delightful wildness about them: They turn our everyday world askew so as to reveal complicated truths beneath the surface. Leyna Krow is the perfect storyteller for this moment, for she so deftly captures the brutality and absurdity of living in what often feels like the end of the world."

—Edan Lepucki, *New York Times* bestselling author of *California*

Fire Season

Longlisted For The Center For Fiction First Novel Prize

"Leyna Krow locates her first novel in a late-nineteenth-century American boomtown that 'prided itself on being wild and rugged.' Washington Territory is on the brink of statehood when Spokane Falls succumbs to the disaster that gives *Fire Season* its title. But rising from the ashes is a process that reveals its citizens to be rather more vulnerable than they'd like to believe. So too are the grifters who will soon find themselves at loggerheads—and over much more than easy money."

—*The New York Times Book Review*

"This feminist, magical Wild West romp is exactly the summer treat we all ordered."

—*Good Housekeeping*

"Evocative . . . The prose is marvelous. . . . Readers will be captivated."

—*Publishers Weekly* (starred review)

"*Fire Season* is uncomfortable and excellent—a story of scams set in the Wild West (Washington not-yet-state in the 1800s). Krow's plot takes off like a spooked horse, running and not stopping, to the delight of the reader. . . . Let this Western take you for a ride."

—*Glamour*

"Calling all Western fans: This debut novel follows three misfits in [the] 1889 American West [whose] lives end up on the same path after a fire destroys the city of Spokane Falls."

—*Apartment Therapy*

"Wholly satisfying."

—*The Spokesman-Review*

"A picaresque story of three schemers whose paths cross in nineteenth-century Spokane just as the Washington Territory is striving for statehood . . . [A] darkly whimsical reimagining of the American West."

—*BookPage* (starred review)

"Part revisionist Western, part meditation on misogyny and female power, it's an appealingly strange, idiosyncratic tale."

—Carolyn Juris, *Publishers Weekly*, "A Summer Reads Staff Pick"

"The prose is incantatory. . . . A novel that makes peace with uncertainty."

—*Kirkus Reviews*

"*Fire Season* is a smoldering visitation of the American West, a novel about three opportunistic figures who converge following the great fire of 1889 in Spokane Falls: a con man, a bank manager, and a woman who can see the future. Sparks fly as they collide with one another, and it's not long before their simmering tensions, attractions, and conflicts lead to a conflagration most might not see coming, and from the ashes of which most will never rise up again."

—Olivia Rutigliano, *Lit Hub*'s "35 Novels You Need to Read This Summer"

"A suicidal banker sees opportunity in an illegal scheme. A new-to-town con man's time may finally be running out. A future-seeing woman entertains both these men with her power. In her debut novel, Krow (*I'm Fine, But You Appear to Be Sinking*) follows these three people as their lives converge and are irreparably changed when a fire devastates their town."

—*The Millions*

"Leyna Krow plays fast and loose with the tropes of the frontier novel, leaning into the notion of the unsettled West as a place where people could reinvent themselves."

—*BookPage*, "The Best Historical Novels of Summer 2022"

"First-time novelist Krow is a keen observer and raconteur of human nature; her characters spring forth fully formed from a few whimsical sentences. The prevailing tone is one of delicious dark humor, along with a touch of the absurd and a dose of spiritualism. The result is a literary conflagration that absorbs down to its cooling embers."

—*Booklist*

"A magic-laced tale set during Spokane's founding days . . . An engaging page-turner reimagining the past with a touch of the supernatural."

—Chey Scott, *Inlander*

"In this enthralling debut, Leyna Krow brings us the story of three misfits, united by fire, each living out a dream (or nightmare) of the American West. It's an arresting take on magic, science, disaster, and salvation that's eerily resonant with the fire seasons we find ourselves living through today."

—Anna North, author of Reese's Book Club Pick and *New York Times* bestseller *Outlawed*

"Devilishly funny and endlessly inventive, *Fire Season* is a remarkable debut novel, a wry alternate history of Northwest schemers, dreamers, and scorched earth. Leyna Krow is a wildly talented young writer."

—Jess Walter, #1 *New York Times* bestselling author of *Beautiful Ruins*

"*Fire Season* sparks to life on the power of Leyna Krow's masterful subversion of criminality. While at first this novel's inferno seems confined to one minor Western outpost, by the final pages, it's throwing light on the unreliable narrators who perpetuate misogyny across America. Riveting, resonant, and charmingly rebellious, *Fire Season* will leave you wanting to read anything by Leyna Krow."

—John Larison, author of *Whiskey When We're Dry*

"Leyna Krow is a master of literary sleight of hand. *Fire Season* will convince you it's a satire of the early American West, while subtly inching into different territory. It's a completely new kind of story: a genre-bender that teases out strange, wry, beautiful surprises from familiar tropes. Imagine Jane Campion taking over a Coen brothers film for the denouement. As in her short stories, Leyna Krow is the usher sneaking you in the side door of a future cult classic."

—Alexis M. Smith, author of *Marrow Island*

"*Fire Season* is fantastic. Here's an old Northwest so full of con men and creeps, the best thing for it is to burn it all down. Here's a heroine only Leyna Krow could imagine—a woman whose transformation over the course of this story will also transform what we think a novel of the West can be. A powerful, absorbing, and incredibly funny book."

—Kate Lebo, author of *The Book of Difficult Fruit*

"Leyna Krow's *Fire Season* is a twisty, beguiling tale that was the most fun I've had in a while. If you love the novels of Patrick deWitt; rooting for an imperfect, sometimes devilish character; 'certain kinds of women'; wildness; and the way wildness tricks us into believing it's tamed, then get ready. This book is quite the ride."

—Lindsay Hunter, author of *Eat Only When You're Hungry*

"Leyna Krow's *Fire Season* is an act of literary magic: a lively historical picaresque about an intertwined trio of schemers, threaded through with a compelling story of a woman forging her own otherworldly redemption out of the crude material of the nineteenth-century American frontier."

—Shawn Vestal, author of *Daredevils* and *Godforsaken Idaho*

"Leyna Krow's debut novel, *Fire Season*, is Karen Russell meets Patrick deWitt meets Katherine Dunn—an edgy, twisty tale of fraudsters, underdogs, and an all-seeing woman who longs to rise above man's greed. Exploding with history, theft, humor, and magic, this incendiary novel is a thrilling addition to the Northwest literary canon."

—Sharma Shields, author of *The Sasquatch Hunter's Almanac*

"*Fire Season* conjures up a dazzling vision of the frontier West, where cunning men can take on new identities as easily as riding into a new town and fortunes can be made or stolen in a single scheme. . . . This is a rich, complex, and riveting book whose magic will start working on you long before you've realized its full power, and will stay with you long after you've finished the final page."

—Kea Wilson, author of *We Eat Our Own*

"In this rare and luminous novel, Krow weaves a fabulist history of the inland Northwest in its rangy adolescence. Against a backdrop of catastrophe, her renegade characters stake everything on games of chance and destiny. *Fire Season* is a testimony to the power of transformation and influence, a reminder that true vision is not about controlling the future, but creating it."

—Megan Kruse, author of *Call Me Home*

I'm Fine, But You Appear to Be Sinking

Finalist For The Believer Book Award

"Krow's stories offer humor, lightness, and a perspective unlike any other in contemporary short fiction. From this collection emerges a wholly original voice, along with a sense of wonder toward the world at large that remains long after the last page."

—*HuffPost*'s "Best Fiction of 2017"

"*I'm Fine, But You Appear to Be Sinking*, by Leyna Krow, will remind you of the magic just waiting to be discovered around every corner of your otherwise-mundane surroundings—if you only keep your eyes open enough to see it. . . . Filled with mystery, intrigue, and humor, each story offers an engrossing journey of discovery and surprise."

—*Bustle*

"[Krow's] writing is fresh and playful. And her experiments with form leave you wondering why we haven't been writing this way all along. Trust me, she is a genius."

—*NW Book Lovers*

"So completely original in voice and concept—smart, humorous, poignant, clear, and meaningful. A fresh, important voice for a new generation of writers."

—Gregory Spatz, author of *Half as Happy*

"Bound by a crackling wit, an inventive vitality, a laser eye for the silent currents between people, and a sneaky emotional power. *I'm Fine, But You Appear to Be Sinking* is a wildly imagined debut, a blast of fleet power."

—Shawn Vestal, author of *Daredevils* and *Godforsaken Idaho*

"Leyna Krow's stories crackle with fearless curiosity and an expansive, embracing wonder toward time and the world. *I'm Fine, But You Appear to Be Sinking* is an antidote to every cynical, self-centered impulse."

—James Tadd Adcox, author of *Repetition* and *Does Not Love*

"What a wonderful book Leyna Krow has written! And what a rare book—innovative, clever, funny, deliciously language-driven, delightful dialogue—but also so very warm and human. It's about humans, it's for humans, it makes me feel better about being a human reading this book about humans. A joy to read."

—Amber Sparks, author of *The Unfinished World*, *The Desert Places*, and *May We Shed These Human Bodies*

PENGUIN BOOKS

SINKHOLE, AND OTHER INEXPLICABLE VOIDS

Leyna Krow is the author of the novel *Fire Season*, which was longlisted for the Center for Fiction First Novel Prize, and the short story collection *I'm Fine, But You Appear to Be Sinking*, which was a Believer Book Award finalist. She lives in Spokane, Washington, with her husband and two children.

ALSO BY LEYNA KROW

I'm Fine, But You Appear to Be Sinking

Fire Season

SINKHOLE, AND OTHER INEXPLICABLE VOIDS

Stories

Leyna Krow

PENGUIN BOOKS

PENGUIN BOOKS
An imprint of Penguin Random House LLC
penguinrandomhouse.com

The following stories were published previously in different forms: "The Twin" in *Tri Quarterly*; "Sinkhole" in *Moss.*; "The Unmatched Joy of Killing Something Beautiful" in *Moss*; "The Octopus Finds Love at Home" in *The Spokesman-Review*; "Chet's Landing Resort and Luxury Cabins" in *Midwestern Gothic*; "The Sundance Kid Might Have Some Regrets" in *Lilac City Fairy Tales*; "Nicholas the Bunny" in *The Massachusetts Review*; and "A Plan to Save Us All" in *The Journal.*

Designed by Nerylsa Dijol

LIBRARY OF CONGRESS CATALOGING-IN-PUBLICATION DATA
Names: Krow, Leyna, author.
Title: Sinkhole, and other inexplicable voids : stories / Leyna Krow.
Description: New York : Penguin Books, 2025. |
Identifiers: LCCN 2024030300 (print) | LCCN 2024030301 (ebook) |
ISBN 9780593299654 (paperback) | ISBN 9780593299647 (ebook)
Subjects: LCGFT: Short stories.
Classification: LCC PS3611.R79 S56 2025 (print) |
LCC PS3611.R79 (ebook) | DDC 813/.6—dc23/eng/20240712
LC record available at https://lccn.loc.gov/2024030300
LC ebook record available at https://lccn.loc.gov/2024030301

Printed in the United States of America
1st Printing

For Scott, Bixby, and Walden

Contents

SINKHOLE, AND OTHER INEXPLICABLE VOIDS

The Twin

Ruby was the first one to use the word *twin*. It was a Sunday and we were all home. I heard the telltale cries from Jace's room, signaling that he'd woken from his afternoon nap. "Coming, buddy," I called as I made my way upstairs to extract him from his crib. When I reached the doorway of the baby's room, I became aware of a second cry, not so much an echo as a harmony. But my brain could not process this sound, not at first, and so it meant nothing to me. It was only once I stepped fully into the room and turned on the overhead light that I understood.

I must have screamed. Ruby and Troy appeared at my side. "What is it?" Troy asked in his worried dad voice. "Is he okay?"

"Look," I said.

In the crib were two babies. Their crying had stopped now that we were all there. They sat side by side. They both looked at us with Jace's glacial blue eyes, which always got him compliments. The babies raised their arms. They wanted to be picked up.

"Oh," said Ruby. "It's his twin." She said it in the matter-of-fact way of young children. She was four, an age when everything in the world is either crystalline in its clarity or totally unfathomable. She went to the crib and reached through the slats for the baby who was not Jace. She squeezed his belly and he giggled. “Cutie-cutie,” she said.

We didn’t know what to do, except the things that always needed to be done. We picked up the babies. We changed their diapers and gave each a bottle. I got Ruby her afternoon snack and turned on cartoons. We put the babies in the playpen and stared at them. They seemed content, as Jace often was on his own, to fidget with the toys and chew on the board books.

“Should we call someone?” I asked. “Should we call the police?”

Troy said no. What would the police do?

I agreed. There was no foul play. In fact, there was nothing wrong at all. The second baby seemed healthy, happy. And clearly he was ours, with his resemblance to Jace. He was fine in every way, except that he should not have been there.

So, we did what all good middle-class Americans are supposed to do when faced with a challenge. We went shopping. We needed another car seat, another crib, another high chair, a double-wide stroller. Ruby led the way, instructing our purchases.

“He likes green,” she said about crib sheets.

“He wants to feel like a big boy,” she said on the subject of high chairs.

“He wants lots of shade, but he still wants to see me and Jace,” she said about strollers.

We took her at her word and bought the things she picked.

Back home, I sat on the couch and held the baby who was not Jace. He was content to be snuggled, a pleasant surprise, as Jace had grown wiggly once he’d learned to crawl, rarely allowing me to cuddle him for more than a moment. This other boy fit well against my body. His skin was soft and his hair fuzzy, same as Jace’s, same as

Ruby's when she was that size. As fine a baby as any. Ruby sat beside me, tracing an invisible picture on his back.

"Ruby, what's this one's name?" I asked.

"Nicholas," she said.

She said it with the same certainty she'd said everything else about him and so I took it as fact and shared this information with Troy. It was not a name he and I would have picked, too long and too formal for our tastes. But I didn't feel we were in a position to argue.

"Shall we call him Nicky for short?" Troy asked.

"No," Ruby said. "Nicholas."

HOW? AND FROM WHERE? *And what for?* The first few nights, after the kids went to bed, Troy and I conferred in a frantic, breathy way, trying to make sense of him. Was he a glitch in the simulation? A government experiment? Had Jace cloned himself like an amoeba? Had Nicholas been there all along and we had simply forgotten? We googled things like "sudden identical twin" and "new baby who looks exactly like other baby," but got no coherent results.

"Is he a miracle?" I asked once.

At this, of all things, Troy laughed, accusing me of religiosity.

"Think of a better word," I challenged him.

"Phenomenon, surprise, curiosity, oddity, wonderment, additional tax credit," he offered.

"How will we decide?" I asked.

We never decided. We were stumped about Nicholas, and the stumpedness washed over us, rendering us victims of inertia. We went about our days. Work and parenting and cooking and cleaning and mowing the lawn.

Early on, Troy did make a phone call—to the county records office, but only to say we had lost the birth certificate for one of our sons. This document arrived by mail without incident. Nicholas's date of birth was the same as Jace's, the time fifteen minutes later. After that, Troy relaxed. If the paperwork was in order, then so was everything else, he seemed to believe. And for a while I think I believed it too.

WE WERE in a good place in our lives for keeping a secret. We'd moved to Spokane just a year prior, shortly before Jace was born. We'd been slow at making friends. Aside from a few acquaintances from Troy's office, we hadn't socialized much. When these people saw us with our kids, their reaction was something like, "Oh, I didn't realize you had twins." Then we'd laugh and say, "Yes, twice the trouble, twice the joy," and the conversation would move on. As for family, Troy was estranged from his parents and brother. My only relation was my mom, who had been living with early-onset dementia for several years and for whom the names and ages of her grandchildren were already a moving target.

Even people who should have been alarmed by Nicholas were not. When it was time for one-year checkups, I called the pediatrician's office and requested appointments for Jace Fenster and Nicholas Fenster, expecting confusion. But the receptionist's only question was if I wanted to bring both boys in at the same time, or separately. On the day of their appointment, the doctor, who had been seeing Jace since he was a newborn, spent a long time staring at her computer screen. When she finally looked away it was just to ask if I had any concerns about either baby. And I didn't, not yet. She examined each boy, showed me a chart with their height and weight, and explained which shots they were due for. All this information she put into her computer, and I read it later online at home as well, Nicholas's name a surprise each time, even though he was sitting in my lap at that very moment.

RUBY HAD NAMED him after a rabbit. I didn't make the connection right away, but once I did, I thought it sweet. Nicholas the bunny was from her favorite book when she was a baby. In it, the cute and dapper Nicholas, dressed in a button-down shirt and overalls, observes the habits of his animal neighbors in the forest. She'd outgrown that book, preferring now Berenstain Bears and Elephant & Piggie. It had been a long time since we'd read it. When I went to her room to retrieve it, it was much as I remembered. The bright illustrations; the earnest, curious bunny. But something about it unsettled me. On each page, Nicholas watches what other critters are doing, but in this, he is conspicuously alone. No rabbit parents or siblings keep him company. He is the only rabbit at all, in fact. Certainly the only character in clothes. He seems a creature without a place, an interloper and an outsider all at once.

JUST AS RUBY was the one to state his name and his place in our family, so too did she give shape to my anxiety. It had been creeping, amorphous and untethered, ever since the day Nicholas arrived. By speaking aloud, she made it manifest. After that, I could not escape it.

"When will he go away?" she asked. A casual question. She was playing roll-the-ball with the boys in the playpen. The ball was in Nicholas's hands. He squeezed it heartily before sending it back to her.

Not *Will he go away?*

When.

Another fact of Nicholas: He was not ours to keep.

I TOLD TROY what Ruby had said. He understood my worry, but did not share it.

"Where would he go?" he asked.

"Back to wherever he came from," I said.

Troy shook his head. "I don't think that's how this works. I don't think people can just disappear."

I countered that we clearly had no idea how this worked. If a person can just appear, why couldn't he just disappear? What was there to keep him tethered to us?

"He's okay," he said. He said it in the same way as when Ruby was a newborn and he would catch me standing over her bassinet, my hand on her chest to feel her breathing. *She's okay.* And she always was. I hadn't done that with Jace. The first one had lived, so I trusted the second to do the same. Now I saw how naive that logic had been. I should have been pressing my hands to all their chests at all times.

WHAT, EXACTLY, was I afraid of? It is difficult to fear an abstraction. Troy was right. In our experience, people did not vanish. My mind needed something familiar to fear instead. Illnesses, injuries, kidnapping, car accidents, food allergies, mass shootings, choking, wildfires. Pesticides on strawberries, flame retardant on pajamas. It can be hard to know where the dangers are coming from, but it's easy to know there are a lot of them. I never wanted to parent in that way—to be a mother octopus who tends so obsessively to her eggs that she no longer eats or sleeps.

But Nicholas really *was* a miracle, wasn't he? A vulnerable, inexplicable miracle. I did not understand him, and so I could not trust the world with him. He needed my constant vigilance.

Ruby's preschool also had daycare and we'd been talking about enrolling Jace, but once Nicholas came along, those conversations stopped. *The cost!* I lamented by way of explanation. I also stopped seeking out our usual sitter, and the teen neighbor girl who, for ten dollars, would walk the kids to the playground for an hour. This left me totally alone with both boys during Troy's work hours. It was exhausting. Even still, I made excuses most nights to sleep on the floor of their bedroom, claiming Nicholas had a cough, or was just in a really needy mood, and I had to stay nearby. At the end of the book, the bunny curls up in a hollow tree to sleep until spring. But I looked it up and real rabbits don't hibernate. There was something particularly ominous about this to me. A warning and a threat.

"IS IT POSSIBLE you're suffering from postpartum depression?" Troy asked one evening.

"But I didn't give birth to him," I said. "There's no partum to be post."

"You gave birth to Jace. It wasn't that long ago."

No, I insisted. This was neither hormonal nor physiological. It was existential.

I knew, when it came to Nicholas, I was being too much. But I also knew I wasn't wrong.

I turned the question back to Troy.

"How can you just go along like normal? How do you live with *When will he leave*?"

Troy sighed. "I get it. I do. And I appreciate that you like to take Ruby seriously. But she's not exactly an oracle. Half the time she doesn't know if she brushed her teeth before school. She ends up doing it twice."

We laughed together at this. Troy asked again what I wanted to do, what might help. I told him I wanted to wait, to be patient. I think he assumed I meant with myself, and with the situation. We were all still adjusting, after all. But really, I meant wait for the true answer for how to protect Nicholas.

I tried to be a kind of cocoon, with Nicholas strapped to my chest in the Ergobaby, snuggled in a blanket on my lap, pinned with an arm to my hip. I wasn't an octopus, though I wouldn't have minded being a kangaroo, with a pouch. Nicholas was attached to me in one way or another with such frequency that Ruby began using him for storage. When she had something to hand me, she would give it to Nicholas instead. An empty snack dish set on his head. Clever, how adaptable we all were. There is an intimacy in keeping someone so close and I did not dislike that part of it. I could have happily spent full days nuzzling the top of Nicholas's head, kissing his neck. I assumed that from the outside it just looked like I was being a really good mom.

TROY WAS PATIENT, as he agreed he would be. I hovered while he gave the babies their bath each night, recut Nicholas's food into smaller pieces after Troy had put it on his plate, double-checked carseat straps, insisted on dressing Nicholas each morning myself to ensure he would be neither too hot nor too cold. Through all this,

Troy said nothing. Until one day when I suggested the call might be coming from inside the house.

Troy was out back playing with the kids while I cooked dinner. The window was open and I could hear their game, which was of the Daddy's-going-to-get-you variety. Shrieks and laughter rolled in. But then the laughter turned to crying, real crying, the scared and pained kind. A thought flashed through my mind: Troy did not want Nicholas. From Troy's perspective, Nicholas had disrupted our family's easy dynamic. And now he had decided to rid himself of that problem. I banged through the door and shouted, "What are you doing to him?"

Troy turned to me, red-faced Jace tucked into his arms.

"Oh," I said, before I could stop myself. "I thought it was Nicholas."

Then I went back inside. Troy followed.

"Don't you want to know what happened to Jace? He tumbled off the steps."

"I'm so sorry. I thought it was Nicholas," I said again. "I thought you had become resentful of him."

Here, Troy's worry cracked into anger.

"What the hell, Jenna? Resent him? He's my son. You're the one who's uncomfortable with him being here. The rest of us have moved on."

I glanced out the window to where Ruby was sitting with Nicholas in the grass. Fine. Then I double-checked to be sure.

"I need you to talk to someone," Troy said. "This isn't healthy for you. Or for the kids. You obsess over Nicholas, but you act like Ruby and Jace hardly exist. I'm afraid it's going to fuck them all up." Then he looked away, knowing there was no greater indictment he could level.

And indeed, I was shamed. I agreed to find a therapist. In fact, I called several offices the next day, but was told none were accepting new patients. They would add me to their waitlist. I never received any calls back, though. Eventually the issue resolved itself. Mostly, it was just the passage of time that did it, but before that, an incident of violence, theft, and calamity.

HERE IS WHAT HAPPENED. On a Saturday morning, Troy and I drove the kids to the park downtown. We had packed quickly, a hustle to get everyone out the door and into the sunshine. After thirty minutes at the playground, our snack supplies ran low. Ruby started to whine and when Jace reached for his sippy cup and found it empty of milk, they made a mournful chorus. I offered to find a coffee shop for provisions. I grabbed my wallet from the diaper bag and loaded Nicholas into the stroller.

Troy squinted at me. "You don't have to take him."

"It's just easier," I said. Though of course what I really meant was *It's safer.* I turned and started walking before he could raise other objections.

The coffee shop was busy. Nicholas was delighted. From his stroller seat, he waved and smiled to everyone who would look at him. "Hi!" he said over and over. "Hi!" Is there anything cuter than a baby who says hi to strangers? I wished he would not attract so much attention. The bunny is so blissfully naive. He thinks butterflies are for chasing, flowers for picking, and toadstools for playing under.

From the cold case I chose milk, yogurt, and a plastic cup of apple slices. Troy would want a cold brew, Ruby a doughnut. Nicholas had struck up a conversation with the woman waiting ahead of us. "Hi!" She kept turning to say hi back. The fifth or sixth time this happened, I too said hi and tried to catch her eye in a thank-you-for-being-a-good-sport-with-him way. But her attention was only for Nicholas. This realization gave me pause. A few more "Hi!"s were exchanged. Then, instead of turning back, she knelt down to be nearer to him. She was an older woman, grandmotherly with short white hair and big circle glasses. She was slim with knuckly hands that shook a little when she extended them to my son. He reached for her fingers and she laughed. She moved those same fingers so they grazed the top of his fuzzy head. "So soft," she said. Still she did not acknowledge me. *Please don't touch my son*, I was on the verge of saying. Then she did a terrifying thing. "Uh-oh," she said, reaching into the stroller, and I heard, before I saw, the click of the buckle undone.

She was trying to take him. Like a fairy-tale witch, she had traveled from her otherworld in search of him. Now she was taking him back from whence they both came, back to his land of butterflies and toadstools, to live forever in a hollow tree without me.

"No!" I shouted. She finally did look at me then, her face a question. She said something. I was already mid-stride. "No!" I said again and shoved her. She tumbled backward, an ungainly slide against the coffee shop linoleum. When I picture the scene now, it includes the faces of everyone else in the store—surprise and horror, some moving to help the woman, others trying to block me. But the truth is that in the moment I could see no one but Nicholas as I took hold of his stroller handles and ran us both out the open door.

"It's okay, buddy!" I called to him as I made a sharp right turn on the sidewalk. Though I had seen her fall, I felt certain the woman would pursue us. A witch spurned is not a witch thwarted. Nicholas was crying, from either the jostling of the stroller or the surprise of our exit. Or perhaps, in hindsight, the loss of his new friend. *Twisted* was the word she said. I would hear it later in my memory. His stroller harness straps had been twisted.

I ran to the end of the block and then another and when confronted with a red light, I veered us left, across the street back toward the park. I was very fast at that time in my life. I was a regular runner, my legs long and summer-tanned. I was wearing good shoes that day. Once I crossed into the park, there was a grassy hill and I built up a good deal of speed between my fast legs and the weight of the stroller and the force of gravity. I crossed the bike path. I had the playground in mind—the safety of Troy and also of other parents, who would surely band together to protect Nicholas from capture. But of course I was actually two blocks east and heading not for the playground but for the river.

It snuck up on me. We lived well north of downtown and had only been to the park once before. Though I knew that the Spokane River cut the park in half, I was unprepared for its reality.

By the time I thought *Stop*, I was already in the muck, my sneakers slick with mud and goose poop. My body and the stroller both were skidding into the water. I tried to gain better purchase on the whole situation, but I was still holding everybody's snacks. Yogurt and apple slices, now loosed from their cup, splashed as I dug my feet in and pulled back hard on the handles.

Then Nicholas tumbled headfirst into the water.

He had been unbuckled the whole time. The whole reason for all of it.

I lurched in after him. A child can drown in less than three inches of water. Two steps into the river and I was already up to my knees. Nicholas was somewhere below me, but where? I reached frantically while counting in my head. How long could he go without drawing the river into his lungs? Four seconds? Eight seconds? My hands swished through the opaque water and hit nothing but more water. He was gone. The witch had gotten him. We were always heading toward this. A child I hadn't asked for and now a grief I'd never escape. Search and rescue would scour the river and whatever they found, body or no body, would be the worst possible outcome.

At seventeen seconds, my hand grazed his leg and I pulled him up by it. Not dead, not even coughing up water. He had never been submerged, only flung out of my line of sight and too shocked to make noise until he was hoisted upside down by his superfun mom. Then he laughed. His hair was still dry.

I responded to this joyful sound by vomiting on both of us.

THIS IS NICHOLAS'S FAVORITE part of the story when I tell it now. He and Jace are thirteen, and inclined toward humor of a visceral nature. So when we are reviewing family history, this is always his request: The Time Mom Thought I Was Being Kidnapped and Launched Me into the River and Puked.

"Did you think you were pregnant with more twins?" he asks, then mimes gratuitous vomiting while also holding a pregnant belly.

"Mom did upchuck, like, constantly when she was knocked with you guys," Ruby confirms.

Not only was Ruby not an oracle, she was not even a child with a particularly good memory. She remembers my morning sickness but she cannot conjure the months of Jace before Nicholas, and so our greatest lie is an easy one. Why are there so few pictures from the boys' first year? We were busy, our hands full.

Nicholas's second favorite part is that I stole all those snacks that fell in the river. "Criminal," he says, tsking.

His third favorite part is that I pushed down an old lady.

"Falls can be very bad for elderly people," Troy always reminds. "She might have been seriously hurt."

"But you don't know because you never went back to check!" one of the kids cackles. This quickly becomes a story told in the round.

I did not go back to check, it's true. For a while, I looked through the paper and online every day for an account of the incident, but there was none.

MY FAVORITE PART is what happened next. Though I don't tell this because it's boring. The family version ends with the vomiting.

After that, I walked back to the playground, Nicholas balanced on my hip. I left the stroller and the coffee shop foods where they were—mud-bound at the river's edge. Troy toweled us off with a baby blanket from the diaper bag, put Nicholas into clean clothes, and asked too many times if I was okay, and did I want to go home. But I was okay, and I did not want to go home. I wanted to sit on a bench and watch my children play, to luxuriate in the moment. Something bad had happened, and I had not lost him. He had not evaporated back into the ether from which he came. I believed we were, for a moment, inoculated against other bad things.

The feeling stayed with me in the days and weeks that followed. Nicholas was sturdier than I had thought. And also more tangible. Realer. Getting realer and realer every day. Or maybe I had just, finally, as Troy suggested of himself and the other kids, moved on.

Still, not everything changed after that. Ruby and Jace have always accused me of playing favorites, of picking Nicholas first, taking his side, giving him the biggest slice of cake, et cetera. I don't. I would never. What is happening is their bodies are remembering something old, making it feel new. There was a time, however brief, when my hand reached for his and not theirs, and that won't leave them. I'm sorry. But couldn't I level the same accusations now? Everyone in this family is always grabbing for Nicholas, that dapper bunny who was never lonesome, only curious, so curious, about his new and bright and glowing world. The other kids want him on their team for all the games, to sit next to him in the way-back of the car, to hustle him into a private corner and share their most important secrets.

"Tell it again, Mom!" Nicholas says of the story. "Or another one just like it." Then he laughs. He is always laughing, pulling our family together, closer and closer, in a joyful spinning. Not a miracle, but a force.

Sinkhole

The real estate agent showed us the house on West Garland Avenue and insisted it had everything we wanted.

"Look," he said, "there's a fireplace, granite countertops, crown molding, and a large sinkhole in the yard."

My husband, Alex, and I laughed because we thought he was kidding.

"No, really," the real estate agent said.

We told him we didn't want a sinkhole. That was not an item on our list. We agreed on this with absolute certainty. Back then, we always agreed with absolute certainty.

"I know," the real estate agent said. "But the house is a steal. Way bigger than anything else you'll find in your price range."

He was right. Besides, size was what we wanted most: a home with more space for our ever-expanding brood of children and pets. So we bought the house and put up a fence around the hole to keep the kids from falling in and for a while after that, we didn't pay much attention to it at all.

But then, one night a few weeks after the move, I asked Alex how deep he thought the sinkhole was. He said he had no idea. We went to look. We climbed our new fence and I held a flashlight while Alex leaned over the edge.

"I can't see the bottom," he said.

I stood beside him and peered in. It was almost as if the light was being consumed by the hole, eaten up. We agreed it seemed sinister.

The beam of the flashlight began to fade and soon disappeared entirely.

"Piece of junk," I said. Overcome by a childish impulse, I pitched it into the hole.

"That's sort of wasteful, don't you think?" Alex said. "It just needed new batteries."

No, I said. I told him it felt good to throw the broken flashlight. The feeling alone was worth the waste. Alex chuckled at this. Back then, he thought I was funny.

Inside the house, the flashlight was waiting for us. It was perched at the edge of the coffee table.

"What the fuck?" I whispered, not wanting to wake the kids.

"Seriously, what the fuck?" Alex whispered back.

I picked up the flashlight. I didn't know if I should be afraid or impressed. A minute earlier I had thrown it into a hole in our yard and now it was here, in the living room, on the coffee table. I turned it over in my hands to test its realness. I flicked the switch and the light came on.

"The sinkhole fixed it," I whispered.

"Wait," Alex said, and for a second I thought he was going to warn me to set the light down and back away—it could be dangerous. But he didn't. What he said was: "Let's try something else to be sure."

He found a picture frame that had cracked during the move. I waited in the living room while he took the frame outside. In a moment, it was back on the coffee table just where the flashlight had been, the glass looking clean and solid. Alex returned and we inspected the repaired frame. We agreed it was incredible.

After that, we used the sinkhole quite often. We dropped in scuffed sneakers, forks with bent tines, books with torn covers. They all reappeared on the coffee table good as new. Soon the sinkhole became just another feature of the house we were grateful for, like the dishwasher and the walk-in closets.

We never considered the effect the hole might have on anything living. Not until the morning our oldest son, Jake, woke me to announce in a tear-ragged voice that something was wrong with his turtle. He was holding the turtle, named Bert, in both hands. I could see the creature was sick. I didn't want to take both boy and turtle to the vet only to hear bad news. So, I led Jake to the yard and helped him over the fence to the hole.

"Put Bert in there and it will fix him," I said.

I thought Jake would protest, but worry for his pet made him compliant. He put Bert into the hole and gasped when he disappeared. Back inside, he found Bert on the coffee table and ran to him. The turtle was much improved. But a pale of concern remained on Jake's little face.

"Is my turtle a zombie now?" he asked.

"No, of course not," I told him. "Zombies are dead things that come back to life. Bert was just sick. The sinkhole made him better."

As soon as I said those words—*The sinkhole made him better*—I felt a shiver run through me. Like I'd just found the answer to a very important question I hadn't even thought to ask.

I began to wonder what the sinkhole could do for me, if I put myself in it.

I wasn't sick like Bert. I wasn't broken like our clock radio. But I wasn't the best version of me, either. I was thirty-eight, my body damaged from childbearing, and before that from alcohol and hair dye and music that was too loud. The usual things. Adulthood wore down my character too. I was impulsive and at times forgetful. No great crimes. But wouldn't my family be happier with an improved me? Wouldn't I be happier?

I suggested this to Alex one night and he said no.

"I like you the way you are."

I thought he was just being kind. Back then, we were always kind to each other.

"But wouldn't you like me better if I was better?"

"No, because then you wouldn't be you."

I didn't see this as the compliment he intended. I felt he was saying my essential nature was a flawed one.

Alex looked into my eyes and I could see the worry creep across his face.

"Please promise me you won't get in that sinkhole," he said.

"Why not?" I asked.

"Because it's weird. It's a weird thing to do."

I promised, but I couldn't help but see this conversation as evidence for exactly why I needed so badly to go through the sinkhole: My logic was flawed, my thinking strange. What kind of woman wants to put herself in a hole? I felt strongly that if I used the hole to make myself better, I would banish such weirdness. I would no longer be the sort of person who wished to get into holes.

Alex kept looking at me. I didn't say anything because I didn't want to lie to him. Back then, we never lied.

I felt ready to get in the hole that night, but chose to wait. I wanted to be certain I was doing the right thing. So, for the next week, I went about my life as my normal, flawed self. I went to work; I visited with friends; I fed, cleaned, and entertained my children. I was kind and agreeable and honest and funny with Alex, like always.

But in my head, I kept a list of each mistake I made, every error a more perfect me would have been able to avoid—a burnt pan of lasagna, a forgotten birthday, a child scolded too harshly. And so on. Normally, I might have chastised myself for these missteps and later recounted them to Alex so he could reassure me they weren't really so bad. Instead I hoarded them almost gleefully. They were the evidence against me. I was building my case for the sinkhole.

I made a habit of visiting the hole before bed each night. I took my flashlight and, dressed in my slippers and robe, stood beside it, looking in. It was a meditative practice of sorts. I tried to think of nothing while I did this—not my flaws, or what a flawless me might be like. I just stood and stared, letting the darkness of the cavern fill my mind with calm and hope. Sometimes I was aware of Alex watching me as I did this, waiting at the bedroom window for me to finish my ritual. But he never said anything about it. Why didn't he say anything? What was wrong with me that my beloved husband could watch me do something that bizarre, night after night, and never feel capable of confronting me about it? Was I so fragile? So frightening? So beguiling?

Then one evening Jake went off for a sleepover and left me with instructions to feed Bert—what kind of veggies and how much. Of course I forgot. In the morning, the turtle gazed out at me from his cage with what I imagined to be a hunger-stricken look. *Never, ever again*, I thought.

I went straight for the hole. As I climbed the fence, I wondered about my entry. Should I dive? Cannonball? No. Such actions suggested a kind of playfulness. But this was not play. It was work—the work of repairing myself. I walked into the hole as if stepping off a curb. I tumbled over once in the dark air, then I was seated, legs crossed, back straight (no more slouching for me!) on the edge of the coffee table, feeling calm and perfect. Like I was someone else entirely. So, Alex had been right, of course. I was no longer myself. But the new and better me didn't care. The better me was content to sit at the edge of the table, waiting patiently for Alex to come home so I could show him all the ways I'd changed.

The Unmatched Joy of Killing Something Beautiful

We were doing homework at the kitchen table when Ron came in with a caterpillar pinched between his thumb and index finger.

"If you see any of these, the fat ones with the blue stripes, I want you to destroy them," he said. He dropped the caterpillar into the sink and turned on the garbage disposal. Ainsley, who was only six at the time, started to cry.

"Jesus fucking Christ, Ron," I said, because I wanted to hear myself swear, and I knew Ron wouldn't reprimand me. "What the hell is wrong with you?"

Mom appeared from the other room and set about comforting Ainsley and scolding Ron and me respectively: me for my foul mouth, and Ron for what Mom called his "total disregard for how to communicate effectively with children."

"That's exactly what I was saying to him," I pointed out.

"Yeah, well, nobody asked your smart-ass foul mouth to say anything," Mom said, and it seemed like that was going to be the final word on the matter.

BUT THEN AT DINNER that night, Ron brought up the caterpillars again. He started with an apology. Ron was always apologizing. His apologies were lengthy and earnest. This was in contrast to my mom, who never apologized for anything. It made Ron look weak, and I wasn't sure whether I should pity him for his weakness or just plain dislike him. So far, in the year Mom had been dating him, and the eight months we'd been living in his house, I'd chosen the second option.

"Girls, I want to say I'm sorry for what I did with the caterpillar this afternoon," he began. "I see now that it was not the right way to convey the information I was trying to share. I didn't mean to scare or upset you." He paused to suck in his breath, a sure sign there was more to come. Ainsley interrupted.

"Why did you kill it?" she asked. "Was it dangerous?"

"Those particular caterpillars are very poisonous, yes," Ron said.

My sister's face grew taut and she looked to be on the verge of tears again.

"Ron!" my mother snapped. Then she said to Ainsley, "They're not poisonous to people, sweetheart. They're poisonous to birds."

"Well, I suppose, technically they're poisonous to anything that eats them, birds or humans," Ron said.

"So don't eat the caterpillars, girls," Mom said.

"Gross," I said. "Ron, why would you think we would eat caterpillars in the first place?"

"I'm sorry. I don't think you would eat a caterpillar," Ron said in his sad, flustered way. "I was only hoping maybe you could help me out if you see them around. If you see them in the yard, or even at school or the park, just tell me, okay?"

"Why? So you can garbage-disposal them all?" This was from

Ainsley, who, despite her young age, was beginning to have moments of smart-assery herself.

"Ron, no more insects in the garbage disposal, please," Mom said.

AS PER MOM'S WISHES, Ron didn't put the caterpillars in the garbage disposal. Mostly, he squashed them with the sole of his shoe, or a push broom if he found them in a group. They left blue smears on the pavement that glistened in the sun until the entrails dried and then it just looked like someone's half-finished sidewalk chalk drawing. Ainsley didn't like this, and ran inside whenever he appeared with his broom. I similarly distanced myself, but not because of fondness for the caterpillars. I didn't want anyone to see me with Ron—who looked like a total psycho, smashing bugs up and down the block until his face was red and he was breathing hard—and think I was associated with him in any way.

And he didn't need us to tell him where the caterpillars were, because within a week of showing us that first one in the kitchen, they were everywhere. Not just on our street, but, as Ron had predicted, in the park and on the playground at school, and in the Fred Meyer parking lot, and on the trees that lined the sidewalks downtown. By mid-April, there were so many, it became difficult not to step on them. But I tried my best—again, not out of affection, but because I did not want to accidentally help Ron.

They were syncathia caterpillars and they weren't supposed to be here in Bellingham. They were, in spring, supposed to be in Manitoba. Each year for the past decade, they had been found farther and farther west. Ron and his colleagues had been tracking the syncathias' movements with growing concern. And now here they were. "It's literally my worst nightmare," he said.

"Isn't that a bit dramatic?" Mom asked.

"Yeah," I said. "What about zombies? What about the apocalypse?"

"That's exactly what I'm saying," Ron said. "Except for birds. We're looking at a potential avian apocalypse."

I snorted at this. "Birds aren't people. It's not the same."

But Ron wouldn't fight with me. He only wanted to explain his science things. I was disappointed.

Ron was a professor of ornithology at Western Washington University. He admitted that he'd never even heard of the syncathia until a few years prior, when they began wreaking havoc on the bird populations in the Dakotas, then Montana. The Canadian bird species who lived alongside the syncathia knew to avoid them, their bright colors a warning of the poison they contained. But birds in the American West held no such knowledge. And when the syncathia emerged from their chrysalises as butterflies, huge and slow-moving, birds plucked them out of the air and gobbled them down. And then died.

"We could be looking at mass casualties," Ron said. "It happened in Grant County last year. They lost seventy-five percent of their alabaster martin population. Seventy-five percent! It boggles the mind. That's a species that's been brought back from the brink of extinction, and now there's this new threat. I'm terrified of what's going to happen here with our pine swallows and bluebells."

To my chagrin, Ron's caterpillar hysteria was not confined to our dinner table. He was quoted in the newspaper in an article about the syncathia. Even in print, I thought he sounded shrill, though Mom snipped the article out and hung it on the fridge next to my math tests and Ainsley's coloring pages. And one night, Ron was on TV. Mom herded Ainsley and me out of our rooms to watch, even though it was only the local news. There was Ron, in his ragged tweed jacket and a red tie that looked too tight. He sat next to another guy, who knew how to dress pretty well and made Ron appear even shabbier by comparison.

The better-dressed guy was from the chamber of commerce. He talked about how exciting the caterpillars were for the city. "Sure, they're a bit of a nuisance now," he said, but once they turned to butterflies, they would attract tourists, who would want to see the splendor of the syncathia. "In Winnipeg, they have a butterfly festival each year that brings in over a hundred thousand people. I was thinking we could do the same, since they're our butterflies now," he said.

Then it was Ron's turn to speak.

"The syncathia are not something to be celebrated," he said. He talked for a while about bird deaths, and he said the phrase "fragile ecosystem," like, forty times. You could see the energy drain from the faces of the news anchor and the chamber of commerce guy. I imagined energy draining from everyone all over town who was watching Ron.

"What a killjoy," I said.

"I know, but doesn't he look handsome?" Mom said.

"I think he looks like a total uggo. Just your type."

"Don't be rude, Kit."

"I'm not being rude. I'm simply pointing out your pattern of dating uggos. You're a serial uggoist."

Mom puffed out her cheeks, shook her head, and with uncharacteristic earnestness, said, "You know what, Kit? You should be nicer to Ron. He's a good guy. We're lucky to have him in our lives." And for a moment, I felt chastened.

But when he got home, I could hear through my bedroom wall the familiar sounds of Mom and Ron arguing in their room. I found

Ron's voice, muffled as it was, indistinguishable from all the previous uggos and good guys.

BY MAY, the caterpillars were mostly gone. Though of course not really gone, only transformed. They had wrapped themselves up in their pupas, which hung like tiny Christmas ornaments from every surface imaginable. They lined fence posts and roof eaves and stop signs. Tree branches sagged, laden with them. Wherever we went with Ron, he'd pluck them like he was picking cherries.

He cleared the pupas from our yard, but when he headed to our neighbors', he was sent away. The same went for the people who lived across the street.

"They say they like butterflies," Ron lamented over dinner. "I tried to explain about the birds, but they don't understand."

"Are you sure they don't understand?" I asked. "Or do they just not care?"

"Kit, I know you're trying to be snarky," Ron said. "But I think you've hit the nail on the head, sadly."

He rubbed his palm across his face and pressed his knuckles into his eye sockets.

My mom reached out and patted his shoulders. "It's hard to be a bird man in a butterfly-loving town," she said, though I couldn't tell if she meant it sincerely, and I guessed by Ron's expression that he couldn't either.

THE FOLLOWING SUNDAY, Ron woke us early and we stood in our bare feet and pajamas on the front porch as the first of the butterflies peeled themselves from their chrysalises. All around us blue wings began to appear.

"My God, they're huge," my mom said. And they really were. The giant caterpillars had fulfilled their promise. The syncathia now looked as if they might be as big a risk to birds by devouring them as poisoning them. Their wings were lined with black and spotted ever so lightly. Each wing came to a gentle point at the end.

"They're gorgeous," Mom said. "I'm sorry. Is it wrong to say they're gorgeous?"

"No," Ron agreed. "Just because something is a disaster doesn't mean it can't be breathtaking."

We watched as they ascended in the early-morning air.

"Now that they can fly, they're really a menace," Ron added. We stood and watched, and for a while no one said anything at all, which in our family was a kind of breathtaking spectacle in and of itself.

It was Ainsley who finally broke our reverie.

"The caterpillars in pupas aren't like chicks in eggs," she said in her little-kid fact-stating voice.

"Yes," Ron said, "that's right."

"Duh," I said.

"It was the caterpillars that hatched from eggs," Ainsley continued, ignoring us.

"Yes," Ron said again.

"Ains, did you swallow an encyclopedia?" I asked and felt Mom swat at the back of my head, but not hard enough to hurt.

"Caterpillar eggs come from butterflies," Ainsley said. "So, the butterflies were already here before. To lay the eggs. But, where did those butterflies come from? And why didn't we see them?"

"That," Ron said, "is quite literally the one-million-dollar question!

What a very perceptive thing for you to ask, Ainsley. Very perceptive indeed."

He went on to explain the work he and his team of grad students would do now, to track the butterflies and figure out how they were seeding themselves so effectively in new environs without being detected, and I felt a burning in my throat from the embarrassment of not having thought to ask the question myself, and also for wanting to have been the one to ask it.

ONE EVENING, later that week, Mom sent me to Western with dinner in a cooler for Ron. He had called to say he'd be working late. Mom didn't want him to go hungry so she packed up his meatloaf and green beans, while telling me some exercise would do me good. I offered a half-hearted complaint. Secretly, I liked going up the hill to the campus. It was just a mile from our house, but the wide courtyards and brick buildings made it feel like it was another world. Plus, the biology building where Ron worked had a hall of gruesomeness that anyone looking for his department was forced to traverse—massive insect collections, pinned snakeskins, and creatures of all kinds in formaldehyde jars. It thrilled me.

When I got to Ron's office, I found him, as usual, leaning on his desk with his face too close to his computer screen.

"Your eyeballs are going to fall out if you keep doing that," I said.

"Hi, Kit! Thanks for bringing this!" He relieved me of the cooler, setting it below his desk without bothering to look at what was inside. It occurred to me that he did not intend to eat. I wondered if Mom knew. In the past, when I'd delivered him food at work, she never asked me, when I returned, if he liked his meal. She only asked if he was there, and was anyone else in his office, and did it look like he was having a good time without her.

"While you're here, would you like to see my northern micro quails?"

"No," I said.

"Come on. You'll like them. They'll nibble grain out of your hand like chickens."

He led me to an unused cubicle. No computer or bookshelves, just a bare desk with a dog crate underneath. Ron bent and opened the crate. He made a series of clicking sounds that it seemed to me a grown-up should be embarrassed to make in front of another person. But whatever he said worked because out of the crate walked three tiny quails, about half the size of any I'd ever seen. They stood on the carpet looking up at us.

"Here," Ron said, producing a handful of loose grain from his pocket.

"You keep bird food in your pants?"

"Usually, yeah."

I bent down and held it out to the quails. As advertised, they ate from my hand.

"I call them Huey, Dewey, and Louie," Ron said. "One of my students found them down by the marina. Most quail species don't migrate, but micros do. They belong in the mountains this time of year. They aren't supposed to be here, ever."

"Not supposed to be here like the syncathia aren't supposed to be here."

"Yeah. I see your point," he said, even though I wasn't trying to make one. "But they aren't likely to disrupt the ecosystem since they don't pose a threat to native animals. In fact, if my student hadn't brought them to the lab they probably would have been eaten by a predator. A great snack for a coyote, or even an ambitious house cat. And you guys are just too cute to be snacks, aren't you?" He petted each quail in turn. I petted them too. They were softer than I thought birds could be.

"Where will they go now?" I asked.

"In the fall I'll take them out to Baker Lake. They gather there on their way south. This has happened before actually. We rescued two micro quails last summer. I tagged them when I released them and they seemed to stick with their normal migration route after that. Hopefully these guys will be able to do the same. Until then, they'll stay here in the lab."

I knew Ron mostly as a dweebish reciter of facts and an embarrassing squasher of bugs. I had not known he was also a rescuer of soft cute birds. Baker Lake wasn't exactly close by. I imagined him in his Subaru, asking the quails what radio station they liked and singing along to songs for them. That was just the dweeby sort of thing he would do. I wanted to tell him I thought it was nice, helping the quails.

Instead I pinched my nose and asked, "Where do they go to the bathroom?"

"In the crate, for the most part. Sometimes on the floor."

I stared at the beige industrial carpet while Rob collected his birds.

"Hey, Kit," he said, "I think I'll call it a day here after all. Let me get my sweater and I'll walk back with you."

"You don't have to," I said. "Mom's not mad, if that's what you're worried about."

"I know."

I did not want his company. I had planned to take my time on the way home, stopping by the gas station mini-mart to replenish my secret bedroom stash of candy and Cokes.

"It's okay if you don't want to be seen with me," Ron added. "I'll stay ten feet behind you the whole way."

I sighed and followed him back to his office for his sweater. He did not bother to retrieve the meatloaf cooler.

Outside, the sun was setting and the sky had turned an exceptional shade of pink, but neither of us remarked on it. Ron kept his eyes on the trees and shrubs, looking for syncathia to swat. Whenever we passed them, he knocked at them with his hands and then stepped on any that fell to the ground.

"I hate this," he said. "I hate being angry at a butterfly. I feel like a child."

"There's worse things to feel like."

I thought he might apologize for demeaning the emotional states of children, but he stayed quiet and toed another butterfly to death.

"Would they kill the little quails if the quails ate them?" I asked.

"Well, micro quails don't feed on bugs this large. They would have trouble getting them into their beaks. But if they could manage it, yes."

I decided I hated *that*. And I was a child, after all.

We were passing a church. Its grounds were ringed with hedges. One of the hedges in particular was covered in syncathia. I looked for something and spotted a cluster of traffic cones in the parking lot. I ran for one and returned to the hedge with it clutched to my chest. Then I swung it like a tennis racket, taking the syncathia from the bush to the ground in stripes. I used the cone to bash them into the sidewalk. It was a real butterfly beatdown.

When I was done, I looked back at Ron, expecting to see the expression of horror adults reserve especially for acts of violence by kids, particularly girl kids. Instead he nodded and went to retrieve a traffic cone of his own.

I pointed to the bush. "They're so dumb. New ones came right back to where I just smashed their friends."

"It's instinct," he said. "You can't fault them for it." Then he used his cone to bash at the bush and squash the fallen. We took turns until the regrouping stopped. Ron put his cone back in the church lot, but I kept mine and two blocks later when we found another bush full up of fluttering blue wings, we repeated the process, passing my cone back and forth. We entered the house sweating and smiling, then retreated to our separate spaces so we wouldn't have to explain to my mom that we'd had a good time.

AFTER THAT, Ron and I went out on butterfly murder walks most nights. I had gone from finding Ron's syncathia-smashing mortifying to looking forward to the thin evening hour when I could engage in it too. I was not bothered by my hypocrisy. I just wanted to crush big beautiful bugs. I kept using the pilfered church traffic cone, though I did try other tools—a flyswatter, a flipper from my snorkel set, Ainsley's Wiffle ball bat. The cone was best.

"What are you two up to?" Mom asked. I had no reason to lie.

"I'm helping Ron with his wildlife genocide."

Mom rolled her eyes—our family's signature response to any and all information for which words might fail us.

"Just make sure you take off your shoes when you come back. I'm tired of cleaning blue goop off the tile."

Ron sometimes tried to make conversation while we walked. He'd ask about school or what I had been watching on TV. I kept my answers minimal. I did not want him thinking that we were friends, or getting all stepdadly. Though sometimes it seemed he did not want to talk either, a heaviness settling over his face as he pummeled syncathia. I wondered if there was more than the butterflies making him sad.

THE CHAMBER OF COMMERCE guy's grand plans for a butterfly festival never came to fruition. By the time Ron and I were taking our nightly walks, everyone else had caught up in seeing the syncathia as a menace. The butterflies descended on gardens like locusts, looking for nectar; they were more than the local flowers could bear. As Ron had promised, bird corpses became a common sight. Swarms of syncathia cruised the city, making walking unpleasant and driving dangerous. A car full of high school students crashed after a cloud of them covered the windshield. One of the boys died. No one could like the syncathia after that. Ron was again interviewed for articles and asked to appear on the news. Now he was treated as an expert, even a local celebrity. He was helping to fight a scourge, and return greatness to our city. Though he confided to us at home that he didn't feel like he was doing any good at all.

"What can regular people do to help?" asked the worried-looking news anchor, leaning closer to him as she spoke. We had gathered in the living room again to watch Ron on TV. He was wearing a tie I'd picked out for him. "This one is your least dweebish," I said, after rifling through his drawers. He rolled his eyes at me, which was how I knew he'd wear it.

"He looks better this time, doesn't he?" I asked.

Mom sneered. "If the anchor bends over any farther, her tits are gonna fall out of that blouse. Who goes on TV like that? Where's her boss?"

The next morning, Ron said he'd be late for dinner because he was speaking to the local Audubon Society, hoping to enlist volunteers to count birds. Mom, instead of offering to send a meatloaf cooler, muttered, "Well I guess we know where your priorities lie."

Ainsley and I began to make plans without being told to. I took inventory of my room—what I would need to pack on my own so Mom wouldn't see, and what was okay for her to help with. One day, I overheard Ainsley talking to a friend at the bus stop, saying she didn't think they would be in the same class in the fall, because she might have to switch schools again. We didn't know the details of what was happening between Mom and Ron. We didn't need to. As Ainsley once put it, "I wish she didn't have to fight with everyone all the time."

One Saturday morning, Ron knocked on my bedroom door to tell me he was going to his office to feed the quails. Did I want to come with him? I sneered and said no.

"Are you sure? I thought we might—" But I cut him off, claiming I was busy with homework, even though I was obviously just reading a magazine.

The following evening we were out on our regular butterfly-killing spree when Ron pointed out the futility of our efforts.

"Kit, cathartic as this may be, it's not actually productive," he said.

There were too many butterflies, he explained. Squishing a hundred or so a night was a drop in the bucket. Not even that.

"So you're saying we need to find a way to kill them more efficiently? More killing and faster killing?"

"Ultimately, yes," Ron said.

I knew exactly what he meant. "Have you considered something like in the end of the movie *Fargo*?"

Ron asked who'd allowed me to watch *Fargo*.

"One of Mom's old boyfriends, before you," I said. "If we could get the butterflies to fly into a wood chipper, that would kill a bunch all at once. Like a giant, ongoing garbage disposal."

Ron nodded. "It's a good idea. You're a very creative thinker, Kit. You know that?"

Ron was on TV again the next day. But this time I was the only one in the living room, and when I shouted, "Okay, he's on!" neither Ainsley nor Mom emerged to join me.

It was for the best. The busty anchor was leaning precariously close again. She was asking about management of the butterflies, by which she really meant eradication. Why couldn't the city just bring in truckloads of pesticides and be done with them? Ron explained that anything that would poison the butterflies would also poison native insects, which we wanted to keep around.

"Any attempts at destroying them needs to be manual, not chemical," he said. "Which is what makes it so difficult. I only wish we had some sort of giant butterfly-chopping gyre we could push them all into."

The busty anchor laughed at this, but I didn't think it was a joke. He'd said my idea on TV, in front of adults. Which meant he must have thought it was pretty great after all.

I started to draw up blueprints. At the school library, I copied pictures of what I imagined to be similarly shaped contraptions—cement mixers and snow machines. I worked on them mostly during English class, which I hated. The final product was a three-paneled drawing depicting the butterfly mulcher from the front, side, and back, with butterflies going in one end and coming out the other as blue confetti. I swiped a manila envelope from the school secretary's desk to keep it crisp in my backpack for the walk home. But there was no need. Mom met me at the end of the block, where the baseball backstop edged the street and I always dragged my fingers across the chain link as I walked by. She was leaning against the side of her car. I could see Ainsley in the back, a big duffel bag and three pillows piled beside her.

"Get in," Mom said. "We're going to Aunt Stella's for the night."

I didn't roll my eyes or say anything smart. I got in the passenger seat, then turned to my sister. "You okay?"

"Yeah. She remembered Wolfie and Greenie," she said, gesturing to a pair of stuffed dogs in her lap, her favorites.

Aunt Stella lived in an apartment complex where all the buildings looked the same. The guest room had just one bed, which Mom and Ainsley shared, while I slept on the living room couch. After three days, Ainsley, over dinner, asked a question I'd been too afraid to. "Are you and Ron just having an argument? Or is this for real?"

"It's for real," Mom huffed, then, looking around the table, she asked, "Don't you girls know me at all?"

In the evenings, I continued my habit of butterfly smashing. But now I concentrated on quality, not quantity. How big of a butterfly smear could I make on the sidewalk? How deep of a blue might I create if I were to, say, stack several butterfly bodies on top of each other and pulverize their sparkling wings with a rock?

At school, I revised my original chipper drawing by adding a funnel and a vat, to safely collect the chopped-up butterfly parts for disposal. Then I moved on to inventing other mechanisms: a robotic arm that would catch butterflies out of the air and pull their wings off; a thousand tiny butterfly guillotines all operated simultaneously by a single string; a giant double boiler for butterfly melting. I put these drawings, along with short written explanations, into an envelope and mailed them to Ron's house. I knew my creations were impractical—fantastical, even. But I wanted Ron to know I was still working on the butterfly problem. I thought maybe he'd respond with his own drawings. I thought maybe he'd find a way to mention one of my ideas on the news again.

IT WAS SEPTEMBER when he finally wrote me back. The butterflies were gone by then, having migrated off to whatever city they would terrorize for winter. He thanked me for what he called "all your ingenious gadgets," and said he hoped I would continue to pursue my interest in the sciences and engineering. I was not aware that I had any such interests. Though after reading his words, I thought I might.

"I'm driving the quails down to Baker Lake to release them next week," he wrote. "Hoping they will find their right path from there."

This was at the bottom of the page and I imagined, as I flipped it over, I might see another sentence inviting me to join him on this excursion. There was only a quick line about wishing me, Ainsley, and our mom all the best and then his signature.

The syncathia did not return, not the next year or the year after. Other awful things happened. But never the butterflies. I wondered if Ron ever found out why. By the time I was a biology student at Western, walking the hallway of animal horrors each day, he was gone, having taken a position elsewhere. I tried to write an essay about him once for an English class (which I still hated), and I intended at first to make it nice. Something about him helping me find my "right path" like he'd wanted to do for the lost quail trio. It didn't land. So I talked instead about how he'd shown me not all problems can be solved. Sometimes, they can only be stomped on, ground up, and dismembered. Sometimes our anger, impotent and consuming, is the best we can offer.

Winter Animals

In the glade, as promised, the jays seemed mournful. They dotted the pine trees, flashes of blue like Christmas ornaments. Bea looked up, but it was difficult to focus her eyes on anything in particular. The green trees and the blue birds and the blue sky all mushed to a turquoise mosaic. She looked at Edgar instead. His facial expression was inscrutable; he gave no clues to how she was supposed to feel. They were sitting together at the base of a tree, legs in front of them with feet tipped to the side from the weight of their snow boots. Objectively, she knew the birds were not crying. But it was impossible to uncouple a sound so familiar from sorrow.

"Why are there so many of them?" she asked.

"I don't know," Edgar said. "They just started coming here."

"Why are they squawking like that?"

"They're sad, I guess."

"Or maybe it's just the noise they always make."

Edgar wiggled his feet back and forth. He reached into his boot to scratch his ankle. Bea looked up again.

"Is it us they're sad about?"

"No. They cry even when no one's here."

"How could you possibly know that?"

"My dad told me."

This seemed to Bea a child's answer. If he had been a boy from school, she would have teased him for it.

"Will they poop on us?" she asked.

"Maybe."

"Have they pooped on you before?"

"Yeah."

"I don't want to get pooped on."

She stood up. Edgar stayed on the ground. The glade was a circle and each direction looked the same to Bea. She wasn't sure which they'd entered from. She didn't want to embarrass herself by picking wrong.

Finally, Edgar stood too.

"I'm bored," he said. "Come on. I'll show you something else."

BEA WAS ELEVEN. Edgar was thirteen. Bea had known Edgar her whole life, according to her parents. Though Edgar had moved away from Spokane, to the mountain town of Winthrop, when Bea was in preschool. The families saw each other once every year or two now, a lifetime in childhood. On those occasions, Bea and Edgar were reminded that they were friends and sent to go play, which they always did. This day at Edgar's house was no different. They ate handfuls of salt-and-vinegar chips in the kitchen. Edgar showed her his sketchbook. The drawings were of animals mostly, some geodes and some dirt bikes. Then he suggested the jays. Bea and Edgar each had a sibling. Edgar's sister was out somewhere. Bea always thought fondly of the older girl who had once, when Bea was in first grade, showed her how to paint her nails and put on lipstick. Now this sister was grown-up enough to be excused from family social gatherings, allowed to leave with her real friends for the day. Bea's little brother didn't want to go outside. He claimed it was too cold, and instead burrowed himself into a recliner with his chapter book and stuffed alligator.

But it was not so cold at all. It was the end of February and though the snow was thick on the ground, the air felt fine. It was sunny. Edgar and Bea had shed their jackets and hats, leaving them draped over the fence at the edge of Edgar's family's property. Bea's snow pants were purple and she was embarrassed by them because they were the bib kind, which she thought were for little kids. Edgar wore the same, only black.

THE SOUND of the birds drained into the distance. Edgar walked fast through the woods but Bea didn't mind. She also liked to move quickly if she had somewhere to go. They had already kissed once. As soon as they'd gotten out of the house, Edgar asked her if they could and Bea said yes. She was very curious about kissing. She'd done some kissing before, with her best friend from school, Anna, and a boy, Perry, who lived in her neighborhood. Those kisses had been like a game, and ended in laughter. Edgar did not laugh when he kissed her. He looked at her very seriously and took her face in his hands. He was an older boy. Bea's mom had advised her of that on the car ride to Winthrop. *Use your best judgment. He's an older boy.*

Edgar led her to a creek, and when they reached its sloped bank, he dropped down to his knees.

"It's a beaver dam," he said, pointing.

"Where are the beavers?"

"They're around. There's a whole family, I think. I saw babies last year. They were really cute."

Bea studied the dam, branches in a muddy tumble in the middle of the water. It looked like a mess that needed to be cleaned up.

"Do you want to see a dead one?" Edgar pointed downstream. "Inside that log. You have to climb on top of it to see."

It felt like a dare. Bea scooted down the bank to the water, then trudged to the log. When she looked back, Edgar was still on his knees. She'd thought he would follow.

"You have to walk out to the middle!" he called.

The log was slick. The creek was still icy at its edges. Bea didn't want to fall in. She also didn't want Edgar to think she was afraid. She put her hands on the cold, wet log, climbed up, then inched forward. As promised, the middle of the log was broken open. She looked inside and saw a curled animal form. She would have assumed it was sleeping. She shuffled backward until she reached the shore. Walked back to Edgar. She wondered how he'd found the dead beaver in the first place.

"I bet it's nice to come to this creek in the summer," Bea said. "I'd swim in it every day in the summer, if I lived here."

"Not every day, you wouldn't," Edgar said. "Last year we had to evacuate."

"How come?"

"A fire got too close," he said, pointing past her. "There was an even bigger one somewhere else. When we were allowed to come back home, the sky was still orange."

"That happens at my house too in the summer. The smoke, I mean."

"Not like this, I bet. It blocked out the sun practically, like an eclipse. You could look directly at the sun and it wouldn't hurt your eyes."

Bea shrugged. "I hate it. Everything gets canceled. Swim team, camp, soccer."

"Yeah, it's pretty fucked," Edgar said.

She liked that he agreed with her. She knew it was a petty gift, and one she should not covet. Still, she felt the muscles in her cheeks wanting to smile.

"Do you want to kiss again?" she asked.

Edgar looked away. "I know of something else dead if you want to see it."

"What?"

"An elk."

"Who's killing all these animals?"

"Nobody. They're just dead."

"Is it far?" Bea asked.

Edgar said it wasn't.

BEYOND THE CREEK, the trees fell away. Bea and Edgar walked through a field of snow.

"Is this for wheat?" Bea asked, thinking of the vast open expanses to the south of her own home.

"It's for nothing," Edgar said. "The trees just don't grow here."

There was a long dune of snow to their right. It was crusted with ice. In the city, on the side of the road, she would have called it a berm. The plows made them as they pushed snow from the middle of the street.

"What causes this?" Bea asked Edgar, pointing.

"Snow," he said.

"Is there anything you actually *do* want to talk about?" she asked. She was mad he hadn't wanted to kiss again.

"I'm thinking about majoring in geology in college."

"Are you even in high school?"

"Eighth grade."

"That's cool. So why does the snow get pushed up like this, then?"

"That doesn't have anything to do with geology. Geology is the study of rocks."

"Is it the wind?" Bea guessed.

"Yes, it's the wind."

Edgar climbed up the snow dune and began to walk along its spine, his arms wide for balance. He looked in front of him and down to his feet like he was concentrating very hard. Bea thought he was trying to show off, to prove himself a daredevil. The dune was only as high as her chest. The icy log she had traversed to see the beaver was riskier, she thought.

"You want to try?" Edgar asked.

She dug the toe of her boot into the snow and scrambled up. Right away, she saw that she had misjudged the situation. They were not in the middle of a field at all. They were on a ridge, at the edge of the tree line. The snow from the dune was blocking her view of a steep hill that tumbled into a glen, with another creek at the bottom. To walk the spine of the dune was to walk the edge of this cliff. Or, not quite a cliff, a slope. But an edge nonetheless. She looked to Edgar and could tell he was proud of himself for this surprise.

"Do you want to hold on to my hand?" He offered his fingers to her.

Bea shook her head. "I'm okay."

Edgar started walking again, one foot in front of the other. Bea followed, trying to match her steps to his boot prints. She imagined these tracks would hold her feet, snug and secure in each groove. This was not the case.

They'd gone fifty yards this way when Edgar's foot slipped. Just for an instant. He did a little hop step and righted himself. The motion startled Bea from her boot-track reverie. She stepped not into

Edgar's next print, but to the side of it. She felt the snow slide out from under her. It went slowly at first, a gravelly crackle of ice, then faster, and she went down with it, her right leg in the lead. *Plunging* was the word that came to her mind. She clawed with her fingers, trying to slow herself. She did not think to scream.

Her foot hit something. It seemed to grab her and her whole body twisted so she was parallel to the creek below. She rolled over once, spread her hands out again, and this time she was able to stop sliding. She held very still. Hurt people are supposed to hold still. She had heard that before. She called out for Edgar, but nothing came back.

She decided she didn't want to be still anymore. She pushed up to her hands and knees. The hill was steep and slick. She could see the thing that had stopped her descent—a branch sticking out of the snow. She shuffle-scramble-crawled toward it. Once she got hold, she was able to pull herself up to standing. Her right leg hurt. Her hands burned from scaping bare along the ice. Dirt and ice were pushed up under her fingernails. She estimated that she'd fallen about halfway down the slope.

The woods below her looked different from those above. The trees were bare. She had taken them at first for deciduous but they were pines like all the rest, only burned. This was where Edgar had pointed from the creek. Had he meant to bring her here, to show her this too? No. He had kept his eyes on the ground as he walked, she remembered. It seemed a mean place, though she knew it held no heat. The fire had come and gone.

BEA LOOKED UP the hill again and saw a gravelly scar in the snow. *Deer trail.* Though she didn't know if it was really something deer used. She could use it. She shuffled from her branch and started to climb, keeping her eyes only on her feet until she reached the top.

Edgar wasn't there.

He went to get help, she thought. She wished he hadn't, though she understood. It must have looked bad, the way she fell and then did not move. They were told also to go get help when someone was hurt. *Stay still. Go get help. Use your best judgment.*

"Edgar," she called again, but not very loudly. It was more of a gesture.

She sat down in the snow to wait. When you are lost, you're supposed to stay where you are. That was another thing.

She wished she was with Anna. Anna was the waiting sort. She was good at that. Not the kind to move quickly just to move, or the kind who asked to kiss. Anna waited to be kissed. She was funny, and would have funny things to say about Edgar, now that he was out of earshot. They would agree he was not so cute as he thought he was, or so brave. Anna would call him a practice boy. *You can practice kissing him, but not for real. Ew.*

But Anna would not have wanted to go into the woods in the first place. Never would have been interested in crying birds, a dead beaver, a dead elk.

Bea had been out with Edgar alone. They'd told their parents they were going to the glade with the jays. That seemed to her a long way from where she was now.

She wondered about the elk. She would have liked to see it after all.

Bea stood up again. She wedged her arms into the bib of her snow pants. She wished for her jacket and also her hat with the little puff ball on the top. Her mittens were in the pocket of her jacket. The sun had moved below the treetops and she was cold. It would get dark. Even if she knew where she was going, it might still be dark by the time she got back to Edgar's house. She started walking.

The dune and ridge had been to their right on the way. She put them to her left now.

BEA THOUGHT SHE KNEW all the awful things that could happen to a person. She had accumulated this information gradually, as children do. She did not remember a time before she understood death, but her parents had a cute story about it. Bea was three, playing with a dead worm, and had said something like *Wormy is so sleepy today.* Her mother had taken the opportunity to gently explain. Small Bea, unfazed, had carried on with her game, simply changing her narration to *Wormy is so deady today.* She understood now, of course, that horrors took many forms beyond a sleep one does not wake from, that death is not just something that happens to the dead person.

She knew two other children who had died. One was a boy from her school who was hit by a car. He wasn't in her grade. She didn't remember if she'd ever talked to him. She could picture his face, but she wondered if the memory was only from the photo that adorned the hallway beside his old classroom. Every time she saw that photo, it knocked the breath from her lungs.

The other was the daughter of one of her mom's friends. She had only met the girl twice, once before she got sick and once after, when her hair was gone from chemo. Bea's mom had talked of her often as her cancer got worse. It seemed obscene to Bea, that she should know so much of this girl, things that were so sad about her. She wouldn't want people to know those things about her, if she was dying. Then the girl really had died. Bea's mom went to the funeral but she did not offer to take Bea and Bea felt something had been denied her.

WALKING HELPED BEA FEEL warmer. She pulled her arms out of her snowsuit bib. The scrapes on her hands stung. She decided that when she reached the end of the snow dune, she would look for her own boot tracks, try to pick them from all the other pocks and ruts in the melting snow. She would follow the tracks through the forest to the creek. She would keep the creek to her right until she got to the dead beaver log. If it became difficult to discern her tracks, she would guess the distance. Count five hundred steps and turn up the hill. The hill would lead her to the glade. She would hear the jays cry if they really did cry all the time. She would not lose the path in the middle, would not be deceived by the ring of identical trees. She would follow it straight back to Edgar's house, where their jackets would still be on the fence. She'd open the gate, fumbling for the latch in the near-dark. She'd see flashlights switching on just past the house, hear the sounds of worried voices before she could make out the words. She'd call to them and see the lights coming toward her. Hear Edgar's dad shout, "There you guys are! We were about to come looking. Where have you two been?"

Then Bea would say it was only her.

WOULD SHE BE ALLOWED to attend Edgar's funeral? He was her friend, after all. Her parents reminded her each time they visited. *Your friend. Go play with your friend.* She was the last person to see him. Surely. Surely, this time she would be allowed to know.

She had not cried, not from the fall or the climb back up, or the walk through the darkening woods, not until she was inside the house, at the kitchen table with a blanket over her shoulders, her parents' anxious faces pressed close. Their lives could have been ruined.

They were all being so patient, asking her gently what had happened—where had she and Edgar gone? Edgar's mother was on the phone, calling neighbors. His father had a map, showing Bea the house and various creeks. *This way? This way?*

"I don't know," Bea said. He seemed so scared and she couldn't bear it. "I could take you. Once I stop shaking, I can take you." Her own parents said *No.* Her brother cowered in the doorway with his alligator until Bea waved to him and he came over, handed her the stuffed animal, then climbed onto her lap and cried too.

Edgar's dad had put on his gloves and taken up his flashlight again, heading for the door, when his phone rang. Bea felt herself suck in her breath. They all must have. It was that kind of quiet in the room.

"Hello," he said, in a flat way, as if he did not trust even this one word. Then he listened and still no one breathed. It seemed like such a long time. "So he's there? He's there right now?" he said finally and Bea felt herself go light, a human balloon, she held to her blanket and the alligator, willing them to keep her in place.

The phone call went on a long time. Why wouldn't he just hang up and tell them what had happened? But his tone had changed. It was just a conversation, like friends talking, like the grown-ups had been that afternoon before Edgar asked Bea if she wanted to see the jays, if she wanted to kiss, if she wanted to see dead things, if she wanted to walk the dune.

"Okay, thank you. We'll see you tomorrow." Then he finally did put the phone back in his pocket.

"He's safe," Edgar's dad said, turning to his wife. "He's at the Platts'. Joel said the boys want to have a sleepover, so he was asking if it was all right for Edgar to spend the night. He didn't even know anything was wrong. They'll bring him back in the morning."

"The Platts'? How did he get all the way to town?"

Edgar's dad shrugged. He took off his boots and gloves and sat across from Bea at the table. "I'm sorry," he whispered to her. Then, to her parents, he explained that Gabe Platt was Edgar's best friend from school. The boys were regulars at each other's houses. In fact, Edgar had asked that morning for a ride to Gabe's and had to be reminded that he had a guest of his own arriving.

Bea's mom went to Edgar's mom and hugged her. Edgar's mom let out a loud sigh. The adults began making dinner. Bea was offered a shower, followed by hot chocolate. After dinner, she went to Edgar's room under the auspice of picking out a board game. She opened his dresser drawers, touched his clothes, rifled through plastic bins containing action figures and sports equipment. She found more sketchbooks and looked through them. Some had words like a journal, but these were mostly an accounting of what was drawn. She was looking for something about her. Of course there was nothing. He hadn't been thinking about her before at all.

She found a checkers board in his closet. She and her brother played three games, then went to bed at the same time. She did not want to be alone with the adults, who seemed to be having a really nice night, talking amicably and laughing, like they always did. Her leg still hurt, but she didn't tell. She did not want to make this about her leg. In the dark, under the blankets, she picked dirt still lodged under her fingernails, clods like small pebbles. She would have to cut her nails to get it all out, she thought. Again, she felt denied something.

In the morning, she and her brother and parents packed the car and drove back to Spokane. Edgar was not yet home from his sleep-over when they left. There were hugs all around and Edgar's dad said again, "Bea, we're so very sorry about yesterday," but there was no gravity to his words. Her own parents waved as they pulled out of the long driveway and onto the forest road.

SHE SAW EDGAR'S PARENTS just twice more during her youth, though never Edgar. Once, they met for a weekend at a ski resort, but Edgar was on a school trip. A couple of years after that, Bea and her family returned to Edgar's house. By then he was old enough, as his sister had been the previous occasions, to come and go unquestioned. He was an honors student with a college scholarship on the horizon. He had a car, purchased with his own money from his own job. On each of these visits, the families cheerfully recounted the tale of Bea's accident, her heroic survival, her abandonment by the mercurial adolescent Edgar. As if it was so long ago, as if they were different people who such a thing could never happen to again. In her adult years, Bea too would tell the story like a comedy of errors, of the hapless grown-ups who presumed cocoa and checkers could make up for being left for dead in the woods. Sometimes she mentioned the elk, how the real tragedy was that she did not get to see the thing she had been promised. That part never seemed as funny to other people, and she wanted the story to be funny. After all, she did not go to Edgar's funeral, and he did not go to hers. But she could never shake the feeling. They had come to a precipice together, all of them. She was the only one who did not walk away.

Egret

Ruby maintained that the accident happened not because she was drunk, but because she so very badly needed to pee. She *was* drunk. She didn't deny that. The arresting officer told her she blew a 0.12 on the Breathalyzer, and she believed him. That sounded about right to her, she agreed at the time, though she knew, vaguely, she should not be talking. There were rules about that—to remain silent, to have a lawyer present, to not just agree with whoever says you've done a crime. But she felt bad. Col. Mustard was dead. That was clear right away. Still, she had this sense, in the moment, that if she could be pleasant and helpful, she might be able to set things right.

She had been out with old friends from high school. They'd started at a restaurant, then they'd gone to a bar, then a party at another former classmate's house. Ruby did not know this other person well, hadn't been to the house before. When she thought back, she remembered she'd already had to pee when she got there, had even looked around for the bathroom but there was a line and she was caught up in conversation as soon as she walked in the door anyway, which was something that always happened to Ruby. She thought she'd wait for the bathroom after she finished what she was saying, after she'd finished her drink. But then her friends said they were bored and tired and so she left too, forgetting, until she was already driving, that she needed to pee.

"I can make it," she assured herself. Home was only two miles away.

The situation was more dire than she realized. She shimmied in her seat, clenched her pelvic muscles, and pleaded with her bladder not to explode. She didn't know if this was a thing that could really happen but she remembered her eleventh-grade physics teacher telling the class it was how the Danish astronomer Tycho Brahe had died. She did not want to go out like Brahe. She also did not want to piss herself. She refused to stop before she got home. She was so close.

She was going too fast when she turned off 395. And still too fast when she made a second left a half mile later onto her own street. She was uncomfortable and distracted and the wheel slipped from her hands, lurching the car to the right. Her foot found the brake but not before she'd punched through the low wooden fence of Danny and Willow Klein, the couple who'd lived at the end of the block for what Ruby assumed was their entire lives.

This all would have been embarrassing, but not so bad, except that moments before Ruby's accident, Willow had let her dog, a sweet-tempered and gloriously curly-furred Bernedoodle, out to relieve himself one last time before bed, which he was doing on the fence when Ruby came through it. The irony of this did not escape Ruby.

She didn't know the dog was there until Willow screamed from the porch. Later, Ruby would learn that Willow's screams were for both the crushed Col. Mustard and also Ruby herself. Willow had assumed her critically injured, the way she flopped unmoving over the steering wheel. Ruby wasn't hurt, only catatonic from the surprise of it all. She stayed like that until the police, and an unnecessary ambulance, arrived.

The worst part was, though her own house was just three doors away, the police wouldn't let Ruby leave the scene. When she finally did get out of her car, she had to ask the Kleins if she could use their bathroom. At the edge of the vanity was a small framed photo of Col. Mustard as a puppy, sitting fluffily in a field of tulips. They really loved that dog.

NO ONE HAD EVER suggested to Ruby that she might have a problem with alcohol. What Ruby had a problem with was taking everything too far. Ruby could not have just a little fun. Ruby could not back down from a fight. Ruby could not jog just three or four miles. Ruby struggled with speed limits, overdraft fees, page counts, and any game that required use of a sand timer. She was twenty-two, a recent college graduate, living back home with her family for the summer.

Her parents, Jenna and Troy, were very understanding about the accident. They offered to pay for the Kleins' fence, and to drive Ruby to essential engagements, like work and court, until she got her license back. Ruby convinced herself this kindness was really an act of financial pragmatism. She was starting law school in the fall, and any money she had was already earmarked for tuition. If she paid for the fence, her parents would end up footing some other bill later in the year. Her education was too important to them, she reasoned; they would not let her squander it on a night of stupidity. So, they swept up her mess for her.

“But what’s actually going on?” her mom asked as her dad stood by with his brow furrowed. A unified front of worry.

“Nothing’s going on,” Ruby insisted. “I just really needed to pee.”

Whether they believed her or not, they let it go after that. The fight had already been worn out of them that year.

HER BROTHER OFFERED to resurrect the dog. But first, he wanted to make jokes.

“I bet it was the best pee of your life,” Nicholas said. Ruby agreed this was true. She’d had to flip over the little framed Col. Mustard picture, could not meet his puppy eyes and pull down her pants at the same time. But after that, it had been an exquisite pee.

“Absolutely transcendent. I would have stayed in that bathroom forever if I could.”

“Truly a moment to savor and to treasure.

“Poor pup, though,” he added, his voice lower. Then, quickly, as if he had forgotten himself, “Sorry.”

Ruby felt her guilt, which had many facets, swell again. Guilt was another thing she often took too far.

“Should I get them a new puppy?” she asked. “We could go to the shelter and see if they have anything cute.”

“I think a puppy would be a distraction. Grief isn’t aided by distraction.”

“Maybe a houseplant?”

“What if I brought Col. Mustard back from the dead?” Nicholas asked.

“How?”

“With magic!” He waved his hands in front of her face like *abracadabra*. She swatted him away.

"Okay," she agreed. "We probably should get a puppy for Mom and Dad, though, right?"

"That's the best idea anyone in this family has had in a long time."

THEY HAD ANOTHER BROTHER. Jace, Nicholas's twin, had moved out ten months prior, decamping not for college, but abruptly and angrily for Denmark. He'd spent nearly a year preparing in secret for his departure, working every day after school his senior year bagging groceries, squirreling money away. Then, once he'd laid his plans—bought his nonrefundable plane ticket, given away most of his stuff to friends, posted an essay on the forum Climate Justice: Action and Accountability Now! about his decision, which earned thirteen hundred likes and two hundred comments along the lines of "fuck yeah, man!"—he begged Ruby and Nicholas and their parents to come with him.

Their dad had been furious. "You want us to just pick up and go? Our lives are here. Our jobs are here. Our home."

"What good do you think your jobs are going to be if your home burns down?" Jace said. "What kind of lives do you really think you're going to be living in five years, ten years? Have you been outside today? We can't even fucking breathe here."

And it was true what he said; the smoke was bad that day, Ruby remembered, that whole summer. But it was Spokane, her parents argued, and the fires would not reach the city, the sea too far away to rise, the latitude too high for extreme heat. The mountains nearest them too low to melt. It was a safe place.

Nicholas and Ruby had said nothing. Which someone might have pointed out as a once-in-a-millennium family record, if they were in a joking mood.

That was in August. He left in September, alone.

NICHOLAS GOT A PEN and a sheet of notepaper, which he labeled *Supplies Needed.* On the first line, he wrote, *Item 1: Puppy for mom & dad to distract from grief about their kid who is not dead, just moved out.*

"You know, Dad's actually more of a reptile person," Ruby said. "Should we consider a turtle instead?"

Nicholas dismissed this. "There's no therapeutic value in turtles. That's a known fact."

Item 2: Supplies for reanimating dead dog—river water; a bunch of pine needles; fur from a different, but similar dog; beer.

"I don't think I should be buying you beer right now," Ruby said, "given the nature of my current trouble."

"It's not for me. It's for Col. Mustard."

"Is there a religious component to this?" Ruby asked.

"Good question!" Then he wrote, *Buddha statue; Old & New Testaments; holy water (do not mix with river water!); kosher salt; halal meats.*

"Are those all the religious things you know about?"

"Pretty much."

As they sat hunched over their list, Jenna came in, home from work.

"What are you two up to?" she asked.

Nicholas shooed her away with a flick of his hand. "Top secret. Out, out."

"Oh, I do love to see you kids hatching schemes together," she said, giving them each a shoulder squeeze before retreating to the den.

Ruby gestured to the pen. "Item three: scheme more often—it makes Mom happy."

JENNA HAD ONCE DESCRIBED Ruby and the twins as the crew of Apollo 11. Ruby and Nicholas were Buzz Aldrin and Neil Armstrong, boldly exploring a new world in search of thrills and accolades, making grandiose pronouncements and inside jokes the whole time. Jace was Michael Collins, who stayed inside the space capsule, alone and silent as it passed around the dark side, losing contact with his colleagues on the moon and on Earth. In interviews afterward, Collins said he'd liked it, the quiet and the waiting.

"Every crew's got to have its likes-to-wait-in-the-dark guy," Nicholas had laughed.

"They'd have died without him," Jenna continued. "If he didn't make it back around, they had no way to return home."

There'd been a time when they were little when they'd played astronauts every day. They called their backyard playhouse a space shuttle and took turns piloting missions, directing the other two on space walks, alien encounters, and vital quests of discovery. There was a three-year age gap between her and the boys, but Ruby had no memories of the time before her brothers. They were her first friends, and for many years she could not tell the difference between the two of them, or between herself and them. They'd been a clump of children, a hydra. It was only in adolescence that she had separated from them, popping fully formed into the world on her own: The loud one! The girl! Still, it was a long time before she recognized her brothers as entities separate from each other. If she was honest, maybe not until a very specific moment her senior year of high school. The twins were just starting as freshmen, and on the first morning of the new school year a teammate of Ruby's from cross country had seen her talking to Nicholas.

"Is that your brother?" the girl had asked. When Ruby nodded, she said, "Oh my, baby heartthrob!" and clutched her chest.

Ruby stuck out her tongue. "That one too," she said, pointing to Jace. The girl, in turn, stuck out her tongue to match Ruby's.

This was confusing because the boys were identical. Nicholas had some semblance of a haircut, while Jace kept his long and ragged. Otherwise, same face, same blue eyes, same laugh—when Jace chose to laugh, which was less often than Nicholas. But no one in human history had ever laughed as much as Nicholas. This, Ruby felt, was ultimately what her friend, and eventually the whole rest of the world, picked up on. Nicholas was the twin who wanted to have a good time, and who wanted everyone else to have a good time too.

Jace wanted the part of the moon where no one would bother him.

They'd all been close in those teen years too. Ruby hadn't really gone away for college, only to Eastern Washington University, the commuter school fifteen miles outside Spokane. She came home most weekends, and some weeknights just for dinner. Her family wasn't perfect; she never said *perfect*. But they were loving, and they were fun, and everyone had their special role, which was even better than being a giant kid hydra, if you really thought about it.

JACE HAD PULLED THEM all apart with the argument, which did not start the day he announced he was moving to Denmark, and did not end when no one wanted to go with him. He hadn't expected them to go, obviously. That was why he'd kept his plans to himself for so long. It was a "tactic," Troy said, something Jace had learned from his "friends" online in order to make a point. Troy used air quotes when he said *tactic* and *friends*. He'd been so angry, and could not help showing his anger when he talked about Jace's decision to leave. This surprised Ruby. While Jenna was prone to mild unpredictability and had a streak of taking-things-too-far herself, Troy was always unflappable. So, whatever its origin, Jace's *tactic* had worked.

They were not safe in Spokane, Jace said. "Seattle thought they were safe. All those lists, top-ten climate-proof cities! Remember?"

Ruby did not remember. She had never read any such lists, never thought to seek out that information.

"The truth is, nowhere in the US is safe, except maybe Traverse City, Michigan. But that's only half the problem. The US is a criminal polluter. *Crim-in-al.* Someday, when The Hague gets its priorities straight, American politicians and businesspeople are going to be hauled into court by the dozens for what they've done, what they're still doing. Anyone living below the poverty line in this country is a victim of those crimes, not to mention basically everyone living in developing nations. Anyone making more than a hundred and fifty thousand a year is inherently a perpetrator."

"I don't think that's fair to me and your mother," Troy said. "We try to be good stewards of the earth, to the best of our abilities."

"I know you do. That's what makes this so sad," Jace said.

"We recycle, we compost, we got rid of all the grass in the front yard and replaced it with those pollinator-friendly flowers. You helped your mom plant the seeds, remember?"

"Those flowers were non-native and died."

"Still, it's drought-tolerant out there now. And we always earmark a portion of our charitable giving for environmental causes. I drove a Prius before practically anyone went hybrid or electric."

"Your charitable givings—where are they going, specifically? Do you have names? Dollar amounts?"

"I can look it up for you. My point is, we aren't criminals. We're people living our lives and trying to do our best."

"And my point is, you're both. It's systemic. Systemic environmental violence. To live here is to knowingly participate in it."

"Come off it, Jace," Ruby had heard herself say. "You make Mom drive you everywhere. At least Nicholas rides a bike."

"Well, in Copenhagen everyone rides a bike," he said. "So I guess I'll learn."

RUBY AND NICHOLAS RODE their bikes first to the convenience store, where Ruby bought them a six-pack, even though she'd said she wasn't going to. Nicholas nestled the bottles gently into his messenger bag. Then they went to the river. They sat on rocks at the water's edge and drank the beers. They filled the bottles with river water and hammered the lids back into place and put the bottles back into the messenger bag. The afternoon nothingness stretched cruelly in front of them. Ruby was working part-time for the summer at an antique shop owned by a family friend, but the man was out of town for the week and the shop closed. She had two more months before school started. She felt itchy for the next thing to begin. A career in law seemed like a natural outlet for her too-muchness. She envisioned herself in a socially conscious specialty, like immigration or labor. Maybe even something to do with the environment. Ruby wanted, more than anything, to be of use. Since the accident, guilt and shame bubbled up whenever her mind was unoccupied.

Nicholas, unburdened, had no summer job. He seemed content to mark time until he returned for his second year of community college, where he was majoring in nothing in particular.

"Let's ride downtown," Ruby said. "Or into Little Seattle. We could do karaoke."

"Only sociopaths do karaoke in the daytime," Nicholas said. "Besides, these bottles are going to leak. Let's go home."

When they got back to the house, Ruby followed Nicholas inside and up to the twins' bedroom, where he arranged the bottles on the windowsill.

"Do you remember in elementary school, looking at river water samples under a microscope?" he asked.

Ruby said yes. She always liked the look-at-things-under-the-microscope projects.

"Do you think they're all still there, the little squirmy guys?"

"The protozoans? Why wouldn't they be?"

"I read this article. No one's seen a beaver on the Spokane River in three years. I just wondered what else was gone."

"They're still there," Ruby said. "We'd know if they weren't. There would have been another article."

Though she hadn't known about the beavers.

Nicholas moved the bottles closer together, a glass wall. Sunlight pushed through them, creating amber shadows.

"Pretty," Nicholas said, his hands on his hips like he'd accomplished something.

"We forgot pine needles," Ruby said. "That was stupid. They were all around us."

"We can ride back tomorrow," Nicholas said.

Did she believe he could make a dog out of water and tree droppings and fur and Bibles and whatever? It didn't matter. She left the twins' room and went to the kitchen in search of something to maintain her buzz. All she found was a bottle of her mom's chardonnay in the fridge. It was already two-thirds empty. She allowed herself a small pour, then put the rest back. Not because she didn't want Jenna to know she'd been drinking in the middle of the day but because she didn't want to deprive her mom of a glass of wine when she got home. Jenna worked hard. Ruby thought she deserved nice things. Her dad too. Together, they'd made a safe and sweet life for their kids. Ruby loved that.

It was what made her mad about what Jace had done. She didn't think he was wrong in the things he'd said. But the way he'd turned it all back on them, on their family, making them doubt the way they lived. When they'd been so happy. When he'd lived his whole safe and sweet and happy life that way.

After the argument where Ruby accused Jace of insufficient bike riding, Nicholas had taken her aside.

"Can you not do that?" he asked.

"Not do what?"

"Not get involved in their thing?"

"Isn't it our thing too?"

"It doesn't have to be," he said. "I don't want Jace to think we're not on his side."

"I'm not on his side," Ruby said, then regretted it.

"You're right," she said. "I'll keep my opinions to myself."

Nicholas had thanked her but the damage was done. After that, he would not confide in her about Jace; not about anything important. She had proved herself untrustworthy. They weren't fighting, she and Nicholas. There was just this gap between them, a Jace-spaced hole. Ruby wondered what Nicholas might have liked to say about their brother but didn't.

NICHOLAS WOKE HER in the morning.

"Come on, we've got to get there early before they sell out of all the good stuff," he said.

When she asked where, he wouldn't say. She didn't care. It was beautiful outside. Ruby had nowhere she needed to be, and she knew the idleness would grate on her.

Nicholas led her a winding six miles on their bikes. She laughed when she finally saw where they were going—a Catholic bookstore on Boone, in the heart of Little Seattle. She'd never been inside but every time her parents drove past it, one of them said, "Can't believe that place is still there," with true reverence in their voices, as if a building from the olden days of Spokane was a religious miracle unto itself. It was wedged between a skinny condo tower and a fast-food hot wings place. Ruby and Nicholas locked their bikes and went inside the store.

"I remembered about candles with Jesus's mom on them," Nicholas said. "We need those."

Ruby drifted toward the artwork—framed samplers, oil paintings, stained glass.

"What if I got the Kleins a stained-glass window?" Ruby asked. "That'd be a meaningful gesture, right?"

"No. You're getting them their dog back. If you can manage to stay focused." He tapped her on the forehead for emphasis, then headed for the cash register but was stopped short by a spinner display of prayer cards. "Gonna need some of these too, for sure!" Hands full of candles, he used one foot to rotate the display.

The woman working the register came over to them then. "Can I help you?" she asked in a voice of mild concern. She was not dressed as a nun but Ruby assumed she was one anyway. A solemn woman who would not tolerate shenanigans in her place of business.

"Definitely!" Nicholas said, turning toward her, blue eyes warm like tropical water. "Do you know if any of these saints are good for dogs?"

"Oh yes," the woman said, smiling now. How quickly her face and her whole posture had shifted. This always happened when Nicholas talked to people. It was as if just by looking at them he was inviting them into a secret club, and they couldn't wait to join. Not even undercover nuns were immune.

"Saint Roch is the patron saint of dogs," she said. "And Saint Francis is for all animals."

"Grand," Nicholas said. "We'll take both. And are these the best candles of Jesus's mom? Or are there some others in the back we could look at?"

The woman laughed a full throaty laugh and Nicholas laughed and Ruby laughed and the woman brought out a whole other box of candles for them to see.

Outside, it was warmer, though still not really hot. Ruby suggested brunch. "Twig and Bean is around the corner," she said. "They have amazing benedicts. We could get mimosas." But Nicholas tapped her on the forehead again. They rode home.

THE NEXT DAY they walked the neighborhood looking for dogs.

Nicholas knew the landscape, announcing the breed and name that accompanied each house. He'd worked as a dog walker and pet sitter while he was in high school. It occurred to Ruby that he had also taken care of Col. Mustard. She'd been walking slightly ahead of her brother, as was her unconscious habit—to always be a little faster than anyone she was with. It sank her, this revelation that her brother himself was another grieving party.

"You miss him," Ruby said.

"Who?" Nicholas asked. His voice had a bristle to it. Not sadness, something else. It made Ruby look back.

"Col. Mustard. You had a relationship. You used to walk him."

Nicholas shook his head, smiling now that she'd met his eyes. "That animal was a dummy. Didn't even respond to his own name. I was never particularly fond. If you ran over Radio Dog, then we'd have beef," he said, referring to a charismatic mutt so named for his sleek, too-long tail that stood straight up at all times.

Then his gaze shifted. "There!" he yelled, pointing to a beige rancher. He bounded across the street and hopped a low fence into the yard. Ruby ran after. She watched as Nicholas chased something into the side yard. He reappeared a moment later, grinning and holding a Pomeranian.

"Quick!" he said, thrusting the animal toward her. "Brush it!"

"It looks nothing like Col. Mustard," she laughed. "It's not even the same color!"

"But he's so fluffy. Feel."

Ruby petted the dog. It was very fluffy.

"What's its name?" she asked.

"I don't know," Nicholas said. "I've never seen this one before."

"Oh my God. You trespassed on a stranger's property and grabbed their dog?"

"Yeah, I'm still doing it. It's still happening. Can you hurry up and get some of its fur? I think it wants down."

The dog had begun to whimper and squirm in Nicholas's grasp. Ruby reached out again, this time with both hands, and swept her fingers through the fur, coming away with a solid harvest of shed. Nicholas set the dog gently on its grass and climbed out of the yard. Back home, he arranged the fur on his desk, between his candles and saint cards. He set the bottles of river water in a circle around these objects, like sentries. He closed his eyes as if in prayer.

"Should we say a few words?" Ruby asked.

"Not yet," Nicholas said.

That night, there was penne Alfredo, one of Ruby's favorites. A salad with mixed greens, and a cobbler for dessert. It was not a special occasion. But there were often favorites lately. The meals were frequently vegan, ingredients locally sourced. These details Jenna mentioned sheepishly but deliberately. The Alfredo was made with cashew cream. Before they sat down, Troy invited Nicholas and Ruby to each choose a record for the record player, like when they were kids.

Conversations too were gentle, supportive. No one bothered Nicholas about what classes he had picked for fall. Instead, did he need new clothes? A backpack? Was his intramural floor hockey team getting back together for another season? After the immediate squaring away, there'd been no mention of Ruby's accident, the money for the fence, or the death of the dog. Ruby and Nicholas did not discuss their project, only that they'd spent the day together, which Jenna and Troy smiled at in tandem.

They were trying so hard. To keep the kids happy. To show they were good people. It was all for Jace, of course, who, had he been present, would have found it super annoying.

MERCIFULLY, her boss returned from vacation, and for the next three days, Ruby was scheduled to work. Though only in the mornings. Jenna gave her rides downtown, then she took the bus back at lunchtime. In the afternoons, Nicholas insisted they look for pine needles. They didn't need to go to the river to get them, of course. Spokane was a city of pines. Half the homes on the block had pine trees in their yards. Pines ringed the neighborhood park and stood watch in front of the library. Their needles were everywhere. But Nicholas had exacting specifications. He said in order to work, the needles needed to be the length from his wrist to the tip of his index finger exactly. Unbroken. Green, not brown. They shuffled through the same streets they'd walked looking for dogs, this time with heads down, slow, pausing frequently to hold a green needle to Nicholas's palm for measurement. It was a pace, and level of attention, Ruby was unaccustomed to. Nicholas bundled what they found with pipe cleaners and put them beside the saint cards.

JENNA AND TROY had made a rule for Jace that he needed to call home every three days. Of course, it was really just a request. There could be no rules for the boy with his own money, living five thousand miles away. He did as he was asked. Jenna always relayed what he'd said to Ruby later, as if a phone call was the only way to get information from out-of-town family. Jace was taking classes in Danish, working as a dishwasher in a café, living in an apartment with three other expats he'd met online. "He says he's good," Jenna added after these reports. Jenna and Troy had asked when they could visit but Jace kept pushing them off, claiming he wasn't settled yet.

"What does that mean? Not settled?" Ruby asked.

Jenna shook her head. "It's his adventure. Let's give him time."

Her use of the word *adventure* bothered Ruby.

"You're proud of him," she whispered, though they were alone in the house.

"I'm proud of all my little astronauts."

Ruby knew her mother meant what she'd said, and it gnawed at her, a jealousy she did not want to admit. Hadn't she alone, not her brothers, done what was asked? Troy and Jenna never said the kids must live a certain way. Still, there were implied expectations. Ruby had gone to college, gotten good grades, picked a path. She was preparing to dedicate herself to a vocation as her mother dedicated herself to marketing, her father to engineering. Her life had a plan, an order, a use.

If she'd known running off to be a hero, or whatever, was an option, maybe she'd have chosen that instead.

WHEN SHE FELT MAD at Jace, she reminded herself that he'd done what he'd done because he was scared.

After the lahar, Jace started wetting the bed. Nicholas brought this up to Ruby and their parents. "That's if he sleeps," Nicholas said. "He's up a lot. I can hear him watching videos of it."

It was the collapse of the largest glacier on Mount Rainer, the crush of water plunging down the mountain's flank, picking up the earth below as it went. This deluge bursting the Mud Mountain Dam and the resulting flood overwhelming the cities south of Seattle—Enumclaw, Buckley, Sumner, Bonney Lake, Puyallup—with little warning. Ruby had watched the videos too. Some were taken by people with their phones, some from Forest Service cameras. The most terrifying was from a research station at the base of Rainier itself. In it, a woman, off camera, had time only to state her name and her location as a wall of mud thundered into view. The camera was consumed, and presumably the researcher as well. She sounded young and brave, her voice unwavering. Ruby could imagine herself in that moment, but also could not.

In those first days after the lahar, Ruby and her brothers had huddled together over their phones, united in their rage. The hydra once more. It had been an unrelentingly hot spring and then a hotter summer all across the state. Part of the glacier gave out. Whole neighborhoods ended up under the slurry, with less than an hour's notice to evacuate. Twelve thousand people dead and ninety thousand displaced. This was the reality of a warming world. They did not want it, had not consented to it, but here they were, watching it unfold. *So, so, so fucked*, they'd muttered.

But weeks had passed and Jace still could not look away.

"It's a sad time," Jenna acknowledged. "Everyone is processing their feelings differently."

This irked Ruby, the soft nothingness of it. "He's upset about this shithole planet you're leaving us with," she said sharply. She had wanted the hydra in that moment, the safety of together. But already her own anger had more or less diffused. Her life, 250 miles from the destruction of the lahar, had gone on unchanged.

"Well, now, I think it's unfair to put that on me," Jenna said. "If you want to blame someone, blame your grandparents and their generation's dependence on fossil fuels."

"Oh, like your generation isn't also dependent on fossil fuels?"

"Only as much as you are, I suppose."

"I'm going to be honest. I don't really know what a fossil fuel is," Nicholas said.

"It's a nonrenewable energy like gas and coal made of hydrocarbons in the earth's crust and extracted through costly and environmentally traumatic means!" This, shouted by Jace, who had been listening the whole time from the next room.

"It's cool that you know that!" Nicholas shouted back.

"You should know it too! We learned it in geology, a.k.a. Exploiting the Earth for Capitalism class! You just weren't paying attention!"

Then Jenna had shouted, "Jace, come in here if you want to talk with us!"

Ruby and Nicholas were both laughing by then, so quickly overtaken by the humor of the moment. But when Jace appeared in the doorway he had tears in his eyes. Nicholas pulled his brother to him, apologized with his mouth pressed to Jace's ear. Ruby and Jenna and Troy wrapped their arms around the boys. Like a geode in a rock, rings in a tree, a nut in a shell—like everything good in nature that comes in layers.

"We're okay," Troy had reminded them.

Jace didn't cry in front of them again after that and Ruby took that to mean one thing but really it meant another.

RUBY NEVER TALKED to Jace on the phone. She'd never talked to him on the phone before he moved either. Instead, they'd kept up the habit from when she was at college—texting random pictures they thought the other would like. She saw little bits of Copenhagen this way, in the background of whatever Jace found funny.

I drove drunk and killed Col. Mustard with my car, she texted him six days after the accident.

The pet food industry generates 120 million tons of carbon dioxide a year, he wrote back.

So you're saying I should run over all the dogs?

Nah. Only some. Nicholas told me about Col. Mustard. Sux.

Of course he already knew. Whenever Ruby saw Nicholas's phone lying around, there was an open chat with Jace on the screen. She suspected they kept up a constant, all-day dialogue, despite the time difference. Whatever Nicholas knew, Jace probably knew too. And vice versa. Which meant Nicholas knew Copenhagen. Nicholas knew about not enough beavers and about too many pets. Nicholas knew all the horrors waiting for the world but, unlike his brother, said nothing.

"I'M READY," NICHOLAS SAID. "I feel like I can conjure a dog today."

This was on a Sunday morning. Ruby and Nicholas had the house to themselves, their parents off at brunch with friends. They'd made pancakes, bacon, and Irish coffee. Ruby cleaned the kitchen afterward, wiped down the sink and counters, swept the floors, and was thinking of dusting the blinds. She wanted to go out but was avoiding her friends, still not wishing to tell them what had happened after she'd left the party. She knew they would laugh about it with her if she told it in a funny way—*I just reeeeallyyyy had to pee*—but she didn't want that either.

"What makes you think so?" she asked.

"It's just this feeling," he said. "It's weird, but I like it. Let's go now, before it goes away." He was already moving toward the door, slipping his feet into his sandals.

"What about our supplies?" Ruby asked.

"Nah, leave 'em," Nicholas said. "I was just messing around. I don't actually need any of that stuff."

"Then why did we spend the whole last week collecting it?"

Nicholas shrugged. "Something to do."

Something for you *to do*, he'd meant. Ruby didn't know if she should feel pride or shame, how well her little brother managed her energy. He'd been playing camp counselor, keeping her busy so she wouldn't . . . what? Drive drunk again? Spend hours crafting apology letters to the Kleins? Move to Europe?

She followed him out the door and down the block. The reconstruction of the Kleins' fence was already in progress. Nicholas stopped when he reached it and patted one of the posts with his hands. "Looks good," he said.

"Do we have to do this right here?" Ruby asked.

"It's the last place Col. Mustard was alive."

"I just don't want the Kleins to see us," she admitted.

"Don't worry. We'll be quick."

They were not being quick, not in Ruby's assessment. Nicholas rubbed the fence post with his hands some more. He looked up at the sky.

"It's a nice day," he said. "It's so clear."

He pulled out his phone and showed Ruby his air quality app. The AQI was 9. "Stupid Jace," he said. "It's been a perfect summer. No smoke at all."

"It's an anomaly," Ruby said quietly. "A lucky year. You know that."

"Yeah, well, we could have all had a good time together if he was here. That's all I'm saying."

Ruby thought Jenna was wrong. It was she and Nicholas who stayed in the space capsule. Jace was the only real moon explorer among them.

"Okay, I'm going to do it now," Nicholas said.

Ruby watched her brother. She waited for him to adopt some sort of absurd pose or sing a song or invoke the name of the handful of gods he could think of. Something irreverent and for show. He continued to look up at the clean blue sky.

No dog appeared. A warm breeze blew. A pine needle fell from a tree and Ruby watched it spiral to the ground. It landed near her sneaker. Out of habit, she assessed its color and length but she could tell even without picking it up that it would not pass muster. She wondered again how long she and Nicholas would stand there. She looked to the Kleins' front windows, then nudged Nicholas with her elbow.

"Wait," he said.

She nudged him again, a little harder.

"Look," he said, pointing over her shoulder to the corner.

Ruby turned and saw nothing.

"Wait," he said again. She followed his gaze, then looked back to his face. His pretty blue eyes could turn cold when he wanted them to.

"Okay, you're creeping me out," she said. "Let's go."

Neither of them moved. They kept looking until a tall, shockingly white bird appeared. It was walking on the sidewalk and came around the corner with a purposefulness like it had someplace to be, its knees bending backward. It had a long beak and tiny eyes nestled cozily in puffs of feathers. It rounded the bend until it was facing them, then stopped. It was a stunning creature, and abhorrent. So many things were not right lately—this, somehow, a culmination.

It looked to Ruby like a stork, a bird she knew mostly from cartoons. She remembered her mother explaining to her as a child that kids were once upon a time told that storks were responsible for bringing new babies to human families. She said this was to protect youngsters from the knowledge of vaginal birth, and also to devalue adult women, their sacred task outsourced to a swamp bird. Ruby remembered her father walking in on this conversation and asking, "Why are you telling her about this?" He'd said it like he was uncomfortable. It had made her wonder if there was more to the stork myth, something sinister.

What has it brought us now? Ruby thought and shivered in the stupid summer heat.

"Is it a stork?" she asked.

"It's an egret," Nicholas said, his voice gone soft, as if the words themselves were something fragile that he did not want to break.

"How do you know that? Did you learn it in geology class?" A thin and desperate joke. When Nicholas did not respond, she said, "They live by the river. It's just lost, that's all."

"Those are herons," Nicholas said. "This doesn't belong here."

He reached toward the bird, beckoning it with his hand outstretched as if he held some offering. The bird bent its knee and Ruby thought it really would come to them, but of course those knees were a trick. It was going the other way, stepping backward, then turning, a quick pivot, and it was in flight, long wings flapping.

Nicholas ran after it. "Come back! Hey, come back!" he called. He ran until the bird was out of sight. Then he stopped, turned, and ran back toward home.

RUBY FOLLOWED him down the block, through their yard, past the drought-tolerant plants. She was faster and could have overtaken him but she was also afraid. The egret had set something off in her brother. He ran up the stairs and into his room, slamming the door behind him like an angry child, which he had never for a moment been. When Ruby opened the door, she found him sitting on the bottom bunk, face in his hands. It was Jace's bed. Nicholas still slept on the top each night.

"Why are you crying?" she asked, sitting beside him, unable to hide her alarm. She did not wait for an answer. She rattled off all the ways it would be okay. The Kleins would get a new puppy, an even smarter and cuter one. Sometimes birds just get lost and don't actually mean anything. Jace was fine. He had made his point about Denmark and would come home soon. The summer would stay nice.

She and Nicholas could do more made-up projects, just the two of them together.

"It's none of that," he said.

"Then what? I can fix it. I promise."

"I'm afraid I'll never see anything that beautiful again."

They were not a hydra. They would never go to the moon. The smoke would come back the next summer, but maybe it wouldn't the year after that. Ruby couldn't really promise much. She was always overpromising. She folded her thumbs together. Her hands made the shape of a bird and she flapped its wings.

"You will, though."

Nell and the Marmot

Nell said she was going to give the marmot to our mother as a present. My sister was always like that, disguising her mischief as kindness.

This was Spokane in June 1910. Not hot yet, but already the days were long and dull. Any idea to leave the apartment was a good one.

Down at the river's edge, Nell stalked the wheat-colored creatures. While I fretted about wet shoes, she removed her blouse. I was about to start in with *Mother won't like it* when Nell pounced, trapping a marmot in the fabric of her shirt, its head and torso covered, feet kicking frantically.

"Give it here." I rearranged the frightened bundle in her arms like a baby in a swaddle. It calmed.

"See, you're already a good mama," Nell said, teasing but not mean.

She carried it five busy blocks through downtown, men calling out from tavern doors, respectable folks with errands pretending not to see. I blushed. Nell stuck out her tongue at everyone. Then four flights of stairs to our apartment. She tried to sit the marmot in the empty fruit bowl. "So decorative!" she declared. Of course it wouldn't stay. It clattered off the table and out our open door, its whistle loud and true. We knew its trail through the building from shouts of "Monster!" and "Rat!" Nell ran after, laughing at the fun of it.

Outside, the marmot had flushed everyone from their dens—the palm readers in the front shop, the day drunks at their card game on the second floor, the whores and their madam on the third, and the family with too many people in too few rooms (which was us) from the fourth. Everybody was arguing over who was to blame for the vermin. Along came a cop, who didn't give the occultists, or the gamblers, or the prostitutes a thought, but glared at Nell and me. "What are you *kids* doing *here*?" Nell told him she just wanted to catch her marmot back.

"What for?" I whispered.

"To let it go again," she said.

We were thirteen and twelve—not little girls anymore. We were supposed to be thinking of the future, of a clean home, a respectable husband, and all the babies he could give us. And I did think of those things, wanting to be good, to do as I was told.

Nell didn't think of them at all. Only of trouble set free.

Moser

The University of Washington conference had been on my calendar for months, but it wasn't until a week prior that I texted Becca to tell her I'd be in Seattle and would *absolutely love* to get together if she and Josh had the time. She wrote back right away and insisted I stay with them. I was hesitant. The university would reimburse my expenses. Plus, it was early May. Becca was expecting her first child at the end of the month. I remembered from my own pregnancy with my daughter five years earlier the discomfort and low-simmering rage of those final weeks before delivery. I hadn't wanted my parents to visit, much less seldom-seen friends from college.

But Becca and I were not the same person. Always a social butterfly, she might be craving distraction in the form of houseguests, I thought. Plus, I felt guilty for waiting so long to text and did not want her to think herself an afterthought in my plans. So I agreed, though I assured her my visit would be a quick one. Just two nights, with most of my waking hours at the conference and therefore out of her way.

Great! she replied. **Send your flight info & I'll pick you up!**

BECCA AND I first met on freshman move-in day. Her dorm room was down the hall from mine. I was nailing a mezuzah to my doorframe and she, passing by, leaned in and said, "Oh thank God, I thought I'd be the only one here." After that first year, we got an apartment off-campus and roomed together until graduation. Becca was the kind of college friend high-school-me had dreamed about. Someone to take me to parties, teach me how to make pot brownies, and goad me into trying improv. Someone with impulsive ideas for fun, like tree climbing and shaving cream fights. Someone to talk about with boys, because they all knew her and wanted to be with her. And when they found out they couldn't *all* be with her, wouldn't at least some of them settle for being with me?

It turned out there was no shortage of other Jews on campus, and so I did wonder at times what Becca got out of our friendship. "There can't be *two* of Becca in one house," a mutual friend once suggested. "So there you are." Even if my main role in Becca's life was only to be reliably *not Becca*, I relished it.

After college, we stayed close, but not the same kind of close. How could we? I moved two states away for more school, and across the country for even more school after that. I met my husband, Mitchell. We married shortly after I finished my PhD, and our daughter, Harper, was born the following year. The rigors of early parenting dovetailed so smoothly with those of academia, I felt them two sides of a coin. Like I had always been slogging up this same hill, sleep-deprived and jittery. Mitchell too worked hard. We had a lot of debt between us, but we bought a little house anyway with the help of his parents.

Becca, like all good free spirits, went traveling. She hitchhiked through Europe, landing for a while in Spain to teach English. She bounced to Singapore, to Beijing. I found this lifestyle very appealing, much more exciting than my reality of data sets and domesticity. *Oh Becca, you've got it right*, I thought. *That's the way to really* live.

As we waded through our midthirties, my mindset changed. I felt that I was now in the enviable position, with a career and house and husband and child. The mutual friend who told me in college that my greatest asset was not being Becca said the same thing again, but in a different way: "She seems lost. I wish she'd come home and settle down."

Then she did. She married Josh, her longtime boyfriend and fellow itinerant English teacher, and they moved to his home state of Washington. Becca took a position teaching at a private high school. Josh was a photographer for an outdoorsy magazine. Now when Becca texted, it was about the dramas of homeownership and petty gripes with coworkers. Much less interesting than dispatches from her globe-trotting days. But for the first time in a long time, we were in the same place.

BECCA MET ME at baggage claim. She was bubbling, full of questions. How was my flight? How was the family? What was my presentation about for the conference? Was I nervous? What would I wear? Did I have plans for dinner?

Her step was light and she moved quickly as she guided me through the parking lot to her car. She offered to carry my shoulder bag, but I declined. I studied her. Becca was always the full-figured sort, her midsection never totally flat. But she wasn't currently bulging either. This was not the shape or movement of a woman who was nine months pregnant.

My first reaction was a vicious sort of relief.

The previous spring I had confided to Becca that Mitchell and I were thinking of trying for a second child. She replied that we ought to get to it because she and Josh had already "pulled the goalie," as she put it.

"We could have kids the exact same age," she said. "Wouldn't that be perfect?"

I agreed it would.

Four months later Becca called to say she was pregnant and encouraged me, once again, to get after it. I too was pregnant by then, but not yet ready to share the news with her. I miscarried a week later. I was grateful not to have to tell Becca. I didn't want her to feel like she couldn't talk about her pregnancy with me. I told myself I didn't begrudge her and Josh their baby. Though as my own null-and-void due date approached, my sadness amplified. It was another reason I didn't want to stay with Becca in Seattle. The reminder of what we'd lost.

Now it seemed she had suffered her own loss. Again, we were in the same place.

How to broach such a subject? Becca continued her rapid-fire repartee. Everything from her mouth was light, cheerful.

Finally, in the car, as we merged onto the highway, there was a lull in conversation.

"You look good," I said. "You look skinny."

"Shut up. You're the skinny one."

"I assumed you would be"—and here I gestured to my own midsection—"great with child."

"Oh," Becca said. "I thought I told you. I had him already. On the first of March."

So, a living baby. A boy. Born nearly three months early. What kind of condition was he in? Was he still in the hospital, in the NICU?

"He's home with us," Becca said. "You'll meet him when we get to the house—unless he and Josh are out gallivanting somewhere."

I told her I was glad to hear it.

"We feel fortunate. It is something of an unusual situation. He was born very small, but fully formed."

"In what situation is a baby born *not* fully formed?" I asked.

It wasn't a matter of parts, Becca explained. She meant that he was not born into a baby's body, but into a man's. A tiny, three-pound man. But in his nine weeks of life since, he had grown considerably. To full size, in fact.

"By full size you mean man-size?"

"Yes," Becca said. "He's six-one, about a hundred and eighty pounds."

BECCA'S HOUSE was in a suburb to the east of Seattle, across Lake Washington. I had been there once before, also on a work trip. A clean and spacious rancher in a pleasant subdivision. The sort of place that would have bored college Becca to tears, I thought.

Josh met us at the front door.

"The prodigal friend returns!" he said, pulling me into a hug I could only describe as overwhelming. "How were your travels?"

"Good," I said.

"Where's Moser?" Becca asked.

"In the kitchen, having his lunch," Josh said.

"Moser?" I asked.

"We wanted an *M* name. After Josh's grandpa Moishe."

"Max," I offered. "Mason."

Becca laughed. "He just looked like a Moser. As soon as we saw him, we both agreed."

"But it's not a nice word, is it? A moser? Like a tattletale. A snitch."

"Well, nobody knows that. Besides, people are reclaiming all sorts of words these days. We call him Mosey for short. Even my mom thinks it's cute."

She waved me toward the kitchen. I followed and there, as promised, was her son. He sat on the counter, legs dangling. He was eating a burrito.

"What you got there, bud?" Becca asked him, wiping sour cream from his chin with her thumb.

"Pork burrito," Moser said. "But don't tell Mommy. Not kosher."

Then he laughed and so did Becca and Josh and so did I. How could you not?

I felt a terrible guilt for having wished him stillborn.

"Mosey, this is my friend Alicia. Can you say hi?"

I could not decide how old he looked. He was, just as Becca had suggested, full-size. This was a man, with broad shoulders, square jaw, and long knuckly hands. Though there was a newness to him, his skin soft and eyes bright. No dark lines or wrinkles. Not even any freckles. I wondered if his face had to be shaved, or was it naturally whiskerless. His hair was the kind of floppy curls sported by toddlers. His demeanor struck me as toddler-like as well, his mannerisms and patterns of speech. I settled on thinking of him as a three-year-old in the body of a twenty-five-year-old, who happened to be only two months old.

Would Moser continue to grow at his current rate? Would he be six and fifty by May? What about at the end of the year?

Or would he stay the way he was now, forever?

Or something else?

I had nothing to compare Moser to. No previous data to draw from.

"Is there a name for his condition?" I asked Becca once we'd retired to the den, leaving Moser to finish his treif lunch in peace.

"Not really."

"But his doctors must have told you something."

"His pediatrician said she'd seen miracles before, and it made her open to seeing them again."

We went back to small talk after that—gossip about friends from college and our vacation plans for summer. Moser wandered in and out of the room, once on his hands and knees pushing a plastic dump truck. Becca kissed him and ruffled his hair each time he passed by. Nothing about the scene was unpleasant, but I was on edge. I felt grateful when it was time for me to meet my colleagues for dinner.

WHEN I GOT BACK to the rancher that night, everyone was asleep, the lights out except for the one in my guest room. But as I returned from the bathroom after brushing my teeth, I saw Becca in her pajamas, standing in the doorway of Moser's room. I touched her gently on the shoulder so as not to startle her.

"I know it's silly," she said, "but I always check on him in the middle of the night to be sure he's breathing."

"Not silly at all."

I still looked in on Harper most nights as well. I told Becca how when Harper was an infant I'd kept her in a bassinet next to the bed and slept with my face pressed to its mesh sides. "Sometimes I got mad at Mitchell for sleeping too loudly. I couldn't hear her. I thought about smothering him with a pillow."

Becca laughed, but softly. A nighttime laugh. It felt good to share these things. We'd never talked of parenting before. Why would we, since for so long I was the only one with a kid? Now here we were, both mothers. It would have been the same had we been pregnant together, I thought. Though I said nothing of this.

We stood looking at Moser a moment longer. He slept in a queen-size bed with safety rails. He was on his side with one arm flung over his head, the other tucked to his chest.

"I wish he'd sleep on his back," Becca said. "They're supposed to only sleep on their backs at this age, you know. Do you think it's okay?"

I HAD MEANT to sleep in. The rare luxury of time away from home. I made it until seven fifteen, when Becca knocked on my bedroom door.

"I hate to do this," she said, "but I need to ask a favor."

Josh had gone out to the mountains on an early-morning photo shoot for work and gotten a flat tire. He had no spare. Becca would have to go pick him up. Could I watch Moser while she was out?

"I'll only be a couple hours," she said.

Why couldn't Josh call AAA? I asked. Or have someone from his office pick him up?

"It's not that kind of office," she said.

I had no idea what that meant. I looked at Moser. He was sitting cross-legged on the living room floor, stacking blocks. Josh and Becca had done a good job of finding the adult equivalent of little-boy clothes for him. He was dressed in a baseball T-shirt and carpenter-style jeans. The day before had been a gray tracksuit. I knew what advice Mitchell, practical and sensitive, would give. Something along the lines of, "Perhaps it would be best to decline the invitation, given your current need for boundaries regarding situations of this nature."

I didn't have to be at UW until the afternoon. I could think of no excuse.

"Great!" Becca said. "Hey Mosey, Auntie Alicia is going to look after you while I go get Daddy, okay?"

So that's how one goes from friend to auntie, I thought. A willingness to be inconvenienced.

I sat and studied Moser while Becca got ready. He paid no attention to me, wholly absorbed in his blocks. How long could he play with them? Could he play blocks for two hours? But as Becca was assembling her purse, Moser grew restless. He knocked his tower over and left the room.

"What other things does he like to do?" I asked.

"Oh, lots!" Becca said. "You guys could go out. There's a playground just down the street."

Her face betrayed her. Even she knew the trouble with taking her son to a playground. She offered no other options for Moser-appropriate activities.

I decided on a walk. I remembered a pond with a paved trail about a mile from Becca's house. I filled a water bottle, helped Moser with his shoes, and led him to the rental car I'd picked up the previous evening. I made him ride in the back because that is where young children are supposed to be, for safety. He sat silent, looking out the window.

But once we parked and I opened the door and unclicked his seat belt, he popped out full of energy. He skip-jogged on his long legs toward the pond. I feared he might jump in. I ran after him, calling his name. He stopped on the trail, hopping eagerly from foot to foot.

"Don't run off like that!" I snapped. "You scared me."

He pointed to the water's edge. "Ducks!" he said.

I felt bad for scolding. I had found myself, in recent months, shorter with Harper as well. Worry would bubble up without warning. Everything felt fragile.

I tried to make up for my outburst by showing an excessive interest in the waterfowl.

"You like ducks too?" Moser asked me, his face full of skepticism.

I assured him I did, and after that he held my hand and no longer tried to run ahead of me.

We walked around the pond. At the halfway mark, we crossed paths with a man and woman, also holding hands. They nodded to us—that particular nod of social recognition among strangers that says *You are doing the same thing as me*. They had assumed us a couple, Moser and me.

I didn't know if Moser had eaten breakfast. I asked if he was hungry and he said yes. I drove us to a nearby shopping district and found a café. I ordered a fruit plate and orange juice for Moser and a Bloody Mary for me. When the waiter returned with our drinks, he mixed them up. I reached across the table to switch the glasses. Moser was faster. He wrapped his lips around the straw in my Bloody Mary.

"It's salty," he said.

"Yeah. It is. Give it here."

He shook his head, pulling the glass closer to him with both hands.

A toddler making a scene in public is one thing. A grown man, another. I did not want such a scene.

"Okay," I said. "You keep it."

So he did.

When his food came, the fruit plate was mostly grapes. I intended to cut them in half for him, but Moser popped one into his mouth right away. He was a fine grape eater. Something about this made me sad. Not sad for Moser, but for Becca and Josh. What good is being a parent to someone if they never need you to cut their grapes for them?

I took a grape for myself.

"What's your favorite food, Mosey?" I asked.

"Burritos."

"I guess I already knew that, huh? What's your favorite animal?"

"Ducks."

"Knew that too. Who do you love more, Mommy or Daddy?"

"Mommy."

The waiter returned, asking if we needed anything else.

"His Bloody Mary looks so good," I said. "I think I'll have one as well."

"Me too," said Moser, holding up his empty glass.

Our cocktails arrived. I drank mine and let Moser drink his. When he went to eat his olive, the pimento fell onto his shirt. I picked it off. A couple next to us witnessed this exchange and gave us a smile. Again, the assumption of boyfriend-girlfriend, not an "auntie" and her young charge.

And wouldn't that be nice, to be out for a brunch date with someone new on a sunny day? It was a long time since I'd been that kind of carefree. So much of me now belonged to my work and to Mitchell and Harper and the gnawing want of a second child. There was hardly anything left.

I continued to view Moser and myself through the eyes of those around us. A little bit of fun, I told myself, just for a moment. The sort of thought experiment Becca might have come up with back in college. "Okay guys, now imagine if . . ." she'd say. And we would. We'd all imagine it, no matter how absurd.

I FELT MOSER could pass for at least thirty if it weren't for his man-boy clothes. What might a new outfit do for him? I decided to be a good auntie and take him shopping.

We left the café and walked to a little clothing boutique. It wasn't the sort of place I would have gone into on my own, but it seemed right for Moser. Inside, I browsed the men's section while Moser studied the window display. After a few minutes, he called me over.

"What's up, bud?" I asked.

He pointed to the seat of the mannequin's pants. "It's got a butt," he said.

"Sure does, pal."

"That's silly."

I agreed that it was and felt a twinge of pride that Moser had thought to include me in a butt joke.

I picked a few items I thought might look good on him. It wasn't hard. Moser himself was a kind of living mannequin, tall and slender in his unblemished body.

I called him to the dressing room and closed the door behind us.

It was there that I worried I might be overstepping my bounds as auntie. He wasn't really a baby, after all. Would he know that an unfamiliar adult shouldn't be asking him to take off his clothes?

"Let's start with your pants," I said. "I'll help."

I undid the top button of Moser's jeans and unzipped his fly. As I began to pull his waistband over his hips, he stopped me. A big warm hand on top of mine.

"I do this part myself," he said. He took his pants down, dropping them at his ankles.

"Okay. You do the rest," he said. I did as I was told, lifting his feet one at a time and extracting them from his cuffs. I folded his jeans and set them on the floor. His briefs were plain white. This made me a little sad again, because of course they were. There can be no Paw Patrol underwear if you're a thirty-two-inch waist.

I helped Moser with his khakis, pausing for him to pull them up himself. He raised his arms for me to take his shirt off. I had to stand on the changing room bench to get the new one over his head.

He looked good. "What do you think, champ? Pretty cool clothes, huh?" He gave a little hop and I knew he was enjoying the way the Moser in the mirror moved.

"Yeah. Pretty cool!"

I combed his hair with my fingers and laced up his sneakers. I thought about loafers or Top-Siders, but his Nikes looked nice with the khakis. Kind of a classy weekend dad vibe.

I told the salesgirl that Moser would be wearing his new clothes out. She leaned over the register with the price gun to scan the tags, then plucked them off and put them in a bag along with his old clothes.

"Very sharp," she said to him, then she gave me a little wink, like *doesn't it feel good to take your man out and get him cleaned up?*

Moser, polite young fellow that he was, said thank you, and gave an extravagant toddler goodbye wave.

"Have a good one, you guys," she said, matching his big wave with one of her own.

AFTER SHOPPING, I checked my phone. There was still no word from Becca. I decided I didn't feel like going back to her house if I didn't have to.

Moser apparently also had little interest in returning home. He took me by the hand and led me down the sidewalk.

"I'm thirsty," he said. "I want more red juice."

We came to an Irish pub with a green sign and dark wood everywhere inside. Perfect for day drinking. I installed Moser in a booth near the window and went to the bar. I ordered another Bloody for him and a Jack and Coke for me.

"Let's see some ID, little lady," the bartender said.

"Do you want to see his too?" I asked, pointing to Moser.

The bartender looked at my license and handed it back. "Nah," he said. "No need to make him come all the way up here."

I brought both drinks back to our table. Mine was adorned with a row of maraschino cherries on a toothpick. Moser grabbed for it, but he misjudged the distanced and overreached, his arm, chest, and chin all landing on the lacquered tabletop. He giggled. "Oopsies," he said.

The mistake of someone not yet accustomed to his own limbs? No. He was already drunk.

"Here you go, boyo," I said, handing him the cherries, as well as his own beverage.

My moment of fun had gone on too long. Anxiety rushed back to me as I thought of taking Moser home in unfamiliar clothes, sauced like a frat boy.

"What the hell is wrong with you?" Becca would ask in her new stern mom voice. Then I'd have to tell her exactly what the hell was wrong with me. And her anger would turn to pity. I could not bear Becca's pity. Wasn't I always the pitiable one, being *not Becca*, after all? Becca, who got what she wanted. All the friends and the attention when we were in college. Then the freedom after. Then the husband and job and the big house as soon as she decided she wanted that. Then the baby. She said she wanted a baby, so there was a baby. She moved through the world as if the seas would part for her, and they always did. Even for little things. That morning she needed a babysitter, and lo, the universe provided me. How could I ever allow myself to be vulnerable in front of someone like that? But here was Moser, forcing my hand.

"Your parents were right," I told him. "You are a little snitch."

Moser considered this.

"Not little," he said. "Mommy says I'm her *big* boy."

I was wrong again. Nobody asks for a baby like Moser. What if this was the best version of him, the good days of which there would be so few? And I was stealing this one, pretending him to be something he was not.

I paid our tab and led him out of the bar back into the daylight. Without any particular direction, we walked, Moser next to me, his hands in his pockets, his stride matching mine. After just a couple of blocks, he stopped.

"I have to pee," he said.

He'd had three Bloody Marys in an hour. I hadn't once suggested he go potty. Another failing.

"It's okay, sport," I said. "We'll find you a men's room straightaway."

I looked around for a restaurant or bar we could duck into, but it was already too late. Moser was unzipping his pants.

"Oh no no no," I said, putting my hand on his arm. "We only do that in the toilet."

He brushed me off, a single move, swift and rough. He rooted around in his fly and liberated his penis. He began to urinate on the sidewalk. I found myself unsure, at that point, what to do.

It was a prodigious stream of piss. It splashed at his sneakers and tumbled outward. The shopping district had grown busy with other pedestrians. Moser—drunk, beautiful, peeing—attracted attention.

It wasn't just that people had to step out of the way. There was something of a spectacle to him. They stopped to watch. A small crowd gathered. "Yeah, man! You go!" someone shouted.

Moser continued to pee. I listened to the chatter of those who congregated around us. There was disgust in their voices, but more than that, there was awe. I wondered if, once he was finished, there might be applause.

I also wondered if there might be a punitive response. Angry shop owners demanding we hose down the sidewalk, the police arriving to issue a citation. I once heard a story of a man receiving registered sex offender status for public urination. I plotted our escape, the quickest route back to the car.

But as I looked around, I realized there was no *us*. The crowd's eyes were for Moser alone. To them, he was an adult, responsible only for himself. And wouldn't it be better if that were true? What use was an auntie like me to someone like him anyway? Some Good Samaritan would help him get home. Then he could tell Becca. He was more than capable of recounting the facts. I wouldn't have to say a goddamn thing about what happened after all.

Tara's Ultraboost™ Supplements for Good Health and Good Times

Look, everyone knows there's a difference between being a supportive friend and being a SUPPORTIVE FRIEND. And we, the women of the West Hidden Pines Phase II cul-de-sac, had vowed to be the latter.

What is it, truly, to be SUPPORTIVE? For us, it always came down to action. That meant not just sitting on Shay's patio drinking wine and listening to her complain about her deadbeat ex who made plenty of money from his swanky restaurant but still refused to pay alimony. No, SUPPORT meant leaving one-star reviews for said restaurant all over the internet, replete with gruesome details of food poisoning and handsy waiters.

It meant attending Cadence's jiujitsu competitions—which she said were the only way for her to release the tension of absolutely fucking nobody listening to her at her firm even though she was a fucking partner—and also sparring with her, timidly fending off kicks and grabs on her front lawn.

It meant someone offering to pick up my kids from school on days I needed to walk out of West Hidden Pines into the real pines lest I walk into traffic or, more likely, just away to somewhere else and not come back. I got like that sometimes.

But the one of us who needed the most SUPPORT, without a doubt, was Tara. She was prone to melancholy. Her parents had bought her a house in our subdivision after she finished grad school, and she'd lived there alone ever since. From the confines of its well-appointed rooms she struggled to make meaning of her days. Or something like that. We went with her to all the protests and blood drives. We'd been the online hype team for her many Etsy shops. We were the setup and teardown crew for her short-lived backyard concert series (apparently against the homeowners association rules). We read several drafts of her novel-in-progress.

So when she said she was going to start selling supplements, we were not surprised. Like Herbalife? we asked. An MLM seemed a reasonable next step for Tara.

No, she said. This was her own recipe. She'd been working on it a long time, the perfect blend. A women's vitamin for *real* women with *real* bodies. That's the way she said it. Tara had no background in nutrition or anatomy or chemistry, as far as we knew. Her degrees were in English literature.

But we said FUCK YEAH. Because that's what it means to be SUPPORTIVE. We said, What can we do to help?

Try them and tell me how you feel, Tara said.

TARA'S SUPPLEMENTS CAME in mason jars, with the word ULTRABOOST Sharpied on the lid. There were sixty in each jar. They were grayish with little flecks of darker gray, and about the size and shape of an adult's pinkie toe. They smelled like vanilla almond milk. We were each supposed to take two pills every morning for a month. Tara said she would be taking them too.

Then we can workshop them! she said.

We did not know what it meant to workshop a vitamin.

THE FIRST MORNING, I sat down for cereal with my kids and shook two pills from the jar. Look, I said, holding them out. Mommy is taking her vitamins just like you guys!

Are yours shaped like Paw Patrol? my daughter asked.

I said they were not and she shook her head. Those aren't good then, she said.

I thought it best not to include this note in the workshop.

A few minutes later, I sent a text to Tara: **Took my sups! Feeling great already—lots of energy! No coffee for me today!**

I knew she had already received two other, similar texts. This was our plan.

But then, the funny thing was, I did feel great. I whirred through my day, and in the evening I was all piggyback rides and wrestling matches and tap dances with the kids. There was a lightness, a buzzing like I was drunk, but I was also somehow totally clearheaded. I did not want the forest or lonesomeness that day, only the tasks of my life and the people I was promised to.

BUT WHAT'S IN THEM? we whispered to each other over the phone. I cut one in half and learned nothing; it was the same inside as out.

We asked Tara, but she wouldn't say, just wagged her finger. We'll talk in a month. No cheating.

After a week, I asked Tara if I could place an order for more. I knew from her previous ventures that her attention span was often short. I felt it was important to strike while the iron was hot, and not get stuck holding an empty bag, or mason jar, as it were.

TARA DIDN'T WANT us to talk about the vitamins until the workshop, so of course, when she wasn't around, it was all we talked about.

I shared my feelings of newfound contentment, my boundless energy for all chores big and small.

Cadence said she suddenly felt seen at work, her opinions sought out and celebrated. Her kids seemed to notice something as well and had taken to calling her ma'am unironically.

Shay, who was the oldest among us, had been complaining of being perimenopausal. Now she said her symptoms had not only abated but reversed.

I feel adolescent, she said, gesturing to her genitalia. And my menstruation! It's positively volcanic!

We suggested that volcanic menstruation was not desirable. Still, we understood what she meant, the sense of renewal and revitalization. But also power. And something about our anger. Not less of it, but a new purity to it, almost playful. A gleeful rage, we agreed.

Shay's daughter, Kenzie, insisted it was GROSS GROSS GROSS when Shay spoke of the vitamins' impact. We encircled the teen, who was eating toast at the kitchen table, and delivered unto her a lecture on the importance of robust sexual health. We weren't usually so forthcoming with the children, but we were feeling sagelike. We wanted to impart our wisdom. This too, we assumed, was due to the Ultraboost.

Kenzie made a show of plugging her ears while singing PLEASE. STOP. TALKING to the tune of "Jingle Bells."

I WAS TORN between the desire to hoard my stash of Ultraboost and to spread its goodwill. Eventually, I did offer some to my husband. He declined.

Honestly, I can't believe you're taking those, he said. I mean, I know it's important to you to support your friend—

SUPPORT! I shouted, so he could hear the difference.

He scrunched up his face. Yes, he said. That. You could be poisoning yourself for all you know. It seems dangerous.

I implored him to think of the potential benefits. When he asked what benefits, I admitted I could not promise specifics. That was the wonderful trick of it, I argued. Ultraboost seemed to affect everyone a little differently. Who knew what it might do for him? Weight loss? Better sleep? Stop burning the pancakes? Less farting? Actually listening when the kids talked to him?

After that he did not speak to me for the rest of the day. In the morning, I ground up Ultraboost and put it into his coffee. He caught me, but he was laughing, so I thought maybe he'd already drank enough of it to undergo an improvement.

I BEGAN TO ENJOY my sparring sessions with Cadence. I was no longer just weakly blocking her attacks, but delivering my own. We met in the early evenings before dinner, while our kids played. It was warm and we were all in bare feet, which made me feel like we might be feral if it weren't for the perfect cool softness of the stupid lawn. One day, I got so revved up that I punched Cadence in the face. A haymaker, I think it's called.

Cadence shouted, THAT'S NOT JIUJITSU, then tackled me. We rolled around, grappling for a long time. When we finally stood up, Cadence's lip was bleeding and my shirt was ripped mostly off. The kids stared at us from the play fort windows. Her youngest, three years old, was holding his juice box upside down, cran-apple dripping down his arm and tears in his eyes.

Oh no, I said, fearing we had traumatized them all. What should we do?

Let's kiss, Cadence said.

So we did. A big mouthy kiss with our hands on one another's faces. The kids cheered.

Then we went next door to get Shay and make her fight and kiss with us too.

MY HUSBAND CONTINUED to express misgivings, or at least conflictions. On the one hand, I was happier. He liked that. And he agreed that the pills I continued putting in his coffee had made the skin on his hands softer, the sensitive spots on his teeth less sensitive, and the slight weird bend in his penis less apparent.

But wasn't I concerned for my friends? he wanted to know. Had I noticed Shay's eyes? They were like goats' eyes now, rectangular pupils. And why were Cadence's children singing the entire *Sound of Music* score on the lawn each morning?

I reminded him that goat shaming was a microaggression. And hadn't he ever wished our own brood might emulate the von Trapp family? Isn't that every suburbanite's dream? Shouldn't we applaud Cadence, and her offspring, for their success?

Neither of us had noted any change in Tara.

OKAY, I ADMIT I was becoming hungry for answers too. At first, I tried to quench this hunger by making whoopie pies and snickerdoodles with the kids. My domestic enthusiasm got out from under me and we made way too many, the kids complaining of hand cramps and sweatshop-like conditions. I halted the assembly line and took the treats over to Tara's house. Shay and Cadence were already there, having wine on the porch. They looked so beautiful under the soft glow of hanging bistro lights. They were laughing about something. I passed around the cookies and laughed for a while too. Then I said, Cut the crap, chuckleheads. Tara, it's time to talk vitamins.

Shay and Cadence agreed.

For example, Shay said, is it possible I'm turning into a werewolf?

Lycanthropy, Cadence echoed. I'm wondering as well about autovampirism. I'm biting my fingertips, then sucking the blood and really enjoying it.

Tara shook her head. Has it been a month? she asked.

We admitted it had not.

Tara's eyes filled with tears. She told us how much she needed us. Couldn't we see that? Couldn't we see how hard she was working to fix her life? Our lives were so perfect, she said. And hers was such shit. Maybe this could be her perfect thing too. But only if we all took this project seriously and did exactly as she asked. It was important. Couldn't we see its importance?

We were surprised by this sudden turn toward emotion. We thought Ultraboost had insulated us against such vulnerability.

We set down our cookies and wine and gathered around her. HUG is not strong enough a word. We were a cocoon from which she could emerge when ready.

When she finally did push out from us, our beautiful supplement-making butterfly, she was smiling and I thought I noticed something about her teeth. Were they stronger like my husband's? Or maybe more jagged, not like a wolf's but a shark's. Or nothing at all, and it was just wishful thinking on my part—wanting that for her.

I'm not criticizing the werewolfing, Shay said. I like it.

Lycanthropy, Cadence said again. Then Shay kicked her in the shin and called her a nerd, and said, What are you, a fucking werewolf lawyer? They fought for a while because by then we were all always looking to fight. Cadence won because Cadence always won.

After that we hugged Tara some more and pledged our ultimate loyalty and SUPPORT to her. We reiterated our agreement on her very good plan. We swore that when it was finally time for the vitamin workshop, it would be the best vitamin workshop there ever was. No more questions until then, and no more doubt, and we really meant it. After all, we loved Tara. And we loved Ultraboost. Loved it so much. To seal the deal, we spat in each other's palms and ran through Phase II stomping everyone's tulips and daffodils with our Chacos even though that sort of thing is definitely prohibited by the homeowners association.

THINGS CAME to a head later that week when Shay drove her Lexus into the lobby of her ex-husband's restaurant. She rolled out of the car, fists up, insisting he had stolen not only her money but THE BEST YEARS of her life. She took all the cash from the register at the bar and was in the office opening the safe when the cops arrived. They had to drag her out. She kept screaming, ULTRABOOST FOR LIFE, folding her hands up like U's.

The same day, Kenzie got caught at school with her backpack full of Ultraboost. She'd been selling them to other kids at ten dollars per pill, calling them grown-up Adderall and mommy-boner pills. She had made seven thousand dollars in two weeks this way. Which gives you some idea of the volume of Ultraboost Shay must have had in the house, that she didn't even notice so much missing.

So, of course, all this led back to Tara.

LOOK, OBVIOUSLY WE KNEW things had gotten out of hand. Still, we didn't want Tara or Shay to get in trouble. This was part of being a SUPPORTIVE friend. So when two police officers approached us in Cadence's yard as we were sparring, we gave each other a nod to say snitches get stitches. And when they recounted for us the details of Shay's exploits, Cadence said, Oh, it's just because of her volcanic menstruation and werewolfism. Then we laughed so hard and for so long that one of the cops said if we didn't stop we would be charged with obstruction of justice. That only made us laugh more. Maybe we should have been nervous. If they searched our homes, they would find Ultraboost there too, just as much as at Shay's house, if we were being honest. But we knew they wouldn't. Not in this neighborhood, not in front of these bright children and these bright cars and all these nice furnishings.

TARA INSISTED to the police that the pills were nothing—just ground-up corn husks with oatmeal, cornstarch, and a little vanilla almond milk for flavor. And that's all they found in her house.

Still, I continued taking them. I took every last pill I had, two each morning, until they were gone. I wanted to keep feeling whatever it was we'd been feeling—the contentment, the renewal, the rage, the sageness, the werewolfery, the vampirosity. I didn't care how I got there.

RIP Kittitas Bong Squad

"My mom's not dying," Ruby says. "I know this makes it seem like she's dying, but she's not. She's actually in really good health."

Ruby and Kavya are sitting on the floor of the nursery, a slim folder of handwritten letters between them. The letters are from Ruby's mother, Jenna, to her future grandchild. This person has not yet been born. They reside, currently, inside Ruby's ever-expanding belly, which Ruby rubs her hand across now, as Kavya reads.

The letters are baffling to Ruby. They tell a family history so totally unfamiliar, she suspects it of being fiction. Their tone waffles between grave seriousness and frivolity. If Jenna were dying, they might make sense. "Her mind was going, there at the end," Ruby pictures herself saying to her child, "but she loved you very much. I think that's all she was trying to say, in her way." But her mom is not dying, just being a weirdo. Still, Ruby has promised to keep the letters safe and give the folder to the child when the time seems right.

"Why can't you give it to them?" Ruby had asked.

"I might forget," Jenna said, with a wave of her hand through the air, a gesture to where all forgotten things evaporate. "And I wish you'd say *her*."

Though Ruby has chosen not to learn the sex of her baby in advance, her mother is certain it is a girl. Her mother is, the letters suggest, certain of lots of things about the baby. Ruby is certain of nothing. She feels only its movements, which are sometimes pleasant but mostly sharp and strange, and even from these she can discern little—not the baby's mood, or shape, or orientation in her body. She refers to it, privately, as Sluggo, imagining it as a large thrashing slug, and is surprised, each time she gets an ultrasound, by its baby-like form.

"These are sweet," Kavya says. "Maybe a bit of an overshare, for a child. But sweet."

"You're not helping," Ruby says. Kavya laughs and Ruby is glad for this. Still, Ruby was hoping for a confidant with regard to the letters, and perhaps a coconspirator, though she has formed no conspiracy yet with which she could co- anyone. She just wants the option. She sets the letter folder aside and picks up a paper instruction booklet.

Kavya takes the hint. "Right, let's hurry up and finish this thing before the baby gets here," she says. Kavya moves her own baby, six-month-old Valor, who has been contentedly sitting in her lap, onto his portable play mat, and picks up a length of silicone tubing with one hand and a mesh baggie of washers with the other.

"Which one?" she asks, holding them up.

"Neither," says Ruby. "We're working on the humidification port. It's all in the green box."

That the FourthTri Chamber requires assembly is both maddening and perplexing to Ruby. It seems like a trap to increase the anxiety of new parents, setting them up for failure before they have even begun to parent. The FourthTri Chamber itself is, ideally, an anxiety-soothing device. The safest of safe sleep options for children in early infancy, and Ruby's most wanted item from her baby shower registry. Jenna hemmed and hawed over it—how neither Ruby nor her brothers slept suspended in any fancy pods and they all turned out fine. But then her mom was the one who bought the chamber for her, saying, "If it helps you feel better, then by all means, you should have it."

All of this Ruby was complaining about in the front office of the law firm where she is a junior associate. Kavya, a paralegal and a mother of four, offered to help, saying she'd assembled a chamber before her first was born and was pretty sure she remembered how. Kavya is the only other woman in the firm near Ruby's age; the rest are all in their fifties and sixties. Kavya and Ruby have always been friendly, though this is the first time they have done anything together outside the bounds of the workday. There is the slight awkwardness of Ruby being Kavya's superior. But Ruby is grateful for the help, grateful for Kavya and all the things she has to say about being a mom. Most of Ruby's friends are choosing not to have kids. And while she's never doubted her and Brayden's decision, she does, now that she is very pregnant, often feel lonesome in it.

THEY CONSTRUCTED the exterior of the chamber without difficulty. But their progress has slowed now that they face the wires and tubing for the various ports—pressurization, oxygenation, humidity. "Honestly, I don't remember any of this," Kavya says. "It was seven years ago. I may have oversold my abilities. I wish I could just give you ours but Valor still sleeps in it. He loves it. I think he's going to stay in there until he literally can't fit anymore."

"It's okay, really," Ruby said. Then, "Hey, do you see piece B17? It looks like a stubby metal straw?"

They take turns sifting through the contents of the green box. They search the floor around them. Kavya lifts Valor and his play mat in case it has rolled underneath. No B17.

"Fuck," Ruby says and can feel tears welling behind her eyes. It is only a little, tiny part. But it is a part of the machine that is supposed to keep her baby safe while it sleeps. Already she is failing it in its safety. She is not good at keeping it safe. This thought feels both absurd and shameful.

"It's okay!" Kavya says. "Really! Have you ever been to MamaBahama? They have parts for a lot of baby stuff. I bet if we go there, we can get a replacement, easy peasy lemon squeezy."

Ruby has not been to MamaBahama.

"Is that at the mall?" she asks, trying not to cry anymore.

"Lord no. It's in Little Seattle. On Sinto, I think."

Ruby sucks her breath through her teeth.

"I can drive," Kavya offers.

"It's just a ways, that's all," Ruby says. "And I think there's supposed to be wind later."

It's late spring. The season of night storms, when lightning, hail, and drenching rain come late in the day, at least once a week. Though it's the wind that's the most dangerous, downing tree limbs and power lines. It does not sound unreasonable to want to be home well in advance of the weather, Ruby hopes. It's not really why she doesn't want to go to Little Seattle. It's the people. So many in one place. Since becoming pregnant, Ruby has felt increasingly vulnerable in a crowd. Large, slow, and emotionally fragile, she does not think she can bear it. Kavya seems to intuit this.

"Don't worry," she says. "I'll keep all the fuckers away from you."

RUBY DOES NOT LIKE this feeling. This tentativeness, this vulnerability. She reeks of it. She is acutely aware of it when Kavya opens the door of her car for Ruby, then takes her arm as if to help her into her seat. She's never done anything like this before. At work, they are jocular with each other. They call each other "dude" and "bro." Ruby brushes Kavya's hand away.

"Thanks. I'm not, like, a total bowling ball yet, though."

"No one said anything about a bowling ball." Kavya fastens Valor into his car seat, takes her own place behind the wheel.

The source of Ruby's disquiet has three tributaries: worry for one of her brothers; anger at the other brother; and the aforementioned frustration with her mother, which honestly ebbs and flows, but today is at its high-water mark.

First there is Nicholas. Her younger brother has spent his twenties working for the Washington State Parks system in varying capacities. With the exception of a brief stint in Omak, he's lived in and around Spokane his whole life. He has never seemed unhappy or wanting of anything grander. Then, last spring, he announced that he was heading to Northern California for wildland smoke jumper training. When he returned, he said he had signed on with a Cal Fire unit for the next year's season. At the time, Ruby said vaguely supportive things, the way one does when they are not actually supportive at all but the situation is far enough in the future that it does not feel real. But the year has passed. In a week, Nicholas will leave again for California.

"There are wildfires here in Washington you could jump into," Ruby said dumbly. She is full of protestations, as if trying to clog the works with petty logistics.

"Sure, but these guys are the best in the whole country. And they asked me to join them. It's crazy. A dream come true."

"But is it?" Ruby cannot square this with the Nicholas she knows, the cheerful young man who bounds through the forest in his green uniform showing her all his favorite edible plants, who prefers watershed restoration to search and rescue. Her best friend, who she speaks to almost every day, even when she was on her honeymoon with Brayden. Even when Nicholas was in California learning to fight fires.

Jenna claims to get it. "I think it's all he's ever really wanted," she said. "To jump from a great height into peril and emerge smiling."

Only the "emerge smiling" part makes any sense to Ruby. Though she is willing to admit that at this moment, with regard to members of her family, she cannot see the forest for the trees, as the saying goes. Cannot see the fire for the smoke.

She is scared for him and does not want him to go.

THEN THERE IS JACE, her other little brother and Nicholas's twin. Whereas she speaks to Nicholas every day, she had not, until very recently, heard from Jace in seven months. No one had. Jenna fretted. Around month four she had become convinced he was dead and started talking about calling embassies, but Ruby and Nicholas stayed her hand. He'd gone dark before. This was no different, only a little longer.

"He's just off doing his crimes," Ruby reassured her. "He'll pop up when he's done. He's a grown man. He knows how to look after himself."

Jace had left the US at nineteen in the name of climate justice, pledging his life to repairing the ravages man had beset upon the earth. This mandate has, in the past decade, taken a number of forms. He's claimed to be employed by a rotation of NGOs, the existence of which Ruby can never verify. She is certain he has become involved in some sort of espionage, or sabotage, to what end and for whom she can't even guess.

But then, the previous morning, Nicholas had texted, **Jace is in Hyderabad. He's doing good. Says he'll call soon.**

As promised, he had. A video chat request appeared on her screen midday. But when she answered, there was no video.

"Have you talked to Mom? She's been worried sick," Ruby said to the black screen.

"I'll call her next," Jace's voice assured her, clear and low. "I'm free all night." He sounded close. He really was safe, she thought. Somewhere with good internet. He could turn his camera on if he wanted.

"What are you doing?"

"Work. I'm on the subcontinent. We're helping relocate heat refugees."

"Who's we?"

"It's boring. It's not why I called. Nicholas told me you're pregnant. I can't not say anything."

In her womb, Sluggo stretched, hooking a limb under Ruby's ribs. She stood up to relieve the pressure. She felt anger come on so quick.

It's not simply that Jace is always critical of Ruby. He has a way of needling into things she already feels uncertain about. When she first moved back to Spokane, she told him about the firm she'd been hired by, hoping he wouldn't remember its name from the billboards and bus stop bench ads. "I never figured you for an ambulance chaser," he said, cutting right to the heart of the matter.

"You have a diatribe on the subject of human reproduction, I assume?"

"I thought you knew better. And if you couldn't resist the siren song of your own hormones, I at least trusted Brayden would be a voice of reason. It's just insane, Ruby."

She expected a lecture about the environmental impact of a baby. She told him she didn't want to hear it.

"No," he said. "I'm thinking about my niece or nephew. How could you do this to them? How could you bring them into this world?"

His voice, which had moments prior been clear, turned jagged. She thought the connection had gone spotty. But then she pegged the change for what it was. He was struggling for control. Trying not to cry. Or trying not to yell. She didn't know her brother well enough anymore to be able to tell the difference.

RUBY AND BRAYDEN had discussed the issue at length: Was it ethical to have a child? They'd convinced themselves yes.

"We're allowed to live our lives," Brayden said. It has become a catchphrase of sorts, and a reassurance when some evidence is presented to the contrary. *We're allowed to live our lives.*

To hear the opposite, put so bluntly by Jace, was unbearable. Because though Ruby does not admit as much to the rest of the family, she's always trusted that he is right on such matters. He would not live as he does if he weren't right.

RUBY AND BRAYDEN have adopted another adage as well. *We'll do what it takes.* This is shorthand. *We'll do what it takes to keep our child safe.* So far, this has seemed reasonable, something that can be accomplished through attention to detail and the spending of money. Sluggo's safety can be bought, if they just know the right things to buy. Like the FourthTri Chamber, the car seat with the best crash test rating, the all-organic cotton onesies. Though most of those items were gifts from their baby shower. They weren't going to have a baby shower originally, thinking it gauche to ask others to pay for their things, especially when they would not be attending showers for their friends—again, the general lack of breeding in their cohort. But another expense had come up, and they felt they could use the help.

It was at an appointment with Ruby's obstetrician. The baby was healthy and growing well by all observable metrics, the doctor in a good mood, chatting amicably. Then the woman's mood had turned. "It is hard on summer babies, you know," she said. "The smoke."

Ruby assured the doctor they had an air purifier for the nursery.

She shook her head. "It's not enough. Those particles are so small. At a certain point, they're just everywhere and the room purifiers only do so much good. If you have the means . . ." She gave Ruby the name of a central home purification system that could be installed in the ductwork and that promised to filter the air throughout an entire house, cleaning it like new every seven minutes. "Just like we have here at the hospital," she said.

Ruby looked it up once she got home and was aghast. To suggest that the safety of a newborn's lungs could not be had for less than the cost of a new car. There was no question in Ruby's mind they were going to pay it. She and Brayden took out a loan. Its installation had just been completed the week prior.

We'll do what it takes, and so far they had not been thwarted. What about Jace's heat refugees? Is he moving them into Hyderabad or out of it? It seems like a hot place but maybe they are coming from somewhere even hotter. Ruby is embarrassed by how little she knows, her inability to keep tabs on all the suffering. Regardless, those people too must have said *We'll do what it takes*, but then found they could not. She feels guilty for her own safety, for the privilege of being able to buy safety, and the fear that that privilege is really just an expensive illusion.

THEN THERE IS JENNA. Jenna and her letters, which she stops by unannounced to drop off, two or three at a time. She usually comes in the mornings, when Ruby is getting ready for work, probably the worst of all possible times for unplanned parental drop-ins. While she is there, she inspects the progress on the air-purification project, pats Ruby's belly, and whispers things to the baby in a voice so small Ruby can't hear.

Ruby is trying hard to be understanding. Her mother is lonely, her mother is worried, her mother is excited. Her mother has few other outlets for these feelings. Ruby's dad passed away two years ago from a sudden heart attack. Ruby has read many things about the longevity of grief since then. The analogy that fits best for her is one of her own making: Long-term grief is like the jelly in a peanut butter and jelly sandwich made hastily by a child. There's a little in every bite but mostly it gets overshadowed by the peanut butter and bread—the constants, the daily life things. Then occasionally you get a bite with no warning that's just all jelly. She misses him a little all the time and sometimes more than she can stand. She knows that for her mother, every sandwich is still mostly jelly.

But the fucking letters. The first ones were vague enough to be inoffensive. Then there were some that, though strange, were funny and harmless. But this most recent batch is, frankly, really pushing Ruby's boundaries. Most obnoxiously, Jenna has given the baby a name. She addresses these new letters to Marigold. This is not a name Ruby has considered for Sluggo. She doesn't know why her mother has chosen it, why she sees fit to call her grandchild—who might actually still be a boy—that. Well, she does, but only because Jenna explains it in the letter. Ruby bites her tongue, lets Jenna do what she wants, but her patience is waning and when Jenna came by (unannounced, of course) three days earlier, Ruby ran out without brushing her hair or packing her lunch, claiming an early-morning staff meeting just to get away.

KAVYA DRIVES THEM south from Ruby's subdivision. To enter Spokane on I-90 from the west is to have plenty of forewarning that a city is near. The highway descends from a forested plateau, downtown growing steadily larger in view. There is the impression of coming in for a landing. Arriving in Little Seattle from the north side of town is the wholly opposite experience. One bend in the road and the long stretch of modest bungalows with rambling yards gives way to the sharp glass of office buildings and condo complexes. Traffic slows. Kavya winds the car through narrow streets while narrating all the sights for Valor. "Do you see the crane, sweetie? So tall! Do you see the truck? Do you see the blue bus? Honk honk bus."

Little Seattle is a lot of things. Most simply, it is an extension of Spokane's original downtown. The true downtown is hemmed in—trapped on one side by the Spokane River, on the other by the freeway and a hill. Its size now is the same as it was a century ago. But in the past twenty years, Spokane's population has tripled. This migration, mostly from the west side of the state, happened in waves, first gradually as people and businesses got priced out of Seattle. Hence the neighborhood's name. But it also speaks to its aesthetic, which feels much like Seattle's own jumbled business district.

The second wave of Little Seattle residents came all at once, uprooted by the lahar. Ruby was in college at the time and she and her sorority sisters had taken up a collection of canned goods and new clothes for the poor souls made homeless by the disaster. But their offerings were not necessary. It turned out the people capable of relocating to a city across the state were those of means. The real refugees were housed for months in camps just outside the flood zone. Though many of them did make their way to Spokane and Little Seattle eventually—a slow third wave, which changed the face of the neighborhood again.

RUBY'S FIRST IMPRESSION of MamaBahama is that it's an upscale boutique. It smells of lavender, with high-end nursery furniture and wooden toys on display. But the store opens into a warehouse beyond the showroom. Pallets of diapers and formula line the walls. Kavya points out a sales associate and beelines for her, pulling the Fourth-Tri Chamber's instruction booklet from her pocket as she walks. The woman is already shaking her head before Kavya even opens her mouth. "B17? We sold the last one yesterday. The manufacturer says they accidentally shipped eleven hundred units without them. There's a form you can fill out online and they'll send it to you for free, but it could be eight to twelve weeks, so that might not fly here." She gestures at Ruby's midsection.

Kavya looks to Ruby and Ruby assumes it is to see if she is secretly crying again.

"Do you know of any other store in town that carries them?" Ruby asks.

"No," the woman says. "We're it for spare parts. But"—she looks around to see who might be listening, though there is no one else in the store—"I know a guy who may be able to help."

"Help how?"

"He's a metalsmith. He could make something the same size as B17."

"Okay," Kavya says. "That sounds good. Why so shady about it?"

The woman shrugs. "He's just a shady dude."

RUBY AND KAVYA ACCEPT the name and address of the metalsmith. The woman has written it down on a strip of receipt paper. Her handwriting isn't great. Outside the store, they bow their heads over it together. It appears to say *Mr. Socks—8888 W. Mutton., back of castle.* Valor, strapped to Kavya's chest in his baby carrier, kicks his little legs in anticipation.

"There is no 8888 West Mutton, obviously," Kavya says. She consults her phone. "But there's a 2688 on West Mallon, so that's probably it."

"Back of castle? Does this really say castle? What could that mean? Should we go back in and ask?"

"No," says Kavya. "We can figure this out. Walk or drive?"

Ruby's feet hurt. The sky has turned dark with gathering storm clouds. Despite what the salesclerk said about B17, Ruby assumes there must be a secondary market for such things online, which she can find if she turns around and heads home. Or she can get Brayden on the project. He'd be back from his own weekend errands by now, and she could take a nap. But she suddenly cannot bear the thought of going back into Sluggo's nursery without the missing part. Though they have only been gone forty-five minutes, it feels to Ruby like their quest has been much greater. She will not return empty-handed. Ruby does not want Kavya to have to pay for parking again. It's less than a mile.

"It's fine," Ruby says. "Let's walk."

THEY WALK and the neighborhood grows denser. Stand-alone businesses give way to office towers.

"You know which of your mom's letters I like best?" Kavya asks.

"Wait, what?"

"The one about the nuclear lab, or whatever, in California? Kind of wild, what your parents were up to back in the day."

"The early aughts were a heady time, apparently," Ruby says, hoping to sound casual, as if her parents' past is old news, rather than something she is just now learning from letters intended not for her, but for her child.

"You're right," Ruby adds. "That's definitely not the worst one. The worst is the one where she talks about me and her being mountains. Did you read that one? Where she tells the baby it should be a lahar, kind of? Who tells that to a child? *Sweetie, my greatest wish is for you to become a giant murder mudslide.* I can't stand it. I might burn that one. Don't tell."

"Your baby's lucky," Kavya says. "I wish I'd had someone in my life when I was a kid who wanted that for me."

Ruby feels shame rise up hot.

"I used to live on this street," Kavya says, and Ruby, surprised, whips her head around, looking for anyplace a person might live.

"Only until I was in second grade. It was all just houses then," she says, and there is something so sad in her voice. Ruby struggles to remember Little Seattle before it was Little Seattle, but she knows this section was a neighborhood called West Central, and that it had other, less kind nicknames. *A beautiful day in Felony Flats*, her dad used to say when they'd drive past. But it was already all offices. Maybe, Ruby thinks, she never actually saw it any other way.

She sucks her teeth, unsure how to phrase the question. She does not know this woman well.

"What was it like?" she almost whispers.

"Honestly, it was the best. Every house on our block had kids and in the summers we'd run all over together, playing in each other's yards. I don't think anyone ever put shoes or sunblock on me. None of the grown-ups cared what we did; no one was looking. I love the cul-de-sac I live on now, but also, sometimes, fuck it, you know? Waverly was playing out in the front yard by herself the other day and one of my neighbors actually came to the door to ask if I knew my daughter was alone, unsupervised on the street. I mean, she's seven years old, and I was right there, inside the house. Just imagine if she'd been barefoot too."

Can we ever truly know what's at the heart of other people's laments? Ruby remembers family road trips to Seattle. Outside Ellensburg, a rail bridge spans the I-5 freeway. *Palouse to Cascades State Park Trail* is what the sign on it has said for as long as Ruby has been able to read. But each time they would drive beneath it, her parents would shake their heads, point upward, lift their eyes as if to heaven. "RIP Kittitas Bong Squad," they'd intone solemnly together. Ruby understood it was a reference to some piece of graffiti that had once adorned the face of the bridge, before it was rehabbed by the parks system. It had been important to her parents, Ruby thought. And they were sad it was gone. When she learned, as a preteen, what a bong was, she'd felt terribly embarrassed—for herself for being tricked by their faux earnestness, and for them, for making the same joke, year after year after year. "Stooooop," she'd moan as they passed the bridge, her parents mid–Bong Squad reverie. "You're being so dumb!"

It was only later, well into adulthood, that she realized maybe it was the loss of the joke itself they were mourning. Something stupid and inscrutable they'd loved together for that very reason.

"But do you remember a castle?" she asks.

Kavya laughs. "No, I don't remember any fucking castle."

A FEW BLOCKS FARTHER and the street's density eases again. There's an apartment building with a grocery store on the bottom, a bar called the Funeral Parlor, an auto parts store, a community garden, then what looks like a vacant lot. But the vacant lot isn't vacant, just large and unkempt. Near the back of it is, unmistakably, a very small and unassuming castle. There is a turret and a wall with arrow loops and a drawbridge. The whole structure looks the size of a two-bedroom bungalow. Behind that, a larger structure: two stacked shipping containers. A line of men snakes out from it and into the lot.

"I think we've found Mr. Socks," Kavya says. "Should we get in line?"

"Absolutely not," Ruby says.

It has started to rain. It was just a spritz while they walked, but now fat drops fall. Valor mewls as they strike his nearly bald head.

"You're right, better just go straight inside," Kavya says, and though this is not what Ruby meant, she follows.

They pass the queue of men. There is one child, an elementary schooler in a Little League uniform. No women.

Up close the castle still looks like a castle, but it is also clearly a house. It has a mailbox and a front porch. Ruby likes it. The shipping container structure behind it is a shop. It has a front door and windows adorned with flower boxes.

"Excuse me," Kavya says to the men waiting at the door, then, louder, "We have an appointment. Step aside."

They part for her. Ruby is grateful to have this person in her life, someone who can clear the way when the way needs to be cleared. Ruby thinks she used to be such a person. Inside the door is a vestibule of a room designated as a waiting area. Two men wait in it already. Somewhere in the shop, a little bell dings, and a moment later a man opens an interior door and sticks out his head.

"There's a line," he says.

Kavya gestures to Valor. "I needed to get him out of the rain. Are you Mr. Socks?"

"No," the man says.

"Can you make something for us? We're missing a part."

"For a HydroPipe, or a Penis Star?"

"Neither." Kavya holds out the instruction booklet for the Fourth-Tri Chamber and points to B17. He takes it from her hands.

"All your other customers," Ruby says, "are they waiting on parts too?"

"Yep. For HydroPipes and Penis Stars," the man who is not Mr. Socks says. He studies the booklet a moment longer. "Okay, I have something that will work." Then he disappears back into the shop.

"What do you think a Penis Star is?" Ruby whispers to Kavya, who shakes her head, covering Valor's ears with her hands in mock disgust.

"I can show you, if you want," one of the men in the room says. He is smiling, leering, his hand traveling toward his pants.

"Take your dick out and I'll cut it off," Ruby warns.

"Jesus, it's not on my dick," the man says, holding up both hands. "It's in my pocket. You don't know nothing about Penis Stars, do you?"

"I'd like to keep it that way, thank you," Ruby says.

The man who is not Mr. Socks comes back. He hands Ruby a metal tube the width and length of her thumb. It is so lightweight, it feels like she is holding nothing besides the sensation of coolness and smoothness. It is a calming feeling—the texture of the object in her hand as well as its significance. She has solved the problem of B17. She is a good mother after all, capable and resourceful.

"Be careful with that," Not Mr. Socks says. "It's just a thin aluminum, like a Coke can. It'll bend. Should do the job, though—it's mostly an aesthetic piece anyway." He holds out the FourthTri Chamber booklet and jabs at the page with his finger. "It's just a casing for these two silicone tubes. You could have used a milkshake straw and been fine. This will look nicer, though."

Ruby thanks him, promises to handle the metal gently.

"It's fifty dollars," he says.

"For what?" Kavya asks. "You said you already had the tube. You said we could have just used a straw."

"But you didn't use a straw. You want the tube?"

Ruby pays. "What's the story with the castle? Is it your house?" she asks.

Not Mr. Socks's eyes narrow as if he didn't expect this from Ruby, as if she was once someone he trusted but now he isn't so sure.

"No, it's no one's fucking house," he says.

Ruby and Kavya leave quickly.

Outside, the rain has slowed but the wind is beginning. Gusts rattle anything that's rattle-able. Thunder grumbles but sounds far off.

"Success!" Kavya says and offers Ruby a high five. "Man. What a weird scene, though." She wraps her arms around Valor to shield him from the wind. They begin their walk back to the car. Hardly anyone is on the sidewalk now and Ruby thinks this is worse than when there's a crowd. She tucks B17 into her shirt pocket and pats it for the feeling of safekeeping.

"I'm really grateful for your help," she says.

"Of course, happy to!" Kavya says. "Remember when you told that guy you were going to cut his dick off?"

"Yes, vividly."

"That's the Counselor Fenster I know! Where you been all day? Don't say hormones or I'll hemorrhage."

Now Ruby unloads.

She tells Kavya about how Nicholas has left his State Parks job to fight wildfires. How Jace turned up after more than half a year missing to accuse her of endangering her baby simply by birthing it. How her mom is lonesome and Ruby is worried about her, but when she wants to express that worry all that comes out is frustration.

She talks for what feels like a long time. When she finishes, she takes a deep breath.

"Duuuuuuude," Kavya says. "That's a lot."

Ruby is grateful. She has said too much, too fast. But her friend has understood. It is, indeed, at lot.

"I know," Ruby says. "Dude, I know. The really fucked-up thing is, I keep thinking if Nicholas dies, I'll name the baby after him. The season hasn't even started. He hasn't jumped out of a single airplane yet. But already I'm envisioning him dead, thinking of giving his name to someone else. Sometimes I catch myself calling the baby Nicholas. Usually I call it Sluggo."

"Not Marigold."

Ruby recalls for Kavya the answer Jenna gave three days prior, when Ruby confronted her about her use of the name. Just before she'd made excuses to leave early for work.

"She said the baby has to be a girl because men die or leave."

"Oof," Kavya says.

"I told her that's totally irrational. Everyone dies! Staying or leaving has nothing to do with gender. But she said it's been her experience."

"Double oof."

"I know she'll love whoever the baby is once it gets here," Ruby says. "But right now she's going through it."

"So am I. I guess that proves her point? We're stuck together. At least we've got each other. My stupid brothers, I could kill them both right now."

"Such is the nature of little brothers."

"Kavya." Ruby looks to the darkened sky. "How do you justify having four? In all this?" She gestures to the clouds, the trees on the horizon, the ground.

"Well, they'll need each other, then, won't they?" Kavya says quickly. Ruby understands this is not a real answer.

"You know, it always seems to me that the people who have the most to say about something aren't the ones doing the most about it," Kavya says. "It's usually the opposite. They're the ones doing the least and they feel super guilty."

"You think that's Jace?"

"Dude might just be on an island somewhere, drinking rum out of a coconut. That other brother sounds like he's doing a lot, though. What does he talk about?"

"Dumb things. Beer and video games. Where to find good bagels."

IT'S RAINING VERY HARD again.

"It was a mistake to have walked," Ruby says.

By the time they reach the car, Valor is wailing from the cold and wet. Kavya dries him as best she can, takes off his wet pants and socks, straps him into his car seat with a blankie. He will not settle and continues to cry. Kavya is unfazed and speaks gently to him as she drives. There is something reassuring in this scene. Steadfastness. Ruby takes the metal tube from her pocket, turns it over in her hands.

She does not think Jace has spent the decade lounging in tropical locales. Whatever he's doing, it's something. He's trying his best. So is Nicholas, and so is Jenna, and so is Ruby. They have each staked out the things that matter to them and they are trying to do right by those things. No one can do right by all the things at once.

She takes her phone from her bag and texts Nicholas.

Sorry I've been a brat. I'm really proud of you.

He texts back right away, **Jace says American firefighting techniques reflect how we value private property over people and the environment. Continued fire mismanagement just means more fires.**

Jace isn't the boss of fires, Ruby replies. **Are you staying home?**

No. I want to go.

Good. Be safe.

She puts the phone away, goes back to fiddling with the tube.

A howl of wind hits the car. Kavya pulls on the wheel to keep them in their lane. Then a tree branch falls into the street and seems to explode, bark launching onto the windshield. Kavya swerves. Ruby clenches her fists. The tube pops under the pressure in her hand. Not Mr. Socks was right. It was thin and she should have been careful. She opens her fingers. The tube is not crushed but pretty thoroughly bent in the middle. It is not really a tube anymore.

"Oh no," Kavya says. "Oh, Ruby. I'm so sorry."

"It's okay," Ruby says. "I'll figure something else out."

"Well, yeah," Kavya says. "Of course."

Kavya drops Ruby off at home. Ruby thanks her profusely for her help, apologizes again for being so pitiful, tells her to enjoy the rest of her weekend. Kavya offers her own goodbyes but does not get out of the car, her eyes on the sky the whole time. Ruby can tell she wishes she was already snug indoors with all her babies or maybe even in the basement if they live near tall pines. Ruby has not seen Kavya's house, and did not think, even as they drove through the storm, to ask what awaited her at home.

INSIDE, RUBY WANTS ASSURANCES but she's not sure in what form. She takes off her shoes and pulls on a sweater even though she's not cold. On the wall, by the light switches, is a dial for the central air purifier. She clicks it once. "Standard clean" is the setting. Its hum is gentle but persistent enough to drown out the wind outside. Is it a crime to be able to twist a knob and feel safe? To want clean air even on a day when there is no smoke?

Brayden emerges from the den. He does not ask why she has turned the air purifier on. He casts his eyes up as if to the ductwork, or to God.

"Sounding good," he says.

Ruby kisses him and grazes his shoulders with her fingers. He asks if she and Kavya finished setting up the chamber.

"Almost," she says. "We had to go to Little Seattle for a missing part."

"Isn't that always the way? Well, do you want help with the last of it?"

Ruby shakes her head. She's got it, she says.

When he has returned to the den, Ruby takes the crushed metal tube from her pocket and sets it on the table. She takes out her phone again, and this time texts her mom and both brothers.

Do you guys remember the railroad bridge over I-90 that used to say "Kittitas Bong Squad"???

The boys won't know what she's talking about, she thinks, but this will make her mom happy.

The phone buzzes while it is still in her hand. The response is not from Jenna but from Jace.

RIP.

She will not feel guilty, she decides. She will not feel guilty for wanting a baby, for having a baby, for doing what she needs to do to keep her baby safe.

In the kitchen cupboard, there are plastic straws in a plastic cup. She rifles through them, finds the fattest one.

"Are you a milkshake straw?" she asks. She measures it against the metal piece from Not Mr. Socks, cuts it to the same length. Then she calls to Brayden, saying she does want his help after all.

Though really what she wants is to tell the story of her trip to Little Seattle. She wants to hear him laugh about the Penis Stars and gasp at the close call with the tree limb. And years from now, when they drive past the place where the castle was—because surely it will be gone for one reason or another—they can tell Sluggo, "There used to be a tiny castle here," and their beautiful daughter, who will not know the world to have been any other way, can roll her eyes and wonder why anyone would care.

Up in the nursery, Ruby shows her husband the straw. "Clever," he says. "We'll find a way," he says. She slides the tubing for the humidification port through. It fits fine.

The Octopus Finds Love at Home

What can I say? I'd always been a solitary creature.

I thought I would spend my life alone, like my mother did, and my grandmother, and really all my female ancestors for the past three hundred million years or so. I won't claim I was happy in my solitude, but I wasn't unhappy either. After all, I was busy. I didn't have time for friendships or amorous pursuits, my nights full of stalking and hunting and eating, then cleaning my suction cups. And that's to say nothing of my den—its upkeep became a constant chore.

It's because of my den that I met Brandt.

My den is in a rock crevice. I took to it in the first season of my adulthood. No longer a rambunctious paralarva, I was ready to settle down with a place of my own. It was a terrific find—not too large, not too small, and with a narrow entrance that I could just barely squeeze myself through so I knew no one bigger would come in and eat me. Really, an ideal location on all accounts.

But then the sea snails showed up. At first it was just a few of them, creeping into my den and clinging to the walls. I didn't mind them initially. I mean, I wasn't looking for roommates, but they weren't a bother. Then one morning I came home, tired and ready just to clean my suction cups and hit the hay, and suddenly there were hundreds of them! I was mad. It was my den, not theirs. I tried eating them, but they were too much effort, so I settled for plucking them from the walls and flinging them out of the crevice, even the few who had been there since the beginning and who, if I'm being honest, I did have a slight fondness for and had even given nicknames. But Ringo, Curly, and Stella had to go. I could not risk further infestation.

The snails just came back. They were tenacious. I did not know where they spent their days, but each morning when I returned from hunting, there they were. Pests. They also posed a risk I didn't realize. You see, just because I didn't want to eat them doesn't mean no one else did.

One morning I came home so wiped out I didn't have the energy for anything—not for cleaning my suction cups, and definitely not for excising the snails. I just burrowed in beside them and went to sleep, cursing their tiny rigid shells. I'll admit that in my frustration, I did almost wish for someone to complain to. But that was not my life.

I was jarred awake by the terrifying sound of something entering my den. It was a giant crab. He had pushed the rock that formed my entryway aside and was snarfing snails like my den was a snail buffet. I shot him in the face with my ink and he freaked out. He flailed his big stupid pincers around, knocking snails from the walls. He scuttled off. I was victorious! A minute later he was back, clawing at the rocks around me. I heard clattering and thought my home was falling down. I fled, a trail of displaced snails tumbling in my literal wake.

I swam around for a while, then just gave up and floated. I was terribly sad. I loved that den. I'd thought I would live there forever. It's where I wanted to lay my eggs someday, all sixty or seventy thousand of them. I had imagined tending to my brood in that cozy space, cleaning them over and over until they hatched and were whisked through the crevice by the current, out into the big wide world. Then I was going to die in that den. It was the perfect dying den!

After a while of floating and moping, I returned home to see what might be salvaged. I thought I could at least gather my belongings: my collection of nice pebbles and a shiny jar lid I'd found. I liked to look at my reflection in that lid. I was amazed to find my den still standing. The crab hadn't knocked it down after all. The big oaf had only scattered some other nearby rocks. I inspected the damage and found the crab's clumsy handiwork had exposed another crevice just inches from my own. I went to look inside and was surprised to see an eye peeking out. It was a familiar eye, the same kind I saw when I looked into my metal lid. I felt my anger flare. Another octopus. Worse than that, a neighbor.

I stared into the eye as I contemplated my rage. This would mean competition for prey, competition for nice pebbles and shiny things. Not to mention the noise. How was I supposed to sleep with the sounds of someone cleaning their gross suction cups nearby? That's when the eye did an infuriating thing: it winked.

In the days that followed, I watched my neighbor carefully. He was not an unattractive octopus. He had reddish skin and long arms. He swam in kind of a jaunty way, bopping along with the current almost as if it was a toy for playing. I hated him with all my three hearts.

He kept to himself at first. In fact, he seemed to go out of his way to avoid me. A smart choice, I thought. After all, it's a known fact that we females can be quite aggressive.

His timidity didn't last. One evening, just as I was waking up, I heard a tapping at my entryway. I looked and there was a single red arm, inching into the crevice: the customary introduction of a male octopus looking to mate.

"Hi! I'm Brandt," a voice called from the new den next door. "What's your name?"

I opened my beak, not to speak but to chomp the intruding arm, which I did, severing it from the rest of Brandt's body in a single bite. I know this sounds harsh, but it is also a customary gesture—a way to say *No thank you*. Plus, he could just grow another one, no big deal.

"Okay!" Brandt said. "I get it! Maybe another time! Can I try you again tomorrow?"

Still I said nothing.

Then after a moment, he asked, "Can I have my arm back?"

This gave me pause. "What for?" I asked.

"I'd like to keep it as a souvenir."

"No," I said. "I'm going to eat it."

"Okay!" he shouted again. "Enjoy!"

He didn't shout anymore after that. Though I was relieved, I also felt something else. Disappointment? It was so unusual to hear a voice in my den; there'd never been one before. Once it was gone, I was acutely aware of its absence.

I looked the arm over closely before I devoured it. The suction cups had been neatly groomed. He was making an effort. For that, I hated him even more.

You see, this was the real source of my anxiety about my neighbor, not that he would take all the good fish and good pebbles. Because there are, as the saying goes, always more fish in the sea. That's even more true of pebbles. No, my real anger stemmed from one simple, selfish fact: I was not ready to mate.

It is true that I had happily imagined the day I would lay my eggs, and the day my thousands of offspring would hatch and make me a proud mama, and the day, very soon thereafter, of my death. But I thought of all that as far off in the future. After all, I was only a year old. If I was careful and took care of myself, I might still have two more good years ahead of me. I didn't want to surrender that time just because some clean, nice-looking guy happened to move in next door. I vowed I would eat all his arms if that was what it took to protect myself from his advances.

He did not send another arm the next evening. Only his voice. Smart, I thought again.

"Excuse me," he said. "I'm sorry to bother you. But do you have snails over there?"

"Yes," I said. "I have several. Would you like some?"

"No. I also have several. More than several. How do you get rid of them?"

I told him about my method of plucking and throwing.

"And do they stay away?"

"No. But isn't doing something better than doing nothing?"

He didn't answer and I wished I had asked a less abstract question. Because even though I didn't want him to keep talking, I really did want him to keep talking. It was confusing.

The following evening, his voice appeared again with an "Excuse me." That was polite, I thought. This time he asked after my collection of nice pebbles and shiny things. He had lost his own collection when he moved dens and missed them. Might he come over and see mine? he asked. I said no, but I did offer to describe each item to him in detail, which he accepted. He was a good listener. After I was done describing all my things, it was well into the night and we were both hungry. We left our dens at the same time to hunt. I thought he might invite me to hunt with him, which I would refuse, but he didn't. As soon as he saw me, he swam quickly away.

For a while after that, we spoke every evening. He asked about my favorite kinds of fish, my favorite directions of current. He asked deeper questions, like did I remember any of my siblings from our hatch day, and what did I think my mother might have been like. We shared our laments about the snails. We schemed elaborate anti-crab defense plans. It was pleasant to have such discussions, and when I went out afterward, I was always ravenous, eager to feast on any being I could fit in my mouth. But of course I knew we would not carry on like this forever.

One night, after talking for some time about our feelings regarding squid (dumb cousins, we both agreed), Brandt said, "I think our conversations have been going well, don't you?"

Then he ruined the very conversation we were having by asking if he might send over a semen-laden arm for the purpose of fertilization.

"Why would you want to do that if you like talking to me so much?" I asked.

"Because I want to mate with you!" he said.

But male octopuses die soon after mating, just as females die once our eggs have hatched. With him dead, we would not be able to talk anymore.

"If you wish for your corporeal end, why not bring your whole body over here and let me eat you?" I asked. "At least then you'd be doing something nice for me on your way out."

Brandt was quiet for a long time after that. So long I thought I might not hear from him ever again—that he would likely pack up and move to another den in search of a more willing female neighbor.

Finally, though, he did speak.

"What if I come over and you don't eat me?" he asked. "I won't bring any semen. We could just . . . hang out."

I tried to straighten my den up quickly. I arranged my pebble collection along the wall. I swept as many snails from the crevice as would go.

"Okay," I said. "I suppose we could give it a try."

I was not prepared for what it would be like to have another octopus in my den. It was, after all, a space intended for just me. We had to press against each other to fit. At first, I didn't care for it. Brandt was firm and squishy all at once. His skin was soft, though, and I liked getting to look into his eyes. I asked him to wink and when he did, I was not angered at all.

We stayed in my den for several hours, not cuddling exactly, just being close. When we got hungry, it seemed only natural that we would go hunt together. We caught so many fish! Brandt startled them out of their hiding places and then I grabbed them. It was so much easier than hunting alone, and so much more fun. Why, I wondered, didn't octopuses always work in pairs? I resolved to share this revelation should I ever meet another octopus.

Though I still did not wish to meet other octopuses. I had Brandt and that was enough.

After that, we always met in my den as soon as we woke each night. Brandt made an effort at eating my snails to be polite. Then we hunted. Eventually, he started coming back to my den to sleep as well. I learned to like the feel of his body smooshed against mine. I still made him leave when I cleaned my suction cups. A lady needs some time to herself, after all. Other than that, we were always at each other's side, arms often entwined. Sometimes I forgot which arms were mine and which were his. And how funny was that? It was good to have someone to laugh with. Someone to swim with. Someone to gripe about snails with.

Would we ever mate? I didn't know. I loved Brandt. That was the feeling, I decided, when I looked into his eyes and asked him to wink. The only thing I felt certain of: I did not want that love to end.

It seemed to me love was always a little selfish. Or more accurately, love was always an act of sacrifice. Sometimes you sacrificed your plans, sometimes you sacrificed your space. Sometimes you sacrificed your offspring and your duty to your species and the implicit promise you made to the millions of strong, beautiful female octopuses who came before you. You gave that all away in the name of something better, something just for you.

Chet's Landing Resort and Luxury Cabins

At first, we assumed the pack of children who roamed the grounds of Chet's Landing Resort and Luxury Cabins belonged to a large family there for a reunion. But when the reunion ended and the family left, the children remained. Some of the little girls wore sundresses, but most of the children were clad only in swimsuits. They played in the pool, chased each other across the lawn, and dug deep sand pits on the beach. They seemed to be very self-possessed children and didn't cause us any trouble, although we had to pay special attention when pulling into or out of the driveway because they never bothered to look before crossing the narrow road. Sometimes they were loud after we'd gone to bed, laughing and shrieking into the early hours of the morning. Other times we'd come back after going for drinks in town and they were nowhere to be found. We had no idea where they slept.

We came to Murre Bay, Oregon, at the end of July. We picked Chet's at random and although it was rustic, we did not regret our choice. Our cabin had three rooms—bedroom, bathroom, and a living room/kitchenette with shag carpet and a sagging beige couch.

The television had rabbit ears and there was not enough space for the stove and refrigerator doors to be open at the same time. Initially, we planned to stay a week, but then when that first week was up we asked the proprietors if we could keep our cabin longer. Though we'd arrived in Oregon with a goal in mind, we'd made little real progress toward it. As if the goal itself was enough. And so we were content, mostly, to spend our days exploring the beaches and drinking in nautical-themed bars. We bought fresh fish and vegetables from the nearby market to cook in our tiny kitchen. We read the local paper each morning and chuckled at the small-townness of it.

The resort's owners—Simon and Felicia Wojcik—were eager to tell us how they'd purchased Chet's when they first moved to Oregon in the 1980s. "We loved the coast so much, we didn't want to leave," Max said. "So we didn't!" Felicia added. It was like they were reading from a script when they said this, but still we were charmed. They were happy to extend the rental on our cabin and even bumped an extra 10 percent off our already very reasonable rate. About other matters, however, the pair was more demure. They claimed not to know who Chet was. When we asked about the children, Felicia looked confused, as if she did not understand the question. Simon simply shook his head. "It's nothing," he said.

If the children seemed in danger, or even simply uncared for, we would have pressed the issue. We weren't monsters, after all. At least, not those kinds of monsters. The likeliest answer was that they were the offspring of local vacation-home owners and they had found, at Chet's, a swath of territory to call their own. Aside from us, there were only ever a handful of other guests, all of whom gave them a wide berth, and clearly the Wojciks paid them little mind. So they were free to swim and dig and run around as they pleased until it was time to go home, whatever time that was (some nights, seemingly never).

Sometimes in the evenings, if we did not feel like walking into town, we would sit at the picnic table in front of our cabin with a bottle of wine and watch the children. They played some games we recognized, like freeze tag and red rover, and others we did not. There didn't seem to be any winners of these games; they just ended whenever they ended. The games were never violent or cruel and none of the kids were upset by the outcomes. We respected what we referred to as their "democratic nature." There was a range in ages, with the tallest kids, including a set of identical twin boys in matching blue-and-red swim trunks, around twelve or thirteen years old and the smallest as young as four. But they all stayed together. We counted a dozen one night and never saw any new ones join after that or were aware of any missing. It was impossible to tell who among them was in charge, and so we liked to assume no one was.

During our third week at Chet's Landing Resort and Luxury Cabins, another couple rented the cabin next to ours, which had been vacant since the family reunion concluded. These new people, Kev and Gina Broadworthy, were our age and looked very similar to us, with their golf shirts and boat shoes. The distinction, we quickly learned, was that they actually played golf and owned a boat. Our new neighbors, however, were not pleased with their accommodations. "My goodness," Kev said the first time we met them, "this whole place looks like the set of a seventies porno." He'd really leaned in to the word *porno* like some men do, and Gina swatted him on the shoulder theatrically. All of this put us off of them somewhat, especially since we had agreed to find Chet's, with its cramped rooms and aged decor, charming rather than shabby. But they'd brought nice booze with them, this new pair, and so we found ourselves having drinks in the evenings at their picnic table. Even if they weren't the best people we'd ever met, their company was a welcome change of pace.

They too became curious about the children. We shared the observations we'd made already—their democratic nature, their inventiveness, their leaderlessness. We felt like proud parents, talking up their better attributes. "Well, they all look like they're sorely in need of a bath and a fresh change of clothes," Gina said. We watched the children, who were playing one of their inscrutable games, a moment longer and had to agree this was true. Their hair was greasy and many of their faces smudged with dirt. Their swimsuits frayed at the edges. Later, back in our own cabin, we conferred about this slovenliness. Was it a new development among the children, or had they always looked this way and we'd simply never noticed before? "And one of them clearly is in charge," Kev added. He gestured to one of the twins, the boy in the blue shorts. "That's the ringleader. It's obvious." We all stared at the boy. He did nothing explicitly leader-like. No shouting or pointing. But the others did seem hyperaware of him in some way. And when he left the lawn, walking toward the pool, all the rest followed. So that was how a game was finished—when he decided.

We suggested that maybe the boy in the blue shorts was only the leader for the day. Maybe each kid took a turn being the leader. Kev laughed at this. "That's not usually how these things work, is it?" We became defensive on the kids' behalf. We wanted to know what he meant by *these things*.

"Oh, cults and such. Children have a tendency to mimic the worst of adult society if given a chance. *Lord of the Flies*, you know."

We shook our heads and insisted one could not conflate fiction with reality in such a way.

"Well, regardless, we'd never let Bucko run around with a crew like this. That's for sure," Gina said, and Kev nodded in agreement. When we asked who Bucko was, Gina told us all about their own four-year-old son, Buckminster, who was spending the month with his grandmother in Olympia, but was such a dear and wonderful boy. We agreed he sounded great and bit our tongues and bid our time until we could be alone to laugh about the kind of life a boy named Buckminster Broadworthy might lead. "Do you think they make him wear a top hat and monocle at all times?" we joked. We whispered and giggled into our hands for fear our new neighbors might hear us through the paper-thin walls of our cabins.

After that, we started referring to one of the littler children as Buckminster Broadworthy. Then it seemed only natural to name the rest of them as well. There was a Timothy and a Megan and a Brittany. There was a Tobin and a Manuel. There were four Sandras. The twins were Zander (blue shorts) and Mikey (red shorts). We prided ourselves on selecting names randomly, not assigning them based on ethnicity or perceived personality traits, or even, in some cases, gender (one of the Sandras was a boy).

The next time we met up with the Broadworthys, they were eating breakfast at their picnic table, and when we shuffled out of our cabin on our way to get coffee from the front office, still feeling a little rough from the previous night's drinking, they called to us. "We've got more muffins and fruit than we can eat over here!" Kev said. We nodded and sat down. We picked at a single muffin between us while they chattered about their various summertime exploits prior to arriving at Chet's. The children were not yet out to distract us and we were sad for this.

The Broadworthys told us about a safari trip to South Africa. "Bucko's just the right age to really appreciate the beauty of wild animals," Gina said. And they told us about a charity regatta hosted by their country club to benefit Doctors Without Borders. "There had to be a hundred yachts out on Lake Washington if there was one," Kev said. "It was a tremendously successful event." We asked if the country club was also a yacht club, but Kev said no, it was a regular country club; it just so happened that almost everyone involved had a yacht. We nodded and underneath the picnic table kicked at each other's feet, a private code. "Anyway, it was a splendid day. We all had the best time. Bucko's first charity regatta!"

Gina was fiddling with her phone. "Would you like to see a picture?" she asked. We leaned over together to look at the screen. Buckminster wasn't dressed like a young Scrooge McDuck, as we'd imagined. Of course not. In the photo, he stood between his parents on the stern of a boat, leaning slightly against Kev's leg. He wore a Buzz Lightyear T-shirt and jean shorts. All three Broadworthys were smiling very earnestly and squinting from the sun. We looked at the photo, the two of us, not thinking the same things about it at all.

THAT EVENING, I didn't feel like talking about the Broadworthys. But James did. To do so had become our custom. We would go to one of the tourist bars in town, order red wine by the glass, and crack ourselves up.

"It's so good of Kev and Gina to raise money for Dockers Without Borders," James said. "No child in the world should go without pleated slacks."

I waited while he chuckled at his own joke.

"That yachting for charity stuff is risky, though," he went on. "Fortunately, in the event of a shipboard emergency, they can just use their inflated egos as life preservers."

When I again failed to laugh, James grew suspicious.

"Okay, what?" he asked, head cocked to the side, an eyebrow raised.

"I just don't want to talk about them tonight," I said.

"You mean you don't want to talk about them? Or you mean you don't want to kill them? There's an important distinction to be made here."

"Neither, I suppose."

"Well, now, that's a pity. Because I thought we finally had a plan."

WE'D COME to Murre Bay, Oregon, to do something heinous.

Not murder, necessarily. At least, not initially. At first, we'd been thinking to rob a bank.

In the spring, we'd heard a story on NPR about a couple from Alabama who'd committed a string of daring midday heists. They sounded a lot like me and James. Affluent white people in their late thirties. Jobs, friends, gym memberships. They hit a half dozen banks over the course of a year before they were caught. It was a rural branch in Louisiana that did them in. The lone teller, the only person inside the bank at all when they'd come in, had managed to slip out of their sight long enough to make a 911 call.

James and I heard the story while driving and we were so enraptured that we continued to sit in our car after we got home so we could listen to the rest. When it was over, I told James I thought the couple's mistake was they hadn't shot the teller right away. "If you've only got one witness, that's like no witness at all," I remember saying. We made love in the parking garage after that. Couldn't even make it up to our condo.

A few days later, I came home to find James huddled over a scatter of papers at the dining room table. "What's up, buttercup?" I asked, even though I could feel his excitement radiating and so I sort of already knew.

"I think we could do it—banks, I mean," he said. He showed me what he had. Printouts of news stories about other successful robberies. He'd jotted a list of supplies on a yellow legal pad. We had sex on the table with all those papers below us.

We'd reached a particular time in our relationship when we needed something like that. Each night after dinner, we'd pour drinks and settle into our project. We never talked about what we'd do with the money. Only how we'd get inside the bank and what we'd do once we were there. We'd always had a dark sense of humor together. I'd never found that erotic before. Now we couldn't keep our hands off each other. We couldn't stop laughing. James bought a slim handgun and put it on my pillow with a red bow left over from a box of Valentine's chocolates. I told him I felt like the prettiest girl at the ball.

We hit a snag pretty quickly when it came to actually picking a bank. We were living in downtown Seattle at the time. The banks in the city seemed daunting. So many people, so much security. Then any bank at all began to seem unrealistic, frankly. And then the game wasn't fun anymore. I put the gun in a drawer and we went back to watching Netflix after dinner. Once, in college, a friend of mine told me that when a couple starts sleeping back-to-back in bed the relationship is dead. I thought it was more likely when they start sitting on opposite ends of the couch.

So James suggested we get out of town. We would go someplace quiet, away from the city and all its complexities. There, we'd make a plan. We'd do something for real. And when we got back home, we'd have the shared memory to rehash in the car or on the dining room table, whenever we wanted or needed it.

We gave fake names and paid for everything in cash. As far as the

Wojciks knew, we were Bram and Elizabeth from Spokane. James suggested we burn our fingerprints off with bleach. I suggested we just buy gloves.

We stuck first with the idea of robbery. We could hit one of the bars, bloated with tourist cash, or a curio shop. But if banks were unreasonable, these places were pointless. There was no thrill for us in a midnight smash-and-grab.

We considered arson, which I liked. James wasn't interested unless we were intending a string of fires. "I'd like to make headlines," he said. "I want someone with a really good public radio voice to talk about us. Lakshmi Singh or Korva Coleman, preferably."

One afternoon we were out for a drive and James said we should kill a hitchhiker. They were plentiful in Murre Bay. We passed three in rapid succession and speculated about how it might go with each. Then we pulled over in a wooded area and made love in the back seat. After that, murder was the only thing that would do.

I was genuinely prepared to kill, I think. And unlike James, I didn't particularly care who the person was. But James needed a reason. The waitress at Man O' War who was rude to us, or the guy who fished from the pier and always hassled us to buy acid from him. For a while, we tailed a delivery driver James said looked just like a guy who'd bullied him in high school. We followed him to his house and everything. He lived alone, not even a dog. He was our top pick, until the Broadworthys came along.

THE BROADWORTHYS, like the Wojciks, knew us as Bram and Elizabeth. Kev had taken to calling me Lizzie almost right away, which, even though it wasn't my real name, I hated. We'd named ourselves after our favorite Victorian writers. Bram Stoker for him and Elizabeth Barrett Browning for me. I didn't imagine Browning ever went by Lizzie and I hadn't intended to either.

James took great pleasure in this. He worked up what he thought was a pretty good Kev impression and in the evenings, when we were alone, would use it to tease me.

"Oh, Lizzie, just one more thing. Would you mind coming back to my cabin and giving an old boy a hand? I seem to have dropped my pipe down my trousers and I'm hoping you can fish it out for me. Yes, yes, there's a dear, just reach right on in and don't mind anything else that gets in your way."

James's version of Kev was part Winston Churchill, part Rodney Dangerfield and, I think it goes without saying, sounded nothing like the real person.

Anyway, James thought that the thing to do would be to drug the Broadworthys first. Share a bottle of wine at the picnic table outside our cabins and send them home all dopey so they wouldn't know what was going on when we snuck in later to do what we liked.

And what did we like? Our ideas varied from a simple gunshot each to the head to bathtub dismemberment.

But where James needed to know enough about a person to decide they had reason to die (even a small or entirely made-up reason), I apparently needed to know as little as possible. I hadn't realized this until I'd seen the Broadworthys' family picture.

"They have a kid," I said.

"Yeah, baby Bucko," James said, miming a child crying and adjusting a tiny monocle at the same time. "That's not new."

"He'll be an orphan."

"He'll live with his grandma. He'll inherit the yacht. He'll be fine."

"I don't think anyone can be fine after their parents are murdered."

"What about Batman?"

"We're not in the business of creating Batmans here."

"I dunno, could be our new thing."

I told him I was serious. I let my face and my body show it. There was no more fun to be had for me with regard to the plan of killing the Broadworthys. I couldn't unsee the child in the picture, no matter what James might say.

James nodded. He seemed to deflate before my eyes. "Okay," he said. "What do you want to do now, then?"

I offered a sunset drive along the shore, or another drink at another bar. We did a good job of entertaining ourselves in Murre Bay, even when we weren't plotting crimes. We read on the beach, hiked, poked through antique shops downtown. Leisurely picnics and target practice in the woods with the gun. In a lot of respects, it was like any other vacation.

That wasn't what James meant, of course. Though I was in a sour mood, I hated the idea of being the one to end our good time.

"We can still hurt them," I said. "What about some light mutilation?"

"All right," James said. "All right, I'm listening. Let's work it through." Under the table, I felt his hand press between my thighs. I reached down and held it there.

"We could cut off their fingers," I said. Not all of them, I went on. Just one finger each. The ring finger, ring and all. Then we'd keep the fingers together in a cute little mason jar of formaldehyde as a symbol of our love. I particularly liked this last detail. As I spoke, I gained confidence in what I was proposing.

"We should definitely still drug them," I added as a concession to James's earlier idea.

AFTER THAT, things started to come together pretty quickly. James, always our research man, dug in on what sort of knife would be best for removing human digits. Reviews online pointed us toward a commercial cooking brand called Choppity-Hop.

We bought roofies from the guy who fished the pier. We asked questions about dosage, as if he were our trusted neighborhood pharmacist. How much to render two adults fully unconscious? How long for it to take effect? How long to peak?

"What are you two getting into?" he asked, only after we handed him our cash.

"Just a boring old married couple looking to spice things up," James said.

"You need another man for the job?"

"Absolutely not."

"Well. You know where to find me if you change your mind." Then he winked because he was the perfect sleaze, and after weeks of being repulsed by him now we agreed he was just grand.

"WHAT DO YOU THINK the Broadworthys are doing here?" James asked one night.

We were at a bar that had become our favorite. Its theme was beguiling. Crab-fishing equipment adorned the walls and traps hung from the ceiling. Lit tiki torches at the doors and inflatable palm trees throughout. Mai tais were always two for one. We ordered four to start so as not to have to rush back to the bar too soon.

"Vacationing?" I ventured.

"But why Chet's? I mean, they're rich. Yacht, country club, so forth. Shouldn't they be staying someplace swanky? And don't say they're slumming it for fun. Because you've heard them complain."

"Hmmmm, what's your hunch?"

"My hunch is they're up to something too! Those shady bastards. I bet Broadworthy isn't their actual name."

"You're suggesting we should watch out for our own ring fingers in their company?"

"I bet it's white-collar crime. Kev was running Ponzi schemes. Now they're on the lam with the money."

"No. It's family drama. They're hiding out from relatives who want their share of the inheritance Kev and Gina stole."

"Then why didn't they bring Bucko?"

"Would you bring Bucko?"

It was a funny thing to think. The Broadworthys concealing a secret as delicious as ours. After that, whenever we saw them around, James put his index finger to the corner of his eye. Look alive. The game is afoot.

Around that same time, the children started building something in the parking lot between the pool and the rental office. We thought it was a fort. It was made of plywood and cardboard, the pieces stacked together like a house of cards.

The structure grew tall, narrow at the top. One morning, after stopping in the office for a paper and a cup of coffee, we looked inside. The space within was small, not the clubhouse we had envisioned. There were no furnishings, not even any toys. In the middle were two sticks, a single carrot, and a hat.

"Like a dead snowman," James said.

The items seemed deliberately placed, the carrot standing on its broad end. *Shrine* was the word that came to mind, but I did not say this out loud.

"I get jealous of them sometimes," James said.

"Why? They're clearly terrible architects."

He didn't laugh. He was lost in his own thoughts.

"I never got to play like them when I was a kid. My own childhood was so . . ." And here he held out his hands, but only a few inches apart. I knew what he meant. His parents were nice people, but they thought life should be lived a certain way, inside and out.

"And now adulthood," he said, his hands still forming their small box of constraint.

Later that same day, while sunning ourselves on the lawn outside our cabin, we saw Simon Wojcik dragging the plywood pieces to the dumpster at the end of the driveway.

"Kids won't like that," I mused.

"Not one bit," James agreed.

"Do you think he ate the carrot?" I asked. "Pity to throw away a good carrot."

We had discussed cannibalism. Should there be a victorious consuming of the flesh we liberated? We dismissed this. But it was a worthwhile thought exercise nonetheless.

IT WAS BY FAR my favorite vacation we'd ever taken together. I recalled our other sojourns over the years: a river cruise on the Rhine, trekking in New Zealand, a culinary tour in Mexico City. How wasteful they'd been when really everything I wanted was a four-hour drive from home.

"We should do this every summer," I said one evening.

James nodded, and made a sweeping gesture to the mild sunset in front of us. But I sensed he did not agree.

In fact, I had begun to notice a certain reticence from my partner in crime.

Not long after that night, James asked, "When do you wanna go back to Seattle?"

We were at our favorite bar with its luau/*Deadliest Catch* motif.

"What do you mean?" I asked. Our plan was to leave the night of the job. As soon as we collected the Broadworthys' fingers, we'd get in the car and go.

"I guess I'm getting a little homesick. It's been nice to get out of the city, but I'm ready to head back. What do you say?"

"I say if you're ready, I'm ready," I said. Then I gave his upper thigh a squeeze.

"Kristen," he said, and I realized it was the first time he'd used my real name in a long time, maybe since the Broadworthys showed up. "I'm having trouble telling what's going on here."

I wasn't sure what he meant. I asked if he was drunk. He said yes. I suggested we call it a night. He nodded and I went to pay our tab, then I offered him my hand. He seemed so tired. We walked with arms around each other. When was the last time we'd just held each other like that with no jokes or plans, quiet and close?

It gave me the creeps.

WHEN WE GOT BACK to Chet's, though it was late, the children were in the driveway playing three flies up. Zander, the twin in the blue shorts, tossed the buoy and the rest of the kids stumbled around, faces skyward, until someone caught it. Instead of that person then being the one to throw it, the buoy was returned to Zander each time. We stood, watching, for a few moments. There was something otherworldly about the scene. The children's movements seemed so smooth, almost choreographed, in the faded glow of Chet's porch lights. Every step, every jump, looked planned and perfect. It was hypnotic. Then, for seemingly no reason, Zander walked over to Mikey and, gripping the buoy with two hands around the rubber nub at the top as though it were a baseball bat, swung back and hit his twin in the face. It was a hard hit and it toppled him. All the other children stood and watched. Mikey curled on the ground, drawing his knees to his chest and his hands to his face. Zander dropped the buoy. He turned and walked in the direction of the pool. The rest followed him. No one stopped to pay Mikey any mind.

I started toward him. James took hold of my arm.

"What?"

"Wait."

"Someone needs to check on him," I said, shrugging him off. His hand returned to my arm.

"I'll do it," he said. "You go back to the cabin."

I did as I was told. It was so unlike James to be protective, it startled me. It was only when I got inside that I paused to consider just who, in fact, he was protecting.

JAMES WAS GONE a long time. I opened a bottle of wine and settled in front of the TV. I forced myself not to look out the window for him, or for the children. I watched a detective show where the protagonist was searching for a serial killer, but I got bored and switched to HGTV.

When James finally did open the door, I refused to ask where he'd been or what had happened. Instead, I said, "I have a theory about the children."

"Hmm, what's that?" he asked, taking his place beside me on the couch.

"They're ghosts."

"Ghosts."

"Yeah. Like, people who died young in Murre Bay. They've come back and found each other here so they won't be lonesome."

In the glare of the TV, I saw James's face twist. "Goodness, K. That's gruesome."

I hadn't meant it so. Though I saw his point as soon as he said it.

"You're right. The kids can't be ghosts because you just touched one of them, like, an hour ago. You can't touch a ghost," I said, thinking of the last thing I saw before I retreated to our cabin—James bending with hand extended to Mikey.

"No. He wouldn't let me touch him."

"Oh. Well, probably because he really is a ghost," I said.

Then James did laugh and I was glad for it.

After that, we split the rest of the wine bottle while watching an old horror movie. We found a set of dominoes in a drawer and tried to play but neither of us could remember the rules, and so after a bit we called it a draw and went to bed. We both said, all in all, it was a pleasant enough way to pass the evening.

IN THE MORNING, curiosity overcame me. I made fried eggs with runny yolk, which we sopped up with toast.

"Come on," I said. "You have to tell me where you went with Mikey last night. Did you see something terrible? Were you sworn to secrecy on an altar made of sticks and carrots?"

"No. There isn't much to tell. I took him back to the rest of the kids. He wasn't hurt, only startled."

"Did Zander say anything? Did he apologize?"

"His name's not really Zander."

I felt myself grow frustrated again.

"Okay. What do you want to talk about, then?" I asked.

"I guess I want to finish our conversation from last night, at the bar."

"About going back home? Pick a day. I'll sharpen the Choppity-Hop."

James pressed his hands into his eye sockets. "This isn't fun for me anymore. I want to just go."

"Just go?"

"I can't figure you out. I thought we were only playing."

What does it mean to know someone so intimately in certain moments and in others not know them at all?

"You bought weapons," I said. "The gun? The knife? You asked a man with a windowless van for roofies. Why would we be playing?"

"Because it was hot. They were, like, props?"

"So you don't actually want to cut off the Broadworthys' fingers?"

"No. Do you?"

"Yes."

A silence overtook us, even though we kept talking.

"But that makes no sense!" James said. "You didn't even want to joke about murdering them because they had a kid. You think it's not going to mess that kid up if his parents get drugged and mutilated? How's he supposed to have a normal childhood after that? How's Kev supposed to play catch with him?"

"You think Kev plays catch with Bucko? Isn't that the nanny's job?"

"Everyone plays catch!"

I pointed out that we had veered away from the central issue.

James pushed the last of his eggs around his plate with his fork. "There are other hot things. Let's go home and find something new."

"Right. Just whatever pops up next on NPR."

I told him our plan was important to me. It had always been real. I wasn't leaving Murre Bay without our souvenirs.

James said he needed to think on it. He wanted to take a walk. I told him to take his time, I would clear the breakfast dishes.

IT DID NOT OCCUR to me that he'd gone to find the children again, though he must have.

This time I did keep my face to the window. Not long after James left, I saw the Broadworthys pass by. They were holding hands, but moving purposefully, their faces pinched as if walking into the wind, though the weather was calm. I wondered seriously for the first time about what James had suggested: that they too were up to something.

"Did you see Kev and Gina?" I asked when James came back.

"Yeah, I saw them."

"Where were they going?"

"I didn't ask."

I tapped my finger at the corner of my eye, but James ignored this. He was pink, sweating a little, like he'd just come in from a jog or basketball at the Y.

"I made up my mind," he said.

"Good."

"I'll do what we said we would do, if you really want."

"Good," I said again.

"But only if you agree that things need to change when we get home. Like, we need to do some serious work."

"Of course," I said, but I didn't understand. Wasn't this supposed to be our serious work?

"When?" he asked.

"Tomorrow night," I said. "I'll invite them for happy hour."

James nodded. Then he was out the door.

THE FOLLOWING MORNING I was busy as a bee, but James was largely absent. This was not what I had envisioned. We were supposed to share this day together, laughing at our dark deed come to fruition, making love on the disposable plastic tarp we'd bought to save the Wojciks' having to replace the carpet in the Broadworthys' cabin. We really had grown to care for them.

I knocked on the Broadworthys' door around noon. I didn't want to go too early in the day, lest I seem eager, but also not so late that they might have had time to make other plans. My offer was simple—drinks at the picnic table at six thirty. I said a box had just arrived from our wine-of-the-month club and we needed help drinking.

"Wouldn't miss it!" Gina said.

"Social event of the season!" Kev added.

James dipped in and out of the cabin all day—for a sandwich, a drink of water, a hat. He continued to look flushed. I thought maybe he had a fever. I thought maybe he was walking in circles around the property just to keep moving.

I told him to be back by six so he could shower.

I packed the car and settled our tab with the Wojciks. I paid in cash just as we had with everything—meals, drinks, roofies, and so on. For people who were apparently only pretending at criminality, we'd been remarkably careful in covering our tracks.

"What have you been up to?" I asked James when he reappeared promptly at six, as instructed.

"Playing three flies up," he said.

We didn't speak again until it was time to meet the Broadworthys at the picnic table. I had the two bottles of wine in one hand. I reached for James's hand with the other.

"I love you," I said.

"I love you too," he said.

The Broadworthys were in a chatty mood. They said they'd spent the previous day at the nearby town of Seaside (a likely story), and were eager to tell us about their adventure—the golf cart they'd rented to cruise the promenade, the little shops they'd stopped at along the way.

"I thought the golf cart would have more get-up-and-go," Kev said. "I bet my own at home has double the horsepower. Double!"

"Now, Kev," Gina said. "It was only a rental. What can you expect?"

I tried to catch James's eye. Wasn't this just classic Broadworthys? But he was looking at his hands.

His mood was so clearly *morose*. He was always reliable for a good show in social situations, even with people he did not like. I feared his sudden shift in demeanor would make the Broadworthys suspicious.

At one point, Kev did ask, "Have you got the end-of-season blues? Not quite ready to return home just yet?"

To which James replied, "No, we're ready."

Kev nodded, but it turned out the remark wasn't an observation about James after all. "Well, I've got the blues for sure," he said.

"We're thinking of staying on a little longer," Gina added.

"What about Buckminster?" I asked.

"He'll be okay," Kev said. "He likes it best at his grandmum's house anyway."

No one could think of anything clever to say after that. Or perhaps the drugs were beginning to take effect on the Broadworthys. Either way, we didn't linger. Once the wine was gone, we all said our goodbyes and headed back to our respective cabins.

"Dinnertime and all that," Kev muttered.

James had had too much to drink. I wasn't paying attention at the picnic table, but once we were back in our cabin, I could tell. He was unsteady, his movements slow.

"They're not even sinister," he moaned. "They're just sad and trying to avoid their real lives like us."

The *like us* stung even though of course that was the whole point of everything.

"Great time to tie one on," I said.

"I need to step out for some air."

I agreed that yes, he did.

How could we ever move beyond this moment? Where he looked at me and saw a monster, and where I looked at him and saw a coward?

He was gone ten minutes, fifteen at the most. When he returned, he was not alone.

His shadow was a boy, skinny and freckled. He wore blue swim trunks only, despite the time of day.

"What's he doing here?"

"He wants to help," James said.

"Help with what?" I asked, my voice more shrill than I would have liked.

James studied the floor, but Zander looked me right in the eye. He flashed a gap-toothed smile, which was not cruel but sweet, really, all Christmas mornings and candy apples.

"I want to help with the thing where you guys—"

"Okay," I said, cutting him off. I did not know how to parse this new development. Never in all our erotic, hilarious planning had we ever discussed adding an accomplice. Certainly not an underaged, shirtless one. Was this James's way of showing he still had some power over the arrangement? I felt to say no to Zander would be to say no to everything else as well. The whole night would grind to a standstill.

"Okay," I said again. "We're wearing gloves from this point on. Let me see if I have an extra pair."

"Nah, don't need 'em," Zander said, and he held his hands out to me, wiggling his fingers, but in the low light of the cabin I could not make out what he was trying to show me.

We found the Broadworthys just as I had hoped—asleep, but not upsettingly so. Gina was curled on the couch, Kev stretched out on the rug, one hand casually behind his head. You really could take them for just having a little nap before dinner. James went to Gina and tapped her on the shoulder. A test.

"Can you move her onto the floor, next to Kev?" I asked.

I heard him suck in his breath, scandalized. Like he had not ever considered that this activity might involve the moving of sleeping humans. But he did what I asked, shifting Gina to the ground so she lay perpendicular to Kev.

"If you can put their hands near each other." And here he turned to me with a look that said, *It is not too late to stop but soon it will be.*

"It will go quicker, I think," I added.

So James shuffled Gina over some more. I readied our supplies, folding the tarp and slipping it under their arms.

Zander stood near the door, watching. I tried not to look at him, but I could see him doing something with his mouth—picking at his lips, maybe?

"Okay," I said to no one in particular. I knelt down again and took the Broadworthys' hands in turn, dosing them in rubbing alcohol. I found I didn't like that either, and suddenly understood James's hesitance to touch Gina. I took up the Choppity-Hop next and held it out to James.

"I thought you would do this part?" I said.

"Are you fucking kidding me?"

I looked at the knife in my hand. I tried to remember how it went when we played this scene out for fun, when it was still fun. Wasn't James the one to do the cutting? . . . *And then I take a big ole knife* . . . I could hear him saying.

"I'll do it."

Zander was beside me suddenly. He was chewing bubble gum. That's what he had been doing by the door—pulling the gum out and looping it back into his mouth with his tongue. He continued to do so now, as he gestured to me with his free hand for the Choppity-Hop. I gave it over.

The Choppity-Hop worked as advertised. It really could cut anything. Zander held it like he was slicing carrots. Had he removed human digits before? There was less blood than I'd thought, but also somehow more. I guess it's just that the blood exited the wounds in a way I didn't expect. I managed the tourniquets, but without grace. Everything felt slick and sticky. I thought I might vomit. James had backed as far away from Zander and me as possible. He was pale and I knew if I could see in a mirror I would find myself the same shade.

Finally, once my work was done, I looked at the fingers, separate now from the people to whom they belonged. I feared they might continue to move, like chicken bodies are said to without their heads. But they were still, and small. So small all on their own, two sad, lost things.

Shakily, I went to retrieve them for my mason jar. Zander was faster. He had been leaning on the couch arm, holding the knife, watching me. Now he swooped to pick up the fingers, slipping them into the cargo pocket of his shorts, then tapping the Velcro shut. He wiped his bloody hands on his bare chest, flashed his Little-League-home-run-champ smile, and made for the door.

"Hey now," I said.

He looked back once, still smiling, then ran. I followed him to the porch and watched him dart across the grass and into the dark. I wanted to give chase, but my legs held my weight only barely. To shout might give us away. I stared, trying to keep him in sight. As he turned small and blurry in my vision, I saw him not as Zander (or whatever his real name was), but as a kid version of James. A James allowed out of the tight carton of his childhood, free to play wild well past dinnertime. I wanted that for him so badly all of a sudden, as if it was the key to everything. I felt magnanimous in that want—how good of me to think it at a time like this.

Meanwhile, the real James had come back to life. He was bent over Kev, fingers to his neck confirming a pulse. His other hand cradled the cabin's phone handset to his ear.

"It's fast," I heard him say. "He's breathing fast too. Like, short little breaths. The bleeding's under control. But it was a lot of blood." The person on the other end must have said something. James said, "Yes, thank you. Yes. Okay."

He moved his hand from Kev's neck to his shoulder, which he squeezed. "It's going to be okay, buddy. Help's on its way."

Then James stood and, taking me by the arm, ushered me out the door. He walked me slowly, like he didn't trust my legs either. But when we got to the car he said he was still drunk and I would have to drive, which I did. Then it was just like we planned, us pulling out onto the dark road in our anonymous rental car as the sirens of the ambulance and police grew and the lights appeared on the horizon.

We caught one last glimpse of the children. They were spread out on the lawn, frolicking, jumping up and down in the moonlight. I thought it was a celebration. They were paying thanks to their leader for his offering, taking turns smearing finger blood on their small bodies, fondling the graying nails and splintered bones.

Or no, their actions had nothing to do with that. They'd seen what Zander had brought back and grown bored, moving on to a new game entirely.

The Sundance Kid Might Have Some Regrets

There are a lot of clichés out there about twins. I never wanted us to fall into that trap. So when Maggie and I are doing a job, I insist on some pretty obvious distinctions. Like outfits or big hats. Even different languages. Mags has to take the foreign tongue, of course, since she's the one who can do that sort of thing. She sticks with Korean or Russian typically. But sometimes I'll say, *Hey, let's get weird with it today!* And she'll shift into Latin, maybe Yiddish. She's a good sport when she wants to be.

It's best if nobody knows what the hell Mags is saying anyway. She's the brain *and* the brawn of these operations, no doubt. But I'm the face. Mags isn't what you'd call the strongest swimmer, socially. We'll be inside a bank, cracking a safe open and all of a sudden, Maggie might start shouting about albino snakes, or biblical floods, or bleeding chandeliers. Any old thing that happens to be on her mind. She doesn't mean any harm by it; she just gets excited in a crowd. So, better I do the talking, and if she does feel compelled to speak, that her words are undecipherable.

We're bank robbers, if I haven't made that clear already. Which our parents think is a waste of our talents. And by "our talents," they really mean Maggie's. We're not identical twins, even though we look exactly alike, sound alike, enjoy the same foods, read the same books . . . you get the idea. Maggie possesses skills I do not. The ability to speak and understand any language ever spoken on earth, for example. Also, manipulating objects with her mind, seeing through walls, superhuman strength, the regeneration of her own flesh, and so forth. So, a life of crime—it's not ideal, I know. But in our case, you can certainly see the appeal.

Our process is pretty simple. First, we case the joint. We stand outside, Maggie looks through the walls, describes the bank's layout, and I draw a map to her specifications. Then she works up a timetable and arranges our getaway. I pick costumes, rehearse my lines. I take my role seriously, even though I'm just following Maggie's lead. That's okay by me. After all, she's the twin with the talent. We learned how to do our robber stuff mostly from watching movies. *Dog Day Afternoon*, *The Italian Job*, *Bonnie and Clyde*. It's corny, I know. But it works for us.

So this current job, it started out just the same. I've got us dressed up—me in a kimono and jackboots (both comfortable and functional), Mags in surfer gear, *Point Break*–style. She's speaking fifth-century Aramaic and I'm giving directions. *Stay calm; This is a robbery; Everyone lie flat on the floor, please; Do not attempt to contact the police; No need to open the safe for us, my sister will do it herself.* I find most folks are pretty cooperative, sometimes downright helpful. Occasionally we get a "good guy with a gun" scenario. Mags subdues them so quickly, it's almost embarrassing. Just wraps them up in her force field like swaddled babies. I've seen grown men calmed so completely this way, they actually fall asleep on their feet.

No such trouble today, though. Everyone is doing what they should. Everything is going according to plan.

Until the moment it's not. I don't know where we lose control. Mags is working the safe—asking it for its combination. I'm making small talk with the manager about security cameras. Mags has rendered them inert, of course. But I like to pretend they are still something I'm worried about, for the sake of the show. To give the poor bank manager some hope that once this thing is done and over, these two crazy bitches in costume will be captured and prosecuted to the full extent of the law. The deception makes me feel like I'm part of some *Ocean's Eleven* caper, rather than what this really is—a smash-and-grab.

All of a sudden the other employees and customers start squirming around, whispering. They hear something we don't. Then I hear it too. Sirens outside, the arranging of barricades, someone saying something through a bullhorn. Mags has got the cash and is ready to go when I point out our dilemma. This has never happened before. Not even close. It's a scenario we should have practiced for, or at least talked about. After all, it's how pretty much all our favorite movies end. But we were cocky. Or maybe Maggie was cocky, and I was just dumb. We're not identical.

"How did they find out?" I ask. "How could they possibly have known?"

Maggie shrugs. I assume this means she has a plan. She already knows how to get us out of here safely. Always two steps ahead of me, my twin is.

First thing she does is open the door and usher out the bankers and customers. We've got no use for hostages.

Then she closes the door back up. Goes over to one of the bankers' desks, takes a spin in the spinning office chair. Seems pleased with herself. I'm at a loss, so I do the same, but get no pleasure from it.

"Mags, what if you, like, made us invisible so they'd think we disappeared? Or, maybe you could fly us out of here. Off the roof."

"Come on, get real. You know that's not how my thing works," she says, still smiling. And I nod, but if I'm being honest, I don't know how her thing works. Never have. Because it's hers and not mine. We're not identical.

There's more bullhorning from outside. I guess what they're saying is *Come out or we'll shoot.* Because then they do. And I realize that's what the hostages are for: to keep the robbers safe. That's why everyone in movies always keeps their hostages.

I hit the deck, but Maggie doesn't. She stays standing. "These guys are being real dicks," she says. The windows around us shatter. I feel exposed, vulnerable. "Maggie, can't you just make them . . ." I start, but I've got no more suggestions. I am not the idea person here.

Maggie gets shot in the chest, to no effect. She just laughs. "They think we're going out like at the end of that movie about Butch Cassidy and what's-his-name! Shows what they know!"

But they do know—for one of us, at least. Unlike my sister, I've been hurt before. Scraped knees and bee stings and hangnails. My flesh is vulnerable, impermanent. As I've said, we aren't identical.

It occurs to me only now, the Sundance Kid might have had some regrets. Dragged to a country he knew nothing about. Coerced into danger. Forced to share his girlfriend with Butch, or whatever that situation was all about. Sundance—second in billing, second out the door—may not have wanted any of it at all. Dude was just looking for some quick cash and a pleasant place in the foothills to hide out.

I turn to remind my sister that I am not impervious to bullets, that we will have to think of a different plan. She's already out of the bank. Running through the hail of gunfire, dancing really, laughing, halfway to freedom. She can't be stopped. And though it won't go the same for me—we're not identical—I feel I've got no choice but to follow.

Outburst

Andi arrived home to Washington on June 30, the last day before Mount Rainier National Park closed the Emmons Glacier for the season, all access to both recreational climbers and researchers suspended until freezing temperatures returned. The glacier had grown unstable in the heat. She spent her single day on the northeastern slope of the mountain in the company of a hired guide dressed in beachwear—seersucker shorts, a tank top, and sun hat—his sole concessions to the glacier his boots and crampons. The only other person with them was the helicopter pilot who brought them up. Andi asked the pilot if he wanted to walk the ice with them, but he declined, muttering, "Not fuckin' with that today. I got kids at home." He waited in the bird. When she and the guide returned, the pilot asked, "Well, Doctor, is the glacier retreating?" and she said yes.

"How quickly?"

Andi said she didn't know. She was not measuring ablation. She was sounding for water.

The pilot looked to the guide, the shared glance of men trying to make sense of a confusing woman. "What water?" he asked.

"All this water," Andi said, pointing to the ice beneath them.

THE GENESIS for Andi's project had taken place a year earlier in the Ahklun Mountains, in southwest Alaska, where she'd stood on a rocky outcropping and watched a different glacier collapse. Andi was a postdoc at the University of Alaska Fairbanks. She was working with her adviser, Dr. Cassidy Randall, to predict the risk of outburst flooding—the sudden spilling out of water trapped behind glacial ice. Cassidy had developed a sensor that she hoped would be able to pick up telling movement in ice in advance of such an event. They had come to this remote peak—where every summer a natural ice dam broke and a glacial lake spilled down the mountain, only to re-form and refill in the winter and spring—to test her prototypes. And sure enough, the sensors had generated sufficient data for her to anticipate the inevitable flood's date. Cassidy had another prediction: this year the whole ice wall holding back the lake would fail. That was exactly what they saw from the ridge. A massive chunk of the glacier shearing from its perch. In its wake, a plume of debris went into the air and a torrent of water rushed down the mountainside. Cassidy took video. The plume settled and the water split for different channels as it plunged into the valley. But in one channel, the water did not taper off like its sisters. It turned darker, and grew wider.

"Lahar," Cassidy said, pointing. The guides nodded.

"Why only there?" Andi asked.

"Because that's where the lahar goes," one of the guides answered, as if she was dumb. "It's always a lahar over there."

Though Andi had not heard of this before, she understood what he meant.

"And it's always the same size?"

"Thereabouts," the guide said, wobbling his hand, the universal symbol for approximation.

"There was an active volcano here at some point?"

"Sure," Cassidy said. "Though wherever the cone was, it's long gone."

"So the size of a lahar from an ancient eruption can determine the size of a new lahar from outburst flooding?" Andi asked.

Cassidy agreed that appeared to be what they were seeing.

"I'm thinking of Mount Rainier," Andi said, "and the Osceola Mudflow from the Holocene era. It flowed out over two hundred square miles. Most of the cities between Seattle and Tacoma are built on top of its debris."

It had been perhaps her first fact in glaciology, learned in her middle school earth sciences course. The volcano, beautiful and ominous, visible from the classroom window.

Cassidy nodded slowly and Andi noted with satisfaction her adviser's pinched half smile, a sure sign something was of interest and more information was needed. But when she looked to the guides, she saw horror in their faces.

"Don't say that," one of them pleaded. "I've got people down there."

LAVA MIGHT SEEM LIKE the scariest thing about a volcano. But if the mountain is covered in ice and snow, which liquefy upon eruption, then the scariest part is mud. Lava is a slow-moving force, and does not travel far. Mud is nearly boundless in comparison. It churns up sediment, dislodging boulders and trees and anything else in its path. A fast-moving river of cement. That's a lahar.

Glacial outbursts can cause mudflows on their own. These are not as large as the ones produced by volcanic eruptions, which inherently provide more water, debris, and force.

But what if some of those elements were already there, just waiting for the chance to go?

This was Andi's hypothesis. That an outburst flood could essentially restart a previous lahar, picking up where it left off. It was what she thought she'd seen in the Ahkluns—the reanimation of a mudflow that had never gone away, only stopped moving and dried out. That lahar had been relatively small. Mount Rainier, which stands over a river valley that's home to more than two hundred thousand people, has a history of very, very large lahars. Most recently, the Electron Mudflow, five hundred years ago, sent a wall of mud almost a hundred feet high out over sixty square miles. Five thousand years before that the mighty Osceola Mudflow—the lahar foremost in Andi's mind—resurfaced everything from the mountain to Puget Sound, decimating the encampments of people living along the Puyallup River. The Tacoma shoreline of today is fifteen miles farther out because of it. The lahar took all that life, then it made new land.

With Cassidy's encouragement, Andi assembled her fieldwork proposal. It was to be her first time leading a team—she'd signed on two grad students and an associate professor to join her in trips up four of Rainier's glaciers: Carbon, South Mowich, and Tahoma to the west; Emmons to the lonesome northeast.

When the permits from the national park had arrived, and her funding was secured, Andi had called her parents, full of enthusiasm.

"We're the first ones to ever look at this," she said. "People always talk about the lahar that will happen if Rainier erupts again, but no one ever thinks of the glaciers themselves as a source. Outburst flooding is still mysterious in a lot of ways."

"You've discovered a new, exciting way for us to die," her dad said.

They'd both laughed when he said it. Her dad, always safe in his home, in his neighborhood, could not fathom any reason for it to be otherwise. And honestly, neither could Andi. She had grown up safe there too. It was only a hypothesis—something to go and see about. She was thinking of the paper she would write when she returned to Fairbanks. The perfect addition to her CV.

But then, all spring, it was too hot. The park announced it would be closing its mountain glaciers a month earlier than it had the previous year. Andi scrambled to remake her plans, to salvage what little time she could, which was really almost none—a single day. She refined her focus to the Emmons Glacier alone and hoped it would be enough. Her team members pulled out. The grad students had intended to use the trip as a jumping-off point for another project and Andi's new schedule no longer fit with theirs. The associate professor announced he and his girlfriend had decided to elope. Cassidy, who was departing again for the Ahkluns, enjoined Andi to defer until the following summer. "Haste does not make good science," she advised. "And Mount Rainier is a young volcano! Just half a million years!"

Andi did not want to delay a year. She didn't know what Rainier's age had to do with anything. Though she was alone, and short on time, she went anyway.

IT WAS INDEED, as she had told the helicopter pilot, a lot of water. Measurements from her ice radar showed an expansive, shallow subglacial lake underneath the Emmons Glacier. The volume of meltwater impounded in the glacier was impossible for her to estimate, but it seemed like too much.

As in, too much to stay contained in the ice for very long. Water seeks *out.* Water seeks *down.* If it did not have a path for out and down, it would find one, a weak spot in the ice where it would bottle up, then burst.

She went to the office of Cory Forge, the park glaciologist and coordinator of glacial research on Mount Rainier. She did not beg, but asked politely, pointedly. Could an exception be made? Could she have more time on the glacier? She would be careful; she knew ice well; she would not make him regret it by dying heedlessly.

"The data I collected yesterday is concerning," she said.

"And that's why the glacier is closed," he said.

"I'm talking about the subglacial lake. Are you aware there's a sizable subglacial lake beneath Emmons?"

"Not really a lake, though. We call it subglacial puddling. It's hummocky terrain under Emmons. The water gets caught in little depressions in the earth. It might seem like one lake from the numbers, but it's a bunch of small puddles."

"When was the last time you surveyed it?"

He chuckled. "I'm not in the habit of dragging an ice radar across the largest glacier in the lower forty-eight. A couple other folks have made reports over the years. It's always the same story."

"But it's never been this hot before, for this long."

"I hear what you're saying. Even with more melt, there's no danger. All the water from Emmons goes to the White River."

"I'm suggesting that there is, in fact, considerable danger."

"Where's the data to support that?"

Andi insisted this was the very research she was there to conduct. "Please, help me out here."

He shook his head. Even if he said yes, no pilot would be willing to land on Emmons after it was closed. No mountaineering company would allow her to hire a guide. "Though I guess I can't stop you if you want to go up alone," he said, and Andi fumed. She felt the threat of tears. She would not let herself cry in front of this man.

"Look, I can't get you the glacier," Forge said, his voice softer now. "But I can get you something else."

WHAT FORGE OFFERED was a field office.

"It has a nice view," he said.

He drove in his truck and Andi followed in her rental car. Forge worked out of a building near the park's northeast entrance and at first they joined a trickle of tourist traffic, but when the rest of the cars turned, heading for the Sunrise Day Lodge and its vistas, they continued on. The road zigged through evergreens, which occasionally broke open to reveal an alpine meadow. Andi was staggered by this beauty. Though she'd grown up in the city of Puyallup, within easy driving distance of the national park, she'd only been twice before. Her parents, suburbanites to their core, were not outdoorsy.

Ahead of her, Forge signaled, then parked in a wide turnout. Andi pulled in behind him.

"Just up the path a klick," he said, gesturing to the other side of the road. They crossed together. Andi saw a trail marker and, affixed below it, a handmade wooden sign. *The Mount Rainier Center for Avian Repatriation*, it said.

"We just call it the research cabin. But these guys have been using it for a long time. Anyway, there's plenty of space for you too. Plus, there's wi-fi. Tell them Cory sent you. And that I said you could have the south-facing desk."

Then he winked and Andi felt in that moment there was nothing she hated more than a wink of unclear meaning. He jogged back to his truck. Andi walked the trail. It was, as promised, just a half mile, but steep.

As soon as she opened the door to the research cabin, she saw that Forge's wink had been well intentioned. A peace offering. Though there were no windows on the front of the cabin, the other three sides had the appearance of a fire lookout—three feet of wood paneling from the floor, then glass the rest of the way up. The reason for the trail's ascent—the cabin was perched on a ridge. To the north and east she could see the White River and beyond into the unbroken green of the national forest. To the south, a straight line of sight up to the mountain. It was a stunning vantage, not just for its beauty but for its view of the glaciers and the mile markers of their geological history. There was Emmons, and its neighbor Winthrop, nestled in the groove left behind when, fifty-six hundred years earlier, the volcano erupted and the northeast flank failed—the starting point of the Osceola Mudflow. She could trace its path, from Steamboat Prow, a rocky outcropping near the glacier's edge, down the river basin, and if she could see far enough, into the valley where she grew up.

There were two young men inside the cabin, seated at a single computer screen. They turned to Andi with twin looks of unbearable enthusiasm.

"Welcome to the Mount Rainier Center for Avian Repatriation!" they said together.

"We're the only facility in Washington state dedicated to monitoring and expanding the habitats of the blacktail sentinel eagle," one of them continued.

"We're doing a public talk at two p.m. at Sunrise," said the other, "but we're happy to show you around now. Would you like to look at our eagle cams? Or I can get out a box of shell fragments for you. They're really neat colors."

Andi shook her head. She explained that Dr. Forge had sent her.

The men seemed confused.

"Cory," she said. "The glaciologist."

"Cory!" one of them shouted. "The Ice Man! Yeah, yeah, he's all right."

The other scrunched up his face. "They said they'd warn us next time they were going to put someone else up here."

They were strikingly similar in their appearance. Young men with shaggy brown hair and red-tinted beards. One was taller. He gave his name as Grayson. The shorter one, who had just expressed misgivings about having an office mate, was Tanner.

"It's no problem," Grayson said, waving his partner's objections away. "There's lots of room. We just haven't had to share it in a while. We're out of practice is all."

He began clearing the desk for her. Its contents seemed nothing of value—paper towel rolls, a case of energy drinks, canvas shopping bags—and the work was quickly done.

"For reals, though," Grayson said, "have you ever seen a blacktail sentinel eagle before? Most people haven't. They're sneaky. But they're soooo pretty. Come look at the cam. You know, when we first got here two years ago, there were only four sentinels nesting in this area. Now there's thirteen."

Andi was unsure what response was warranted.

"Which is absolutely phenomenal," he prompted.

Andi went to the screen. There were three live feeds, Grayson explained, two from cameras in the woods, monitoring active nests, and one at the cabin's window to watch the birds' flight patterns. He clicked to one of the forest cameras. The nest was empty. "Dang," he said, "she was just there a minute ago."

He asked Andi about her own research.

She thought she was giving her quickest explanation, limiting the number of times she said phrases like *lateral moraines*, *hydrothermal alteration*, and *reduced channel gradients*, but still she could see the men's eyes glaze.

"That's cool," Grayson said when Andi finished her spiel. "Seriously, that's rad."

"Yeah," Tanner echoed. "So cool."

"It's not cool, though," Andi corrected. "It's actually terrifying. "

"Oh," Grayson said. "I'm sorry."

They turned their attention back to their screen and Andi went to the south window and looked out at the glacier and the groove of earth below it for a long time.

ANDI DID NOT THINK she would return. She had a fine desk in her motel room and she intended to sit at it the following day and make phone calls.

She called Forge again, who was eager to know what she thought of the research cabin, but he remained steadfast in his refusals of everything else. She called people in the geology departments at the University of Washington and Central Washington University. Names Cassidy had given her as local contacts, "in case you get into trouble," she'd said. But the ones who did answer the phone dismissed Andi's concerns as logistical. "Rules are rules," and "a matter for the park." Mostly, they were not there at all.

She called Cassidy, knowing she would get no answer. She and her field team would be out of cell range. Andi called her own former team. The grad students could not be reached. The associate professor answered, but said he needed to keep it brief—he was picking up his wedding tux.

"How big of an outburst is a big enough outburst?" she asked.

"That's the question you're there to answer, right?"

"The park glaciologist says Emmons is fine."

"Well, it's been a pretty stable glacier for a long time. I figure the western slope's where the real action is. But it's a young volcano, you know?"

"Why do people keep saying that to me?"

Then his tux was ready and he had to go.

THAT EVENING, Andi saw her hired guide. She was staying in the tiny town of Pinestack. It was just outside the boundary of the national park, on Highway 410, a single street of amenities populated almost entirely by park employees and other seasonal workers. The northern side of the park was more rugged than the south, and not as enticing to tourists. Everyone looked to be in their twenties, suntanned and cheerful.

Her guide was coming out of the post office when she spotted him. She waved heartily, grateful just to have someone to wave to. She was immediately embarrassed by the extravagance of this gesture. He not only returned her big wave but came jogging over. Ricky was his name. He was large, easily a foot taller than her. She hadn't noticed that before. Glaciers, in their vastness, have a way making the people on them seem all the same. But here now on the street, she had to raise her face to see his grin.

"Good to see you again," he said. "I had a nice time on Emmons."

Andi took this for sarcasm, a knock at the slow work of pulling the ice radar.

"Well, it needed to get done, so I appreciated your help."

"Such great weather. Really, a beautiful last day for the season," he said, and Andi realized it was not sarcasm at all.

He asked her where she was headed and when she answered to get groceries, he asked if she'd like to go out for dinner with him instead.

"I'm all dressed up with no place to go," he said, gesturing to his faded North Face T-shirt.

There were two options for dining in Pinestack, he explained. Ranger Danger, a decent Tex-Mex joint with trivia on Wednesdays and karaoke on Fridays, or Grizzly Bar, which served wilted pub grub under the gaze of taxidermied bears. "Like, way too many dead bears," he said. "So many dead bears it should be illegal."

They went to Ranger Danger.

He was charming, easy to talk to. From his easy grin and manner of speech, she had assumed him younger than her. He was actually two years her senior. He'd been in the wilderness recreation industry for over a decade. He wanted to be outdoors, to show the outdoors to other people and delight in it with them, especially if they would pay him money for that delight. He lived nowhere, really, moving up and down the state with the seasons for work in the mountains, on the rivers, on the coast.

They had fajitas and beers, then went back to her room at the motel. She found it necessary to be on top of him so as not be overwhelmed by his body. It felt good to have a problem like that—something tangible and solvable.

After sex, Ricky turned conspiratorial. He put his mouth to her ear and she worried he was about to divulge something emotionally intimate.

"I can get you on another glacier, if you want." They were alone, all but one light out in her motel room, and he'd whispered this like a dirty secret, which she realized it was.

"Here? On Rainier?"

"No. Mount Hood."

"At that latitude and altitude? Those glaciers must be closed as well."

"They are. But it's national forest. Not as much enforcement. I know a guy who works out there. I could put you in touch, if you're looking to climb."

"That's nice of you, but I'm here to conduct research," she said. "I don't climb."

"That's too bad. You really should. Everybody should climb."

ANDI DID NOT CLIMB, but she did hike. She stalked the debris of the Osceola Mudflow along the river basin. It was not difficult to find. There were the random exposures of boulders, as if the rocks had been thrown into the hillsides by an angry child giant. Also, the ground had a pinkish-orange tint—a chemical coloration left behind from the minerals in the lava. The dirt was dry from the hot weather. It came away easily in Andi's hands. When she poured water on it from her canteen, it turned to clay, slippery to the touch. Later, she texted pictures of this to the associate professor. He responded, somewhat irritatingly, in rhyme:

Hey, hey!

What do you say?

Is it clay?

How fantastic.

It must be . . . pyroclastic!

One morning, she hiked to the terminus of the Emmons glacier. There were mountain marmots and signs of bears. There were wildflowers in pockets, stunning in their yellows and purples. They should have covered the entire meadows that time of year. The heat had set them off course—they'd peaked early. Now, in July, only the dregs were left.

She wanted to see where the glacier ended and the White River began. The last miles of the hike were slow going across the scree of moraine. The river flowed from a collection of ice caves. It was more water than Andi had seen a glacier let out before. But as Forge had said, it all went nice and neat downstream. There was nothing alarming about the scene. Except she knew there was so much more water that wasn't making it to the terminus.

"Just tell me," she whispered, then looked around, embarrassed. She had never spoken to a glacier before.

IT SEEMED GRAYSON and Tanner had also not expected her to return. Her desk had been re-cluttered with their stuff, which they quickly moved for her. She'd come back to the research cabin for the promise of wi-fi, and she wanted to look at the glacier while she used it. Specifically, she wanted to compare satellite images of Emmons to what she could see from the window, and what she had seen on the ground.

She soon discovered how Grayson and Tanner had run afoul of their previous office mates. They weren't rude to Andi. On the contrary, aside from pleasantries and apologies, they left her alone. But they occupied the space as if it were their birthright, or their living room. Andi—with her eyes on her laptop, her phone, her binoculars—intuited their activities mostly through sound and smell.

There was frequent high-fiving and exclamations of "Dude! Dude! Look! Dude, you missed it!" There was a moderate amount of farting and laughing about it. Once, Grayson spread his arms out and ran the length of the cabin, presumably pretending to be a blacktail sentinel eagle. Every so often there was the sound of clattering aluminum, a can flung from across the room into a cardboard box by the door. The cans were all the same narrow bright red tubes. When Andi asked what they were, Grayson said, "Panic." The best, and most caffeinating, of all energy drinks.

"They're illegal in Washington, though, so we have to stock up every time we go home to Boise. You can get pretty much anything in Idaho."

"Except weed and abortions," Tanner said. "People in Idaho hate weed and abortions."

Grayson play-whacked him on the head.

"Oops, sorry," Tanner said. "I know I shouldn't be bringing up politics in the workplace."

She was looking for recent changes in the glacier, signs of weakness. She was particularly keen on an ice wall just above the area she had surveyed, but she acknowledged this was mostly a function of having witnessed the collapse of the wall in the Ahkluns in all its drama and violence. An outburst on Emmons could come from anywhere. She had sought out satellite images of Rainier's glaciers while she was still in Alaska, but her patience for the task was limited—weather was often in the way and she had to scour months' worth of pictures to find just a handful with good visibility. Now, though, she was willing to put in the time. There were also radar satellite images she could use for calculating change in ice volume, and optical satellite images for measuring crevasses. A person with no other obligations could spend hours each day on this, and so Andi did.

IN THIS WAY, her days formed a triangle: hiking around the basin in the mornings; poring over satellite photos and making agitated phone calls to people she'd already called in the afternoons; meeting Ricky in the evenings.

Still, she had trouble accounting for herself, for what she was actually doing there. Ricky asked where she went when she wasn't with him, and she muttered, "I have a spot at the research cabin."

"What's that?"

"The Mount Rainier Center for Avian Repatriation," she tried.

Ricky's face lit up. "Oh! With the Bird Bros! I fucking love those guys!"

It was also unclear to her what Ricky did in his daytime hours. With the glaciers closed, he was out of work. He spoke of signing on in the fall with a whale-watching outfitter in the San Juan Islands. Until then, though, he appeared to simply be loitering in the company of the mountain. In fact, it seemed to Andi that a lot of the young people living in Pinestack were just hanging out, enjoying the scene. There was a low-key party atmosphere to the place at all hours. Music played from open windows and people walked the street with beer cans in hand. Were they too mountaineers with no mountain? she asked Ricky.

"They're waiting," he said cryptically. Then he shrugged. "But yeah, some people like to have a good time while they wait."

Most nights, Andi and Ricky went to Ranger Danger or they got tall boys and sandwiches from the market and picnicked by the river. Once, they went to Grizzly Bar. Over limp cheesesteaks, Ricky speculated about the species of each taxidermy.

"Such magnificent creatures. They deserved better than this," he said.

She thought him sweet and dumb. They always went back to her motel room. When she asked where he lived, he said, "Oh, just staying with some people." She wondered if he was camping, but didn't pry. He referred to her at times, playfully, as "the woman who saved my life," a joke she didn't get until he reminded her that on Emmons, she'd prevented him from stepping in a hidden crevasse. She'd seen the subtle difference in the surface of the ice and said, "Hold on," while she poked it with her pole and found nothing underneath. The moment didn't strike her as significant, just one of a hundred small decisions during a day on a glacier. She thought he was teasing and she didn't mind it. Most important, he spared her lonesome nights—the time when her mind most wanted to make plans. When to give up, when to go home. Her plane ticket back to Fairbanks had been for the previous Saturday but she'd canceled it.

ONE DAY SHE DROVE an hour to the Mud Mountain Dam, a structure entirely dedicated to preventing snowmelt from overflowing the banks of the White River. It stood four hundred feet tall and carved a stark figure through the dense forest, otherwise broken only by the river itself. The river was running high with early-season runoff. The reservoir level looked high as well.

She went to the dam office and asked to speak to an engineer. A young man ushered her into a cubicle and Andi peppered him with questions. How rapidly could the reservoir be drained? What sort of warning systems were in place in the event of overflow? How much impact by volume and force could the dam's core sustain? But after just a few minutes he held up his hands. He was only an intern, he said. Better that Andi meet with the chief engineer, who was currently away on vacation. She could leave her name and number. He would call her when he got back.

Andi called the associate professor. He was on his honeymoon, visiting the Postojna Cave in Slovenia, but he picked up.

"I thought it would be romantic to see this with her. One of the geological wonders of the world! But two of the largest caverns are totally closed because of flooding. The ones that are open are significantly drippy."

"Significantly drippy?" Andi asked. "Where's the water coming from?"

"Nobody knows," he said. "But it isn't good. It really freaked me out, honestly. Then we got into a big fight about whether or not we want to bring children into a dying world. Anyway, we're okay now but I think we're going to head home early."

Andi said she was sorry to hear it. She told him the reservoir at the Mud Mountain Dam was three-quarters full.

"They should drain that," he said. "A dam won't stop a flood of any kind if there isn't an empty reservoir to catch it, much less a lahar."

"They are draining it, but they have to do so gradually. Snowmelt has come so fast this year."

"Well, what do you expect?" the associate professor asked. "That dam was built in the 1940s. If it was seventy-five degrees on a summer day, it was hot. No one could imagine any different."

TEN DAYS AFTER she'd arrived, a voicemail popped onto Andi's phone screen as she returned to cell range from her morning hike. It was Cassidy. "Andi. I got your message. I'm on the move, in Togiak for the night. Call me immediately."

Andi felt the whole of herself lift, like a kid with a scraped knee suddenly pulled into her mother's arms. Help had arrived.

"Tell me what you know," her adviser said when she answered.

"I don't know anything. That's the problem," Andi said. She told the whole story—her scant hours on Emmons, the radar's readings, the shallow expanse of water, the heat that would not relent, not even at night. "I'm afraid it's a time bomb," she said.

"Wonderful," Cassidy said. "This is wonderful."

It was not the reaction Andi had expected.

"I'm sending you three sensors," Cassidy continued. "This is the perfect opportunity to test. You'll need new permitting from the park office to place devices. Just go through whoever you're already working with."

"Okay, thank you! And I'll be able to get the data from the sensors directly to my phone?" Back in Fairbanks, Andi was the one who recorded the sensors' outputs, but Cassidy never allowed her, or anyone else, to view the raw data. The algorithm she used was proprietary, she explained.

"Well, no," Cassidy said. "It will come to me like always. Until we can build out a user interface, I can't have it just floating around with anyone."

"But how will I know if the glacier is at risk?"

"I'll have the data. It'll be there. We'll figure it out. I'll be in touch. Let's just focus on getting the sensors dropped first."

She wasn't worried about the prospect of a lahar. She wanted a new scenario to test her sensors: an impending outburst with no clear time frame. Andi had always admired Cassidy's clear-eyed empiricism, as well as her ambition. She wondered if this time that ambition was misplaced. Weren't human lives at stake? Still, the sensors were coming and that was a good thing, Andi thought, whatever her adviser's motivation.

SHE TOLD FORGE she had devices that she wanted to drop on Emmons, and she filled out the permit request while standing in his office.

"All good?" she asked. "I need to arrange a helicopter. We won't land. I can throw the sensors from the air."

He said he needed to look it over. He called the next day while she was at the research cabin. The Bird Bros were playing a game called "tooth tap," where they tried to touch each other's teeth. One point for each successful tap with an index finger, "No tongues, no gums." Andi hated that she knew the rules. "Dude, no way dude, duuuude," Grayson said as Andi's phone buzzed and she made the universal symbol with her hands for *Tone it down*.

"I have some questions," Forge said. "First off, what the heck is an ice magnet?"

It was Cassidy's term for the means by which the sensors stayed affixed to the surface of the glacier. Andi did not know how, only that there was a gyroscopic component to it. She had never seen inside the body of the sensors. Cassidy was cagey about their workings.

"I don't have the details," Andi admitted. "It's proprietary."

"Is there any way for you to find out? I can't just let you toss things onto my glaciers without knowing what's in them."

This irked Andi. "They aren't your glaciers."

"I get that," he said. "But, if I may offer a counterpoint, they *are* my glaciers."

"Ha. Ha." She thought he was only being obstinate.

"Look, I know I can't protect them from much," he said. "But I can protect them from you."

Andi felt herself shamed into silence.

Over her shoulder, Grayson shouted, "Is that Ice Man on the phone? Tell him we say hi!"

THE SENSORS were not perfect. They were temperamental, sometimes mistaking wind or rain or the boots of the glaciologists placing them for ice movement. There was an averaging of their data required to get useful readings, which was why multiple were necessary for any section of glacier being monitored. The ice magnets, whatever they were, did not always stick and sometimes the apparatuses slid and were lost.

Still, they did work. Andi had wanted to bring them with her to Rainier from the start. Cassidy had gently dismissed the idea as a not-ideal use of resources. At the time, Andi had felt somewhat spurned by this, but chose not to linger in that hurt.

Andi expected Cassidy to overnight the sensors. She checked the motel office where she received her mail each morning. No packages arrived for her. She called Cassidy but the phone went straight to voicemail. The spurned feeling needled back in and lodged.

She called the associate professor. She asked him if Cassidy was back in Fairbanks. Had he seen her in the office?

"Just for a hot second," he said. "But now she's out again."

"Did you happen to see if she mailed anything? She was supposed to send me sensors."

"Man, I don't know what anybody around here does."

He asked her if she might be interested in purchasing some property in western Colorado. "The missus and I are looking to build a climate compound," he said. "I mean, she's not totally sold on it, but getting there. We'd love to go in on a parcel with a few other folks. Think about it."

"FORGE DOESN'T CARE that there's a whole subglacial lake under Emmons," Andi lamented to Ricky one night. "He calls it *puddling*. My adviser only wants to help because she thinks she'll get famous for her invention, which hasn't even shown up yet, and Forge doesn't want to give me a permit for it anyway. The only one of my colleagues who regularly answers his phone is having some sort of existential freak-out. And literally everyone else who could help me in any way is on summer vacation.

"I'm feeling really lonesome in this," she whispered.

"I'm here," he said, kissing her forehead.

"Thank you. I guess I mean I'm lonesome for geologists."

Ricky snapped his fingers. "Oh! We have some of those! Gem Girls are always down to hang out! I can't believe you haven't met yet. It's Friday, so they'll definitely be doing karaoke at Danger."

Andi allowed herself to be hustled from the motel down the road to the bar. Ricky found who he was looking for—three young women in a booth, dressed in ranger uniforms, their hair pulled into ponytails of varying length. Ricky introduced Andi as "a brilliant glaciologist, with a PhD and everything, and a really good friend of mine." But the women regarded her skeptically.

"Why haven't we seen you around?" one of them asked, and Andi realized she'd been committing a cardinal Pinestack sin. She was living in town, but she was not, as Ricky had put it, *down to hang out*.

"Andi's been pretty busy with her research. She's super tight with the Bird Bros, though."

The women brightened. "Bird Bros!" they said in unison. "They're the best!"

Andi learned that the Gem Girls gave daily "Rock Talks" at the Sunrise Day Lodge. They were geology undergrads at the University of Washington, working at the park for the summer.

"I've got several phone calls in to one of your professors," Andi said and gave the man's name. "He won't call me back."

The Gem Girls laughed. "Yeah, you're not going to hear from him," one of them said.

"He's supposed to be my adviser and I've legitimately never seen him in person," said another.

"He might be dead," said the third. "Tenure is so dumb. I mean, he could really, truly have died in his office and it would take years for anyone to figure it out."

Andi laughed too. Ricky was right. Here in the camaraderie of women who could not find a man whose help they'd been promised, she felt less alone. But when she tried to tell them about her own research, and the other human obstacles she faced, they turned cold again.

"If that was really a threat, someone would have said something," one of them said.

"Yes," Andi replied. "I'm saying something."

They studied their hands. She'd broken another Pinestack rule. Never harsh the vibe.

Finally, a Gem Girl ended the silence. "Let's do tequila shots," she said with deep seriousness. So they did. The girls and Ricky sang karaoke.

"You should come give a Rock Talk with us sometime," the Gem

Girl who had suggested tequila shots said, grabbing Andi by the shoulders. She was back in their good graces, thanks to the magic of alcohol.

Andi shook her head. "Nobody wants to hear what I have to say."

"Well yeah. Not about *that*. But you must know some nice stuff too, right?"

IN THE MORNING, hungover, Andi called her parents.

It was never a laughing matter.

"I thought there was a warning system for lahars," her dad said.

"Yes. If the lahar is caused by an eruption. The monitoring is for volcanic activity. If it's started by the glacier itself there's no way to know about it until it's happening. You may not have time to leave."

"What about your sensor?" her mom asked. "Did you put it on the glacier? What does it tell you?"

Andi fumbled. The sensors weren't hers, she explained. They were Dr. Randall's project; she hadn't brought any to Washington. Some were on their way, but there was a lot of red tape and she didn't have access to the data they generated, "for proprietary reasons," she muttered.

Finally, she said, "I'm afraid the glacier will collapse before I get the sensors running. I don't want to have to worry about you. Is there somewhere else you can go for a while?"

Her parents said they appreciated her concern.

"We leave August tenth for our big Europe trip," her mom said in her most reassuring mom voice. "We'll be gone the whole rest of the summer after that."

That was two weeks away, Andi pointed out.

"I know!" her mom said. "So soon! I still have so much to do to get ready!"

SHE CALLED HER SISTER. Selena was three years older than Andi and lived with her husband and infant son just a mile from their parents. Andi refined her pitch, stating her case clearly and succinctly.

"It might not happen," Andi said. "But it also might happen literally any day."

"Okay. Okay, I hear you," Selena said. "Let's make a plan. I'm thinking Oakland."

Oakland was where her husband, Theo, was from. His parents still lived there.

"I'm seeing tickets available for a flight tomorrow morning. I can book it now. You'll meet us at the airport, or do you need me to pick you up?"

"Oh," Andi said. "I wasn't—"

"Bullshit you weren't." Selena cut her off with such force Andi wondered if her sister had known all along she had no intention of leaving, the whole conversation a setup for this moment.

"You want to save everyone else, but you won't do anything to protect yourself. Typical Andi, always the martyr."

"I have work to do here. I can't leave yet."

"What work? You just said you're not even allowed on the glacier."

Andi had no answer for this. "You're still going, though?" she asked.

"Oh, we're going," Selena said. "Not gonna just sit around and wait to die like some people."

ONCE ANDI HAD MADE the decision to warn her own family, she felt obligated to do the same for others. She called newspapers and television stations across Western Washington. She was put on hold, forwarded to full mailboxes. Told someone would call her back and she already knew what that meant.

She got a text from Selena.

Sorry I got mean. You scared me. It's hard now with the baby. I feel like there's so much to keep him safe from. The rules keep changing. We're in Oakland. I looked for you at the airport even though I knew you wouldn't be there. Maybe you can come in a few days? Stay safe.

She got a text from the associate professor.

W/R/T property: Now thinking Michigan instead of Colorado, per wildfire risk. Let me know.

She got a text from Ricky.

If I enter a hot wings eating contest at Danger, will you cheer me on? I can't do this alone, babe.

One morning she arrived at the research cabin to find it empty of Bird Bros. They'd taken nothing with them, so she understood their departure to be temporary. Still, she was overjoyed.

First, she cleaned. She swept up snack package corners and sunflower seeds. She removed from the wall a line of curling scorecards, left over from some game that preceded tooth tap. She emptied the overflowing recycling box, hiking the Panic cans down to her car. She moved the Bird Bros' portable telescope over to her side of the cabin, as well as the best desk chair, which Grayson usually occupied. These were things she deserved—a pleasant workspace, a telescope she did not have to ask permission to use, a good chair—and she would take them now. But after a few hours the silence settled and she felt, as she looked out at Emmons, that she was more alone with it than ever.

THEN, AFTER FIVE DAYS of quiet, they were back. She opened the door to the sound of a Panic can being tossed into the recycling box. There was a smell to the cabin that was new—something musty like dirt and coppery like blood. Grayson greeted her from his reclaimed good chair and she saw what she assumed was the source of the smell—a bird, wrapped in a towel, on his lap. It was not a small bird, but she knew by its downy feathers and nearly bald head that it was a young bird. It was about the size of a bowling ball, dark gray with flecks of black.

"You shouldn't be holding that," she said reflexively.

Grayson laughed. "Sure I should. What do you think avian repatriation even means?"

Andi had assumed it to be little more than compulsive birdwatching. She shrugged.

Grayson explained that he and Tanner had first come to Mount Rainier after it was discovered that the critically endangered black-tail sentinel eagles of Oregon were moving north into the Cascades and seemed to be thriving. To assist with this population shift, the Bird Bros transported chicks born in captivity in Boise to be rehomed in the national park. This was their fourth such trip in two years.

"This is Kokomo," Grayson said of the bird in his lap.

"Nader and Rhapsody are chilling," he continued, pointing to what looked like a row of small dog crates under the desk. "They have climate control and on-demand mealworm dispensers in there, so it's pretty lux. And Tanner's got Velma."

Tanner turned, revealing a BabyBjörn strapped to his chest, its contents fully concealed except for a puff of downy gray feathers poking out from the top.

Their employer was a nonprofit dedicated to protecting birds of prey. In the coming days, Grayson and Tanner would place the new eaglets into nests of existing sentinel pairs.

"Then we move the cameras in, yes we do," Tanner said in a sing-songy voice to the chick in his BabyBjörn.

"When there are babies in nests, our view numbers go bananas. Right now there's, like, twenty thousand people a day checking the live streams, but once they can see the chicks it'll be two million, easy. That's when most of our donations come in. Good press helps too. Last year we got interviewed by *The New Yorker*!"

"Gotta get that sweet donor money," Grayson said. He offered his fingers to Tanner and they wiggled them together, a maneuver between men Andi never ceased to find off-putting.

"Yeah, Andi. You need to get yourself into the private money game," Tanner said. "It could really help move along your . . . ice . . . mud . . . project."

Her anger felt so close to the surface as to make her physically hot. Millions of views a day for fewer than two dozen birds. Ugly birds. Birds no one would notice if they were just flying overhead. A platform in national publications, money for whatever they needed. And no matter how loud she shouted about the prospect of entire neighborhoods leveled by boulder-strewn floods, no one gave Andi the time of day. If she too were a Bird Bro, she wondered, then would someone, somewhere, call her back?

She tried to think of something safe to say.

"Why is that one in a baby carrier?" she asked, pointing to Tanner's chest.

"She likes snuggles," he said, as if nothing could be more obvious.

BACK AT THE MOTEL, Andi ran through her call list. The only person who answered was the associate professor.

"Andi," he said as soon as he picked up, "I'm worrying about ice worms. Their populations must be in shambles. They don't live anywhere on earth except glaciers, you know. Do you think there's anything to be done for the ice worms?"

"Maybe repatriation," Andi muttered, which sent the associate professor into a tizzy of ideas, and Andi had to make an excuse to get off the phone before she'd even had a chance to say why she was calling.

Not long after, Ricky came by. He shed his clothes and lay on her bed, face propped in his hands. "What do you say, lover?" he asked.

She was not in the mood for sex.

"'S cool," he said. "We'll just hang out." He put his shorts back on but left everything else on the floor.

"Hey," he said. "I've been meaning to ask you, are you still going to be around the weekend after next?"

Andi didn't know. She had no clear reason to stay but she could not bring herself to leave.

"Well, if you are, do you want to come to Mount Hood with me? My friend I told you about, he's getting a crew together, gonna try to summit if conditions are good. Two days up and back. You should join us."

She felt her anger peak again. Why did no one listen when she spoke?

"I. Don't. Climb." Each word punctuated with a pointed finger and spoken at a volume just below a shout. She wanted to get so much louder.

"Okay. I hear you. Sorry. You don't climb," Ricky said, his hands up like he was backing away from an unpredictable animal. "But do you still drink?"

It occurred to her on the walk to the bar, in the safety of outside, the warm wind nice against her face, that she had missed what was important about Ricky's question. Not the part where he had forgotten what she'd already told him. The part where he liked her enough to want to take a trip with her. He was holding her hand as they walked, easy and kind, even after she'd been harsh with him. "It's okay to have a little bit of good," was something her mother would say to her when, as a teenager, she grew morose, refusing even basic human niceties like dessert or new nail polish. She'd been one of those adolescents whose thoughts tended toward doom, a *the-world-is-ending-so-why-should-I-bother* sort. It was rocks that had saved her from that. She'd taken a geology class her junior year. It gave a knowability to the world. To see things in the earth, learn their names, and understand that they had been there for an incredibly long time. Then she'd found glaciology as an undergrad and loved it for the exact opposite reason. Mountain glaciers change every single day, advancing and retreating and sliding. They are at the whims of weather and of the landforms they sit on. You could study one for your entire career and learn nothing lasting. "Of course you would fall for the most angsty of the sciences," Selena had teased her. Andi didn't think glaciers were angsty. They were just being honest. When she said this to Selena, her sister laughed. It's okay to have a little bit of good.

BUT AT RANGER DANGER, there was no more good. Ricky drank one beer and was obviously drunk, which meant he'd probably been drinking all afternoon. It shouldn't bother her, she thought. He wasn't her boyfriend. But still. She didn't like being the last stop on his Pinestack booze cruise. What did he even have to drink about, this man-child whose lazy charm was enough to buoy him through life, his worries nothing more than deciding which outfitter to sign on with for his next season of wilderness adventures?

It was Friday and so they fell in with the Gem Girls even though Andi was not in the mood for their company. The girls had been drinking for some time already too, plotting a weekend float on the White River.

"It's been such a perfect summer!" one of them said. "So pretty, and not even any big fires yet. But I feel like we've been going a hundred miles an hour. I need time to slowwww down. I need a day on the river so bad, you don't even know."

"Don't," Andi mumbled. "The water levels are extremely high for this time of year. It's moving faster than you think."

The girl who had spoken made a pouty face and flashed a thumbs-down sign.

"No, dudes, listen to her," Ricky said. "She knows these things. For real, though, you guys have to get up the ice with Andi. Next season we'll all go together. She's, like, a glacier Jedi. She just senses the crevasses."

A realization came to Andi. He hadn't invited her on the illicit Hood climb out of infatuation. He invited her because he thought she would protect him.

She excused herself to the restroom but headed instead for the door. Out of the corner of her eye, she saw Ricky wave her back. She ignored him. He caught up when she reached the end of the block.

"Are you okay?"

She stopped walking and turned toward him. "You only asked me to go to Oregon because you think I can keep you safe. But let me tell you something—it's August. Nothing will keep you safe."

"That's not why I invited you," he said.

"Then why?"

"I thought you'd like it. I thought you'd want to see it, before it—" He took his hand and made a downward arc. A smooth sweep to suggest water into water, as if it could always be so peaceful. All her anger from the day slid into exhaustion.

"I'm so sorry, Ricky," she said. "I think I just really need to focus on my work. Let's call it for now, huh?"

THAT WEEKEND, something unexpected and awful happened: Andi's mom and dad showed up.

They arrived at the door of her motel room dressed as if they had gone to REI and asked for *one of everything*. Andi thought she was past the childhood feeling of being embarrassed by her parents.

"We were worried," her mom said. "The things you said on the phone. And now Selena's in Oakland with Theo and the baby! She said you were supposed to meet them and never came. She's worried too."

"You guys should also go to Oakland."

"You've been here over a month and you haven't visited," her dad said. "We wanted to see you."

Then he added, "We wanted to see for ourselves," and gestured to the mountain behind them.

"So pretty," her mom said. "We really ought to come out here more often."

Andi did what adult children must always do when parents visit—she took them sightseeing. She drove them first to Sunrise Day Lodge, where they joined the tourists to gawk at the view and buy snacks. Then for a hike so her parents could use their new trekking poles and CamelBaks. She pointed out the leavings of the old lahar—the dirt with its unusual colors. She did the trick with water of turning it to clay.

"During a flood, these pyroclastic deposits make the earth slick and slidey," Andi explained. "It's one of the reasons lahars have the potential to flow so far. *Flow* isn't even the right word. Actually, lahars pulse. The mud runs down the mountainside picking up debris, and at some point as it goes along, the debris gets stuck, creating a bottleneck. The force of the lahar pushes the bottleneck open and it takes whatever stopped it in the first place along. So now it's got more material and more power. The bigger it gets, the more it bottlenecks and pushes free. At its zenith, the Osceola Mudflow was over five hundred feet high, traveling nearly fifty miles per hour."

"It went like that all the way?" her dad asked, pointing in the direction of Puyallup, Tacoma, Puget Sound.

"All the way," Andi confirmed. "The ground under your house is like this too."

"Under," he repeated, in a voice that suggested he was actually thinking *Over.*

"It's really not very sturdy, is it?" her mom asked, picking at the mound of dirt in question with her trekking pole. "It just sort of comes apart."

Back in the car, her parents were quiet, their mood turned somber. Andi felt bad. She wanted to impress upon them the importance of her work, but they were still her mom and dad, and she also wanted them to have a nice time. She thought, begrudgingly, of something they might enjoy.

AT THE RESEARCH CABIN, Tanner and Grayson could not contain their excitement.

"Welcome to the Mount Rainier Center for Avian Repatriation!" they shouted, throwing their hands in the air. If they'd had confetti to toss, they would have.

The Bird Bros did not disappoint. They explained that Nader, the sturdiest of the chicks, had been placed with a surrogate family that morning. But they brought out Kokomo and Rhapsody from their crates for introductions and the feeding of mealworms. Tanner even took Velma from her BabyBjörn and nestled her in a towel on Andi's mom's lap. She petted the chick, speaking gently to her. They handed out shell fragments from the egg box and explained their size and unusual colors. They looked at all the live cams, including the one Grayson had set up to monitor Nader with his new family.

"He seems good," Grayson said as they watched the chick poking around the cliffside nest. "He seems happy."

And they all agreed he did.

Grayson offered them a round of Panics for the road, which Andi and her mom laughed off, though Andi knew it was in fact the greatest compliment the Bird Bros could bestow, a gift from their coveted stash. Her dad accepted. On the way down the trail he confided that it tasted like cherry juice mixed with paint thinner and he was worried he might need to go to the hospital.

Andi had thought at some point in the cabin she would give her parents the binoculars and direct their eyes to the route she and Ricky had walked along Emmons. They would be impressed, she knew, to think of her so far up the mountain. But the birds and their high-spirited Bros had brought such joy, she did not want to dampen the mood again.

She took her parents to dinner at Grizzly Bar. Though neither the food nor the atmosphere were ideal, she assumed she would be safe from bumping into people she knew, namely Ricky. She was wrong, and just as their meal arrived, he came loping through the door with one of the Gem Girls and another woman she didn't recognize. Andi tried to make herself small in her booth. Ricky spotted her right away. She assumed he'd be mad, or sad, to see her, the way she'd rebuked him. But he came right over, introducing himself to Andi's parents. They invited him to sit and he accepted, waving his friends off. *He's only doing this because he knows they'll pay for his food*, Andi thought, then caught herself.

He was, as the Bird Bros had been earlier, friendly and charming. He regaled them with stories from the mountain. He talked about how most guides preferred leading groups up the southern routes of Rainier because they were less technical, and therefore more likely to end with a successful summit. But he liked the Emmons route. Longer, slower, more consuming. He told stories about making camp in whiteouts and about rescuing a fellow guide from a crevasse that had opened where the previous weekend it was solid ice.

"Emmons is just so big. There are spots where, no matter which way you look, all you can see is glacier. It makes you feel like you're on a forever thing. Like it's always been there and somehow always will be."

Then he looked sheepishly at Andi. "Even though, you know, obviously that's not right."

"It's a young volcano," Andi whispered and looked away.

Such a nice young man, her parents agreed after they had parted ways.

"What luck to be friends with someone who knows your glacier so well!" her mom said. "Has he been helpful to your research, those eyewitness accounts?"

Andi lied and said yes, hoping her embarrassment did not give her away. She had never thought to interview Ricky about his time on Emmons. She had assumed herself the expert, treating him as only a hired hand, a quick lay, a distraction. She'd underestimated him from the beginning.

Back at their car in the motel parking lot, Andi hugged her parents and wished them a safe drive, even though it was only an hour and a half home.

"This was a nice day, kiddo," her dad said.

"We're so proud of you," her mom said.

"But you still don't believe me."

"Of course we believe you."

"Just not enough to change your plans."

Her dad sighed. "Life is long, Andi, and you're still so young."

In five days, they would leave for London. They would be fine. They told her to go to Oakland with Selena, or back to her friends and colleagues in Alaska. They too wanted her to leave, but not for the same reasons.

IT WAS A YOUNG VOLCANO.

Volcanic cones have a lifespan of about two million years. In that time, they may erupt frequently or infrequently. Then they grow dormant and sink back into the landscape. Mount Rainier is a half a million years old. If it were a person it would be in its twenties. It is known to have erupted on five occasions in the past six thousand years. It is thought that the next eruption will come from the western flank. There is evidence to show that side is now more vulnerable.

It is thought that Rainier was once a thousand feet taller. That its peak was a point like a jaunty gnome's cap.

Andi wondered if she was also a young volcano, her vulnerabilities constantly shifting and she too ignorant of herself to notice the change.

Always the martyr, Selena had said. Andi lamented the lonesomeness of her knowledge but she also coveted it. She claimed to revere Cassidy for her genius and her resolve, though it was the woman's lone-wolfishness that she'd wound up emulating. She wanted to be the one, the only one, with the right answer. It was the real reason she stayed while telling everyone she loved to go.

ANDI CHECKED the motel office each day. No sensors. She called Cassidy and got no answer. She called *The Washington Post*, *The New York Times*. She called *The New Yorker* and said she loved the article on the Bird Bros of Mount Rainier and had a great idea for a follow-up, but the person she spoke to said they had no idea what she was talking about.

HER MOM TEXTED: **The Gerrys want to know if they should leave town too. Will the lahar reach Woodland Ave.?**

Andi wrote back **Yes and yes. Tell all your friends to go.**

ANOTHER WEEK PASSED BY, another weekend. Her parents left for their trip to Europe. Selena was getting restless with her in-laws in Oakland. She wanted to know when it would be safe to come home. Ricky, presumably, decamped for Mount Hood. She hadn't spoken to him since dinner at Grizzly Bar. The Bird Bros placed the remaining eaglets and set up their new nest cams. Back at the research cabin, they hovered around the computer screen, scrutinizing their care.

Andi understood that she should return to Alaska. The new semester would start in two weeks. She needed to prepare for the classes she was teaching. She needed to begin her job search. Her postdoc position would expire in the spring. She felt she had little to show for her time in Fairbanks—her role with Cassidy's sensors marginal, and her own project at Rainier a total bust.

The associate professor texted her a picture of his penis. When she responded with dissatisfaction, he claimed it was an accident, that he'd meant to send it to his "wife." He put *wife* in quotes. He then said they were living separately, her in their apartment and him with a friend. He could really use someone to talk to, he said. Could he call Andi sometime, just to talk?

And now I have to deal with this shit, she thought. She called Cassidy again, intending to detail the incident for her voicemail. This time, she picked up.

"He's been a fissuring ice sheet for quite a while now, if you catch my drift," Cassidy said of the associate professor.

"I haven't received the sensors yet," Andi said. "I'm having trouble getting permits to place them. Can we talk through the data component?"

"They should be there. They should already be there," Cassidy said, then her connection cut out.

AT THE RESEARCH CABIN, Andi arrived to a scene of grief. The Bros sat huddled on the couch, quiet as if deep in thought. That was how Andi knew something was wrong.

"What happened?" she asked.

"We lost one of the babies," Grayson said. "Velma's surrogate parents rejected her. They pushed her out of the nest."

"I knew they were a bad pick," Tanner whispered like he did not trust his voice. "The feeding in that area's no good this year. The vole population—" Grayson put his hand on Tanner's back and the smaller man fell silent.

"I'm sorry to hear it," Andi said. "She was a really nice eagle."

"Thank you," Tanner said. Then he began to cry in earnest. He reached for Andi and pulled her into a hunched hug. He pressed his face into her shoulder and she could feel the wet through her shirt. He stopped as abruptly as he'd begun.

"I'm so sorry. I didn't mean to do that," he said. "It's just, no one else really knew her, you know?"

THAT EVENING, IT RAINED. The weather had been so constant since Andi arrived at Rainier, the sunny days and the dry afternoon heat. But she wasn't a regular in that place, and didn't realize how much anxiety the sameness caused. The rain arrived suddenly. Andi was at the market when it started. The girl at the cash register shouted, "Rain! It's finally fucking raining!" Everyone went to see, Andi with them. Down the street, people were spilling out of Ranger Danger and Grizzly Bar and the post office and the ice cream shop. Andi looked to the clouds. They were darker to the south, Rainier totally obscured. The storm was coming down from the mountain.

"Thank God," she heard one young man say. "Thirty red flag days in a row, I thought I was going to go out of my skin. Pray there's no lighting."

"All it's going to do is rain," the man standing next to him said. "I can feel it in my foot when there's going to be lightning."

"Remember three summers ago when we never saw the summit?" a young woman asked. "Clouds every day. I miss that kind of summer."

People stood on the sidewalk, catching rain on their tongues as if it were snowflakes. It was like a party, a holiday. Andi felt a deep cut of fear.

Nothing melts ice like water.

She ran back to her motel. She tried with her phone to check the digital thermometer at Camp Schurman, at the edge of the Emmons Glacier, but couldn't get a reading. The weather was in the way. Outside, the rain had intensified and Andi heard a crack of thunder. The man's foot had been wrong. She imagined the mood on the main street of Pinestack swinging from elation to worry, everyone heading back into the bars, or home to their rented rooms. She called Forge's cell phone and when he did not answer she called again and again. Finally, he picked up.

"To what is this in regards?" he asked, his voice small and sounding very far away.

"Dr. Forge, do you have current ground and air temperatures at Camp Schurman? I'm unable to access them."

"Dr. Carling, I am also unable to access them."

He was matching her in formality and honorifics, like he too was trying to mask his fear.

"Dr. Forge, what is the likelihood of freezing temperatures at the summit? Is there any chance this is snow?"

"Dr. Carling, we haven't seen freezing temperatures at the summit in two months. All precipitation will fall as rain and it will all flow straight down."

It might be time to go, Andi thought. But flash flood warnings had already been issued. To drive either direction was ill-advised. The devil you know versus the devil you don't. She stayed put.

IN THE MORNING, all was well in Pinestack. Another bluebird day, already warm and breezy. Outside, Andi could see plumes of smoke rising to the north, evidence of lightning strikes. They looked small. The mountain looked the same as always.

She called Forge again. "Are you planning to survey any of the glaciers after last night's rain? If so, I'd like to come along."

"I don't know, Andi. I might go up by helicopter next week. Right now, all our air resources are going to the fire in Silver Springs." He said this in a single exhale of frustration. Gone was his fear from the previous evening, and Andi missed it.

"A week's a long time to wait."

"Look, I appreciate your commitment to answering the academic question you have posed, but—"

She cut him off. "It's not academic. How is the safety of two hundred thousand people academic? You were frightened too last night. I know it."

"I was worried about the health of the glaciers, yes. And about the capacity of the Mud Mountain Dam. But I spoke to the chief engineer and he said everything is fine—the reservoirs are full but not overflowing."

"He's back?" Andi said. "He was supposed to call me when he got back. Can you please ask him to call me, when you speak to him next?"

Forge sighed again. "Are you still staying in Pinestack?"

She said she was.

"You should be prepared to evacuate," he said. "If the wind shifts south there will be an order."

Andi went back outside. The air smelled like a campfire. She felt the weight of the smoke with every inhale. She could see now one of the smoke plumes was larger than the others and observably closer. She had mistaken the quiet on the streets for peacefulness when actually this was what Ricky had meant when he'd said everyone was waiting. Why hadn't she realized it sooner? The cheerful young people of Pinestack were a wildlands firefighting battalion, search and rescue crews, wilderness EMTs. Their whole reason for being on the unpopular side of the mountain—to wait for disaster. Here it was, and they'd all gone to meet it. She'd underestimated everyone.

In the motel parking lot, a handful of other guests were loading gear into their vans and trucks. Not panicked, but purposeful. Andi followed suit. It took her less than ten minutes to pack her belongings into her rental car. On the way out, she checked the office one more time. There, finally, was the package from Cassidy.

AT THE RESEARCH CABIN, Grayson and Tanner stood at the windows, highly agitated.

"Dude," Grayson said to Andi when she came in. "Everything is just really fucked right now."

"Yes," Andi agreed. "Everything is really fucked."

They both started talking at once. Andi about how the warm rain might have rapidly degraded spots of vulnerable ice, bringing Emmons closer than ever to a cataclysmic outburst, not to mention softening the earth along the moraines and filling the reservoir behind the dam to capacity before said cataclysmic outburst even happened. Grayson about how if the fire spread west literally at all it would burn the areas where their eagles were doing their best feeding. And much beyond that, it would destroy nests.

They stopped talking and a sort of vacant sound took over the cabin, like the whole forest holding its breath; the way of places near but not yet inside calamity. A waiting silence.

"It's just been hot for so long," Grayson said, quietly now. "I'm afraid everything is going to go really fast."

"Me too," Andi said.

SHE SCOURED the surface of the glacier with her binoculars. She couldn't tell anything. She turned her attention to Cassidy's package. She decided she didn't need Forge. She could hire a helicopter to fly her over the glacier and drop the sensors without him ever knowing.

The sensors were the size and shape of two frisbees in the act of mating. Andi sheared through their plastic casing to separate the outer pieces. The inner workings were less intricate than she imagined, but still, she was out of her element. Cassidy, brilliant and secretive, had designed the sensors on her own. The device was hers and all the glory for its success would be hers. Andi was tired of being held at arm's length. Once she figured out how to access the sensors' data, she wouldn't need Cassidy either.

The Bird Bros continued their watch, saying little. Tanner stood with the telescope while Grayson toggled between the camera feeds on his computer, looking for signs of the chicks.

"If the adults are smart, they'll have fled," he said mournfully.

"Cut the streams, will you?" Tanner said. "We don't want donors logging on to empty nests."

Grayson shot him a look like *How could you think of money at a time like this?* but dutifully closed out the program.

FINALLY, JUST BEFORE NOON, Tanner banged his palm twice on the desk.

"There! It jumped the road!"

Grayson and Andi joined him at the window.

"It's moving east," he said. "If it jumped the road, it's definitely going east. The wind made the decision. It's moving away from us."

They high-fived each other. Then they high-fived Andi. She returned to her own task. The direction of the fire had no bearing on her work. But the mood in the cabin had shifted so thoroughly she couldn't help but feel lightened too. Nothing bad had happened. There was still time.

"Do either of you know anything about hacking?" she asked. "Specifically how to jailbreak a satellite transmitter?"

"Heck no," Grayson said. "But it's pretty punk of you to try."

Around her, Tanner and Grayson made plans to visit the nests of the eaglets, and for what to do if they found them empty, or the babies alone. An hour passed and the Bird Bros, declaring themselves famished, plundered their snack cabinet, piling jerky sticks, chips, and packets of nuts onto their desk. They invited Andi to join them in their feast. She selected some cashews and sat listening to them tell stories of other encounters with wildfire, the happy bravado of a near miss.

Tanner got into an altercation with a candy wrapper. "Hold on," Andi laughed. As she reached for her daypack, intending to offer him her multitool, there was a trembling noise, a rattling of the ground.

"Whoa, earthquake," Grayson said, his voice tinged with excitement. Andi turned to see him holding on to the arms of his good chair, smiling like he was on a ride. Behind him Tanner scrambled for cover under the desk. Andi stayed as she was. The tremble did not stop. Through the window, a gray cloud of airborne debris came into view. Grayson's expression twisted. "Ehhhh, what the fuck?"

Andi stood to test the floor, which did not roll but only grumbled. She felt something shoot through her like fear and also righteousness.

"I believe the ice wall has given way," she said.

The whole time they'd shared the cabin, she thought they never listened to her. So she was surprised now to see the speed with which they moved. Tanner rose from his crouch under the desk and swept its contents into his hiking backpack. Grayson grabbed his water bottle. Andi snagged him by the arm.

"You can't outrun it. This is Emmons." She had to shout this. The din of the grumble was rising. To make any other sound heard from here on out would require a fight.

He shook her off and headed for the door.

"Wait," she called.

Tanner brushed past them, out of the cabin and presumably down the trail, which would lead him nowhere. But Grayson turned back to her.

"What's the password to the cameras?"

He blanched.

"Now!" she shouted, snapping her fingers.

"BigOleTitties3!" he shouted back. "Ole with an E, not a D. I'm sorry!"

Then he ran out the door, but not before closing it behind him.

Andi went to the Bird Bros' computer, opened the application, entered the childish password. Turned on streaming and recording. Then she pulled the camera from its perch at the north-facing window and held it so it looked to the debris cloud instead. She had the idea that she would narrate what was happening. She would explain—to anyone watching, to anyone who wanted to know later—the conditions of the outburst, and the generation of the lahar, this thing both new and repeating, more than five thousand years in the making. The young volcano fulfilling its destiny even when it didn't mean to—humans had done so for it.

The sound was so loud as to be no sound at all. Through the debris cloud she could see the wall of water, already turned brown, not a flood but a churning, pulsing beast. It would eat and grow. She bent her head to the camera so her mouth was right at the microphone.

"This is Dr. Andrea Carling at the Mount Rainier Center for Avian Repatriation," she began. But after that, she found she did not want to talk anymore. She stood up straight, pressing the camera to the window. She let the glacier speak for itself.

Nicholas the Bunny

Nicholas is filthy. He knows this from the faces of the men he is with. They are painted with dirt and ash from the brims of their helmets down to their necks. When they pull their respirators off, there is a muzzle of clean. He thinks they look like cartoon dogs.

The three of them—Nicholas, Skylar, and Declan—hiked out from their camp that morning to investigate a report that a previously contained area of the fire had broken out. It was true. They should have called for support as soon as they saw it, but resources are spread so thin. They spent several hours digging new lines, felling and back-burning what vegetation remained. Then the wind changed and the fire headed toward them fast. They had to go, their work mostly for naught.

Now they are hot and discouraged. It is a long walk back—the fire cut off the route they took from camp. The extra miles feel heavy with the weight of their gear and the afternoon heat. The grime from their digging and then the sudden influx of smoke turns cakey as they sweat. Overhead, air support carries water to the place they just were. They have ducked back into the burn area; the fire can't get them where there's no fuel left.

Skylar leads them to a clearing. He gives the hand signal for *Sit the fuck down for a minute and eat a snack*. Declan takes his helmet off to pour water on his head and steam rises. Nicholas follows suit, but feels no better. It is the beginning of November, and he is afraid this season has no end. His family and friends back home in Spokane have stopped asking how things are going. He assumes they know from the news.

No one says anything. Nicholas remembers, at preseason training, when he called these men his friends. When they were all full of bravado and energy, eager to tell stories and make each other laugh. They didn't have to prove themselves tough. They had to prove themselves fun—the sorts who could keep up a good time under any circumstances. A promise none of them, ultimately, have been able to keep. In July, two jumpers from their unit died in an accident—not from a jump but from a tree felled the wrong direction. Then another in September, a man who walked off from camp. Never returned and could not be found, so they assumed the worst. There was no break to mourn. They did not train for this, Nicholas thinks. The part where they would have to hold each other up through despair. He knows it is childish but he wants the fun back, the excitement and optimism of his first weeks in California. He eats his jerky stick, looks at his crewmates' faces.

"I know a trick," he offers.

"Yeah?" Declan walks over to Nicholas. Skylar joins them as well. They are all desperate for something.

He points into the burnt expanse of the clearing. Then he says nothing and does nothing. This part takes a minute. He worries that Sklyar and Declan will get bored and sit back down. It is a trick easily missed without strict attention.

About thirty yards in front of them, a seagull drifts up from the space between the ground and the sky.

"Hold on," Nicholas says. "Sometimes I can get a bigger one."

Then, a pelican. The bird stands still on long legs for just a second. It gets a running start and takes off. The seagull has already flown out of sight.

"There," Nicholas says, and smiles, tracking the pelican with his finger. But the mood of his companions is heavy. He worries he has made an error in judgment. He has never shown anyone his trick before, except his sister, Ruby, but she didn't really understand it was him who had done it. He didn't either, at the time.

It's always birds. For a long time, he would get a feeling and then if he focused on the feeling, he could make a bird. Later, he learned to bring the feeling on whenever he wanted. He just has to search around in his mind for it. Though his desire for birds is occasional at best.

"Never mind," Nicholas says. "It's nothing."

"Now do deer," Skylar says.

Nicholas is surprised when a doe and a buck appear. He did not know he was susceptible to the power of suggestion. The deer look confused in a way birds never do. They turn tight circles. The buck tosses his head theatrically like he's trying to prove something. He bolts in the direction that the fire is not. The doe pursues.

"Now do butterflies."

A puff of monarchs, maybe a dozen. They fly up and away with no consideration to landing.

"Are they real?" Declan asks.

"What else would they be?" Skylar says.

"Now do a rabbit," Declan says.

Brown-furred and white-tailed. Its nose wiggles as it sniffs and sniffs and sniffs at the blackened ground.

"You fucking asshole." Skylar takes a running start at Declan and shoves him hard enough to topple him. His helmet and respirator pop from his hands as he hits the ground. "It's just going to die out here."

"I'm sorry," Declan mutters, crawling to retrieve his gear. Neither of them seem to consider Nicholas's role in this.

Skylar helps Declan to his feet. He checks his watch. He does not apologize.

"We need to get to the drop spot," Skylar says. A plane with fresh supplies and four more crew members is on its way. "Newbie cooks dinner," he adds, pulling on the collar of Nicholas's shirt like he doesn't trust him to follow.

NICHOLAS DOES NOT COOK dinner. He passes the task off on another man so he can return to the clearing. He brings with him the satellite phone. It is dedicated solely for communication with base and other hotshot units—no personal calls, ever. He sneaks it into his pocket when no one is looking. He brings water and a small bag of peanuts.

The rabbit is mostly where it was when he left. It has dug a half-assed warren. More of a divot than a burrow. It huddles there, exposed, nose and ears alert.

Nicholas scoops it up. He sits on a downed log with the rabbit in his lap. He offers it water, poured into his cupped hand, and it drinks a little. He offers it a peanut, which it ignores. It makes no effort to move from his lap. He's always been good with animals.

He takes out the phone and dials his sister.

"I need your help with something," he tells her.

"Are you okay?" she asks.

"I need you to say the word *trees*."

"Are you okay?" she asks again.

He knows he can't do this on his own. If he could, he would have already, before. He doesn't know when, but he would have. He tells her again. He wants her to say *trees*. Once every sixty seconds or so.

She hesitates. He is going to have to explain. She of all people will understand, he thinks. But he doesn't have the energy for it, the capacity. He has been in the field for fourteen days with no plan for when the team he jumped with will return to base. The new jumpers who arrived that afternoon are not replacing anyone; they just need more bodies on the ground. "Do you remember," he starts, "that time I—"

"Trees."

They come two at a time. Big-leaf maples. White alders. Incense cedars. They are lush and healthy, and almost unbearably green in this landscape of black and brown. He asks her to slow down. "Say it every two or three minutes." He is tired. They don't talk in between. After three quarters of an hour, she says she has to go; she needs to feed the baby. He wipes at his eyes. His sister's whole life has changed and he hasn't even met the baby. He knew this would be the case when he left in spring. But now everything important feels so far away.

"Is Brayden there?" he asks. She says he isn't back from work yet, but their mom is over.

"Do you want me to put her on?" Ruby asks, skeptical.

Nicholas says yes. He hears the muffled sounds of his sister and mother conferring. Then his mom is on the line, her voice full of parental cheer. "So, we're talking about trees?"

He doesn't want to worry her. He doesn't want to stop yet, either. He tells her what he needs her to do.

"Oh, I get it," she says. "I see what you're up to. I think it's wonderful."

He has no idea how this could possibly be true, but he appreciates the sentiment.

They finish out the hour. His mind drifts; the trees get smaller, more shrublike. The rabbit still refuses its peanut.

He does not, here in this particular moment, think this is a solution to anything. Later, people will argue otherwise. The situation will become complicated, fraught; everything Nicholas hates.

What he has made is not a forest. His new trees cover just half of the clearing. He can't even fathom the area of the fire his crew is working to contain. It is just one of eight hundred currently active across the state, nearly five million acres burned since the start of summer, a number that is so large it means nothing to him. But this is a nice glade.

"Say toadstools," he tells his mom.

"Say grasses."

"Say wildflowers."

"Say pond."

"Say lily pads."

"Say bullfrogs."

"Say strawberries."

He knows it's too late in the year for strawberries. Still, they look nice. He sets the rabbit down near them; it nibbles. This, now, is a place it can live.

A Plan to Save Us All

The first of the Meyersville time travelers arrived on October 4, 2003. It was late afternoon and he materialized out of nothing into a field, spooking a cluster of cows. I wasn't there, but Mrs. Anderson, who owned the field, the cows, and the surrounding property, was, and the next morning at church, she told us all exactly how it had happened. In fact, she told the story so many times, and in such detail, that I felt I was picturing the scene from my own memory. It went like this:

Mrs. Anderson had just finished brushing Gravy, her favorite horse. She bent down to put the brush back in her bucket, and when she stood up again, there was this man. He was smack-dab in the middle of the pasture. He had just *appeared* there, and he looked it too, turning his head every which way and dusting himself off even though he wasn't dusty. He was dressed all in black, including black glasses and a long black jacket, "like one of those young men from *The Matrix*, but not as handsome," Mrs. Anderson said. Or as athletic. He'd stumbled several times trying to navigate the muddy, rutted topography of the cow pasture. Mrs. Anderson's take: "I think he's the kind who spends his time inside with his video games, instead of outside breathing fresh air." He seemed wary of the cows, but they paid him no mind. Mrs. Anderson, who trusted the instincts of her animals, assumed him harmless, and waved him over. When he finally reached her, he extended his hand (pale, weak) and announced, "I've come from the future where a deadly pathogen that originated in this very town has annihilated ninety percent of human and animal life on earth. If nothing is done to stop it, it will, within a decade's time, kill you and everyone you know. But don't worry; I have a plan to save us all."

Mrs. Anderson did not know what to make of this. Was he crazy? Was he an alien? Was he a messenger from God? She had no room in her home, small and already full up with children and grandchildren as it was, but she offered him the barn. She gave him a sleeping bag, pillow, and electric lantern, and helped him turn the hayloft into a cozy, if rustic, guest room. She felt it was the Christian thing to do.

How long would she let him stay? someone asked.

"As long as he likes," she said. Though she'd want him to chip in for groceries if he was there more than a week. Extra mouths don't feed themselves, and all that.

"What's his plan?" another person wanted to know.

"What plan?"

"His plan for saving everyone."

"I didn't think to ask," Mrs. Anderson admitted.

MRS. ANDERSON may have thought him harmless, but the congregation, on the whole, was wary. We children and teens were warned to stay away from the time traveler, what with his odd style of dress and apocalyptic ramblings. So I sought him out at the earliest possible opportunity.

I was seventeen and equal parts bored and angry. We'd moved to tiny Meyersville that spring from San Diego so my dad could take a job as senior pastor at the one and only Baptist church in the county—a big change from his previous post as fourth-in-command at a beachside megachurch. Dad had hyped the move, extolling the virtues of Northern California: the slower pace; an escape from traffic; a chance to spend time in nature each and every day, to "really get back to the land," as he put it. As if we were exiles, awaiting our glorious return to the countryside.

I had no such interest in getting back to the land, nor did Mom. We liked our city life, and our relative independence from Dad's church. In San Diego, we accompanied him to services on Sundays and the occasional fundraiser or family night, but our presence was superficial. We played the parts of the dutiful wife and daughter and then went back to doing what we wanted. I dated and went to parties and to the beach and skipped school, but not enough to get caught. I rode in other people's cars and never minded the traffic. Mom went to art classes and yoga and volunteered for a host of progressive causes, including raising money for abortion clinics in rural communities, which Dad said was fine as long as she didn't talk about it at church, and of course she never did—why would she? We lived fifteen miles away, in a suburb where men came to mow the grass twice a week, and there was little overlap between the two worlds.

Now we lived across the street from Dad's church in a hundred-year-old house where everything was broken and there was no one to fix it except us. The kids I saw at school were the same kids I saw in church, and everyone from church knew me everywhere I went and wanted to know my business. More important, they wanted to know if my dad knew my business, as in, "Young lady, does your father know you are out here on a school night?" Mom also felt the loss, her world having shrunk down to the church social club. Even getting out of town was an ordeal. Meyersville, with a population of thirty-five hundred, was located midway between Sacramento and absolutely nothing.

I had finished out my sophomore year at Meyersville High School with grades that would have drawn no attention whatsoever in San Diego. But now, under the scrutiny of teachers who were also my dad's congregants, they caused great concern and gossip. My punishment was two sessions at Bible camp. There, I whiled away the days smoking cigarettes behind the kitchen and trying to take the virginity of boys who had just sworn purity pledges. I wanted to shock people, to scare them, to show I was the opposite of all things Meyersville. In hindsight, I suspect my neighbors found me pitiable—a lonely city girl, turning toward minor sin to fill the void.

BUT HERE NOW was someone who really was the opposite of all things Meyersville. The time traveler dressed different, talked different, lived in a barn, and most important, drew considerable scorn from the Meyersvillians. He was the talk of the town, none of it good.

I went to the Andersons' barn after school on a Wednesday, and found the time traveler receptive to my company. I opened the barn door and as soon as he looked at me I said, "My name's Mercy and my dad is a pastor. I'm seventeen. Wanna fuck?"

I had never seen a face as grateful as his. I thought perhaps sex was a scarce commodity in the future. We did it on his thin sleeping bag in the barn attic. There was less hay around than I had imagined there might be, though more cobwebs.

Sex was different with the time traveler than with the Bible camp virgins. Though not so different than with the wannabe skaters I'd hung around with in San Diego. It made me wonder if there's no such thing as sexual expertise—only minimal proficiency. Because why bother being an expert when being just okay still gets you laid? I found this idea discouraging. I was young and wanted more out of life. But I wasn't so disappointed that I did not continue to sleep with the time traveler regularly for the next ten months.

His name was Todd. I would have expected people from the future to have exotic names, maybe even unpronounceable ones. They all ended up having names like suburban boys—uniform and sunny and hollow. Anyway, on our first afternoon together in the barn, following our adequate but unremarkable lovemaking, Todd told me why he'd come to Meyersville. It was just like he'd said to Mrs. Anderson: A new mutation of a very old bacterium, called *Actinomadura umbrina*, was perhaps at that very moment gaining hold in the offshoots of the Meyersville River. In a little less than ten years, it would infect its first human host, a fourth grader named Lewis Leroy. The boy would be medically vulnerable in some way, something wrong with him that made him an easy target for disease. Maybe his parents had spurned all immunizations in favor of essential oils. The point was, though many people swam in the river, it was in young Lewis that *A. umbrina* would find an agreeable home. Then, once acclimated to life in the mammalian body, the bacterium would spread to any human or animal the boy came in contact with. Within a week of that, everyone in Meyersville would be sick in a fainting/vomiting/diarrhea/internal bleeding sort of way. Then, in another week, everyone in Meyersville would be dead.

"The bacterium degrades extracellular matrices. This allows it to migrate through the hosts' cells very rapidly, gets it into the lymph nodes, the bloodstream. It contains an enzyme that converts plasminogen to plasmin. So there's sepsis, but also hemorrhaging. If that makes sense," Todd said.

I assured him it did not.

"It's pretty similar to how plague functions," he said. "You remember your plague studies? Usually first or second grade for the basics, right?"

I shook my head and watched a shadow of concern cross his previously blissed-out face. This was perhaps his first of many, many disappointing realizations about our era.

What about a cure? I asked, trying to right the conversation. What about a vaccine?

There was none, he said, though certainly not for lack of effort. *A. umbrina* was hearty, and sneaky. Drug-resistant and constantly mutating. For generations, it would munch away at Earth's population, until, by Todd's time, humanity's only hope was to intercept the pathogen at the source, before it got into little Lewis Leroy, and all the rest of us.

I shook my head again. I told Todd I knew the Leroys. There were a bunch of them in town. But there was no kid named Lewis.

"Right," Todd said. "Because he won't be born until next year. His parents are Raymond Leroy and Chloe Brown. Perhaps you know them?"

And I did. They were a grade above me in school, newly in love and obnoxious.

"Yeah. They are one hundred percent the type to inadvertently bring about the apocalypse," I affirmed.

Todd didn't think this was funny. He only nodded.

"So what's your plan?" I asked. "You gonna shoot Raymond's nuts off so he can't have kids, or what?"

"I'm going to study the Meyersville River in hopes of determining the conditions that allow *A. umbrina* to thrive, and then develop a method for subverting or eradicating these conditions."

He was a hydrobiologist, he explained. He had degrees from one of Earth's few remaining universities. He had just finished his master's when the government announced its time-travel program and began a nationwide search for participants. He applied, and had been selected as the first to make the journey.

"So there are going to be more of you coming here?" I asked.

"Unfortunately, yes," Todd said.

We were still in the barn, and still naked. I pressed my hand into the pale skin on Todd's chest then let go just to see a red mark appear and fade. Did the man never take his shirt off outdoors? Not even at the beach? Were there still beaches, where he was from? I didn't ask. Instead, I climbed on top of him and fucked him again. I was tired of talking, and besides, I had to be at church by five for teen Bible study.

FOR ALL HIS SUSPICIOUS statements and behavior, Todd turned out to be a likable guy. He was grateful to the Andersons, pitching in for groceries as requested, and even helping out around the farm. In town, he was chatty with the shopkeepers and flirty with the old ladies. He worked to engage civic leaders in his water studies (though they never shared his sense of urgency and therefore offered little real support). He bought all his supplies from a local hardware store, and whatever he needed that they didn't have, he ordered special from them despite the cost. He visited the elementary school and gave presentations on the habitats of the Meyersville River, bringing with him a half dozen bullfrogs and a jar of crawdads. After a couple of months, he became a Meyersville fixture. People still talked about him, though now it was with affection. No longer a stranger to be wary of, but a lovable local oddity.

Did my neighbors believe he was really from the future? I have no idea.

Did I?

Initially, I did not. I assumed he was a con man with a big plan. Or an insane person. But then it became clear he wasn't either of those. The way he talked about his life and his work was so consistent, so serious. I found myself, when I was with him, accepting his statements as fact, taking him as seriously as he took himself. To spend time with Todd, one had to give in to the conceit that he was from the future.

The year he'd traveled from was 2210. I quizzed him on what the world was like then, as if he were a human Magic 8 Ball. His answers came back hazy.

Had contact been made with intelligent life on other planets?

"We've really been too busy just maintaining life on this one."

Were there self-driving cars? What about flying cars?

He said some cars drove themselves and some didn't, but none of them flew. Most people couldn't afford cars of any kind, though, so this too was sort of a nonissue. Todd didn't even have a driver's license, and none of his friends did either.

"The Institute has cars," he said, referring to the government organization that contracted him to travel through time. "Sometimes I can get a ride in one of those." Otherwise he mostly took the subway or the bus.

What about housecleaning robots?

These, also, were a no-go.

"But I heard that rich people"—and here he lowered his voice like he was sharing a nasty secret—"pay other people to clean their houses for them."

I made my eyes go wide, as if I too found this notion alarming.

I saw him once or twice a week. Typically, there was sex, but sometimes we just talked. He offered to take me out on dates—the Institute, seeking to sustain his research for a decade, had sent him with a considerable amount of money. He had more than enough for entertaining, he said.

"Then why do you live in a barn?" I asked.

"Where else would I live?"

At first, I paraded Todd around Main Street on my arm, enjoying the concerned stares of the townsfolk. Word got back to my dad and he put his foot down. "Mercy, you cannot be seen in public with that man," he said, and threatened all manner of sanction, like taking my cell phone, laptop, Discman, et cetera. This reaction pleased me, but I needed my stuff. So I split the difference, following Dad's instructions to the letter—I was not *seen in public* with Todd. But I was seen going in and out of the barn all the goddamn time, and I was happy to imagine the rumors that persisted about me and him. How interesting and dangerous and worldly (even otherworldly) I must have seemed.

THEN, IN JULY, Preston showed up.

The morning of his arrival, Todd was agitated. We were in the barn, naked, but nothing was happening. Todd had turned from my body in order to review his notes on the river. There were papers spread all across us and everywhere else.

"Your filing system is not the best," I pointed out.

"I asked the Institute to send an intern with me," Todd said. "But there were liability concerns."

"I could be your intern," I offered.

Todd shook his head. "I don't know how we'd get you the application paperwork. HR would have a fit if they ever found out."

I thought this was funny, but Todd was too far up his own butt to see the humor. He burrowed through his pages like a rat until ten a.m. Then we got dressed and went outside.

A man was standing in the middle of the Anderson cow pasture, looking a little disoriented. After a moment, he spotted us. I waved. He waved back. He jogged over and when he got to me, he extended his hand.

He said, "I've come from the future where a deadly pathogen that originated in this very town has annihilated ninety percent of human and animal life on earth. If nothing is done to stop it, it will, within nine years' time, kill you and everyone you know. But don't worry; I have a plan to save us all."

Then he added, "Hey, Todd. How's the river-purification thing going?"

TODD WAS EAGER to show Preston his work. He rambled through his pages of research. He brought out water samples in tiny jars, and explained filtration options and cleaning agents both chemical and biological.

"The blackgill trout has a microscopic alga that lives on its skin, and which uses microbes similar in structure to *A. umbrina* in its respiration," Todd said. "They live in Wyoming and Colorado primarily, but I think they could be transplanted here. I'm working with the city to apply for a grant."

Preston listened, but I could feel his impatience. He looked a lot like Todd—same style of clothes, same pale complexion. They both wore their hair short. Preston was bigger. He was more muscular, but also just a larger presence. He stood with his feet wide, unafraid to take up space. I found this attractive.

"Okay, Todd. Okay," Preston said, finally. "This all sounds great, but you've had your time. It's my turn now."

"But that's what I'm trying to explain," Todd said. "This is a long-term plan. I'm not finished. I never intended to be finished so soon."

"Right. That's fine. My plan is a short-term plan. You keep doing your long-term plan and I'll do my short-term plan. No reason we can't have both."

This sounded reasonable to me. I asked Preston what his plan was.

"Simple," he said. "I'm going to neutralize the host."

I didn't know what that meant.

"Lewis Leroy will be born this afternoon," Todd explained. "My colleague here intends to kill him."

I laughed. "After that are you going to go back and kill baby Hitler too?" I asked.

But Preston didn't get my joke. I was beginning to worry the future was a humorless place.

"My mission doesn't involve Hitler," he said.

Todd, drained of his morning nerves and left only with frustration, lit into Preston. His face flushed and his hands got all jumpy as he talked. He called Preston a monster and a murderer and asked how he could claim to be humanity's savior if all he aimed to do was kill. He then turned his ire from Preston to the Institute, saying how stupid, how misguided they were for not sticking to *his* plan, for stacking plans on top of plans. "Think of what I could do if I had the full support and attention of the organization!" he shouted.

"But what if you fail?" Preston asked.

"My plan's a good plan."

"Sure. All our plans are good plans. And if we try them all, then maybe something will work. Can't put your eggs in one basket, buddy boy. That's not good egg keeping."

"Shut up," Todd said. "You've never seen an egg in your life. They have real eggs here and I help collect them in the mornings sometimes. You can put them all in one basket just fine. What do I need to be carrying a bunch of baskets around for?"

I gathered that the future was hedging its bets—firing off multiple time travelers to attack the disease and its spread with different weapons, hoping something, anything would work.

"Okay, let's go," I said.

The men stopped their quarrelling and looked at me.

"Go where?" Todd asked.

"To the hospital," I said. "If Lewis Leroy is being born, he'll be at the hospital. Let's go."

Preston blanched and Todd glowered, but in the end they agreed to wait while I went to get my dad's car. They rode in the back seat together, faces to opposite windows, like I was a taxi driver and they were two strangers forced to split a fare.

AT THE REGIONAL county medical center, I asked about the new parents, claiming to be a close friend. The baby was just born, the woman at the front desk told me, but once they'd been moved to their recovery room, they could have visitors. I relayed this information to Preston and Todd, and we took seats in the waiting area. Not long after, Chloe Leroy (née Brown) was pushed past us in a wheelchair. She was smiling, holding a tiny sleeping infant in her arms.

The proud, dopey father followed close behind. I gestured toward them to let Preston know that was his mark.

"Well," I said, "will you kill the baby right now, or what?"

Preston chewed one of his nails for a moment, then studied it. Then he stood up and asked if we could leave.

NOT LONG AFTER THAT, maybe a day or two, I started fucking Preston. He was staying at one of the two hotels on Main Street (Todd having decreed he could not share the barn). It was the fancier of the Meyersville hotels, rumored to have a Jacuzzi tub in every room. I thought that sounded nice.

I had become frustrated by my acquaintance with Todd. After all, he was no longer considered threatening by the Meyersville citizenry. He'd been accepted and embraced. My dad even suggested that we have him over for dinner.

"I thought I wasn't allowed to be seen with him," I said.

My dad rolled his eyes, as if my whole affair with Todd, and his previous prohibitions against it, had never happened. How could it, with a solid citizen like Todd involved?

Preston dressed identically to Todd—long black jacket, big black glasses—and so distinctive was the costume, I had momentarily seen them as doubles. It turned out that was where the similarities ended.

For example, I asked both men on separate occasions why they never made the switch to contemporary styles. Todd had explained the disease that terrorized future humanity could be contracted through any skin contact. So people covered as much of themselves as possible. And black was simply the fashionable color of the day. He continued to sport this garb in Meyersville because, though he knew it was not necessary, it gave him a feeling of protection against the world—a wearable security blanket, he had said.

When I repeated the question to Preston, he looked confused. "But these are my clothes," was the only answer he'd give.

I assumed him dumb. I assumed him a professional killer, sent from the future for his dumb, blunt, violent nature to do a dumb, blunt thing.

He was actually a doctor of philosophy. He was thirty-seven years old, more than a decade Todd's senior. He headed a team at the Institute responsible for working out the metaphysical and ethical concerns related to time travel. This was why he'd volunteered for the task of ending Lewis Leroy's life as soon as it began. If his team determined such an end justified such a means, then he needed to put his money where his mouth was, so to speak. To do the job himself.

Except he couldn't. He couldn't bring himself to murder a newborn. He lamented his shortcomings, moping around his hotel room, and on the bed, and in the Jacuzzi. I enjoyed this angst and made efforts to soothe it. Plus, though Todd may have earned his place in Meyersville, the appearance of this second time traveler did not sit well with the community. Preston, mired in self-loathing, was not outwardly charming or sociable.

"What's that one up to?" people muttered, suspecting rightly that he was in some way a nemesis of their beloved Todd—an adversary from another time and place, like the other terminator in *Terminator 2*. I was pleased, for the time being, to side with the bad guy.

"Are you still going to kill baby Lewis?" I asked Preston one afternoon. I was lying on his bed eating a room-service quiche. I always ordered room service when I went to see Preston. Sex with him lasted longer than with Todd. He was more practiced and more confident. I appreciated his skill, though I did find my mind drifting to the amenities I would partake in once we were finished.

"Yes, but also no," he said. "I absolutely have to. But I absolutely can't."

He was a lost man, unable to acclimate to life in a new town, in an old era, with a problem he could not solve. This, ultimately, was more angst than my teen attention span could manage. My visits to the hotel slowed.

I found myself drifting back to the barn on lonely afternoons. Todd forgave all.

Until Brendan and Brody and Cody showed up.

Todd and I were helping Mrs. Anderson shoe the horses when they popped into the field.

"We've come from the future where a deadly pathogen that originated in this very town has annihilated ninety percent of human and animal life on earth. If nothing is done to stop it, it will, within nine years' time, kill you and everyone you know. But don't worry; we have a plan to save us all," they announced in gleeful unison.

Todd rolled his eyes. Mrs. Anderson shrugged and said, "Yeah, tell me one I haven't heard before." I looked them up and down and tried to imagine what their bodies were like under those long black coats.

THESE THREE were the youngest of the time travelers, just twenty-two and fresh out of college, with degrees in public health, social work, and nursing, respectively. They had come to Meyersville to embark on a pediatric wellness campaign. It was assumed that Lewis Leroy, in his first years of life, would suffer some sort of deficit, weakening his immune system enough to allow *A. umbrina* to make him its original host. If he was healthy as a boy could be, perhaps this would not happen at all. Keeping other kids healthy would prevent them from taking his place. This plan included but was not limited to: distributing pamphlets and hosting town hall forums on the importance of regular exercise, yearly checkups, and a balanced diet; planting neighborhood vegetable gardens and repairing playground equipment; and offering free head lice checks and routine childhood vaccinations.

They didn't want to stay in the barn (not that Todd was offering), or the hotel. Instead, they rented a house at the edge of town and set up a makeshift clinic in its garage. They received no customers.

This did not seem to concern Brody, Cody, and Brendan, at least not at first. They were in Meyersville to do a job, yes. But they also allowed themselves, far more than Todd and Preston, to indulge in the sights, sounds, and amusements of early-twenty-first-century rural California. To put it more succinctly, they were ready to party.

I was ready too.

I took these young men under my wing, letting them buy me beer from the convenience store and showing them good places in the woods to drink it. I showed them how to build a bonfire and how to skinny-dip in the river.

"Isn't this *the* river?" Cody asked with mild concern. The others shushed his worries with more beer.

And I did wholesome-young-person things with Brody, Cody, and Brendan that I'd never bothered with before, like going to the Meyersville movie theater, and the roller rink. We went to the soda fountain for ice cream, which really was fun, and I felt dumb for avoiding it for so long, for acting too cool to enjoy ice cream.

I was eighteen then. I still lived in my father's house, but his power over me was diminishing. When I announced one night I was going to the grange hall dance with the new time travelers, my dad began to hem and haw and "No daughter of mine . . ." but my mom cut him off. "Jesus Christ, Richard, let the girl live her life."

I was fucking all three of the new time travelers. They must have known they were sharing me, living in the same house and all. But they never complained. They were indistinguishable from one another in bed, just as they were everywhere else, except Cody's penis was the largest, almost twice as long as any other penis I'd ever seen, in fact.

When Todd found out about me and Brendan and Brody and Cody, he took it pretty hard. He said he understood what had happened with Preston, that he could overlook one mistake, but not four. This made me mad. I hadn't made a mistake. What I had made was a decision. I decided I wanted to sleep with Preston, and so I did. Then, when I didn't want to anymore, I stopped. I tried to explain this to Todd, but by then we were both mad. After that, it was a long time before we talked again.

Around that same time, Brody, Cody, and Brendan started having their own troubles. They'd tired of partying and resolved to get down to the work of educating the public. But the public did not wish to be educated, and they certainly did not want twenty-two-year-old time travelers inspecting their kids' scalps, much less giving them shots. Their efforts were met at first with polite indifference, then outright hostility. Who were these outsiders to tell Meyersville how to raise its youngsters? My father spoke about the situation at church in his usual impotent way, urging tolerance, but also vigilance.

"That's not helpful," I chided him after the service. "You aren't saying anything at all."

"Then what do you suggest?" he asked, and for the first time in a very long time, I felt bad for him. The weight of an agitated community squirmed on his shoulders.

The situation came to a boil one afternoon when Brendan, the nurse, frustrated by his inability to inoculate even a single Meyersville child, tried to lure an elementary schooler into the clinic. The boy was walking home from school, a route that happened to take him past the time travelers' rental house. Brendan stopped him and said something to the effect of, "I'll give you a Snickers if you come inside the garage, take your jacket off, and hold still." The boy ran home instead.

Word spread quickly. The police were called and Brendan was arrested, then released on his own recognizance. A citizen task force called Save Our Kids from Time Travelers, abbreviated to the hard-to-say acronym SOKFTT, was formed. Signs appeared on front lawns that read, "Time Travelers Not Welcome Here," and "Go Back to Your Own Era." An ordinance passed that no time traveler could be within five hundred feet of a school or playground. Though Todd and I were no longer on speaking terms, I knew this would be particularly hurtful to him. He'd always enjoyed his visits, bullfrogs and river water samples in hand, with the students of Meyersville Elementary.

I asked Brody, Cody, and Brendan what they would do now. Would they redouble their efforts? Form a new plan? Give up and go home?

No, they said, none of that.

"We'll wait," they said. "Then, when everyone calms down, we'll try again. That's the only thing we *can* do."

SIX MONTHS LATER, Jackson showed up at my front door. I knew him by his style of dress, and by the way he introduced himself: "I've come from the future where a deadly pathogen that originated in this very town has annihilated ninety percent of human and animal life on earth. If nothing is done to stop it, it will, within eight years' time, kill you and everyone you know. But don't worry; I have a plan to save us all."

But why was he at my house? I asked.

"Todd sent me. He said, 'Go see the slut who lives by the church. She'll show you the ropes.' So, I'm here for the ropes."

Our nearest neighbor, Mr. Walsh, a widower, had a spare room. He agreed to rent the space to Jackson so long as he "didn't try any weird stuff with any kids" while he was there. Jackson, unfazed, agreed.

He was in his midforties, tall, and lean. He gave off a vulturish vibe. When we fucked, he exerted a sort of effortless control over me, which was thrilling, and also deeply unsettling. I told myself I would not be returning. Jackson intuited this.

"It was too much, huh? It's okay to feel that way. You'll grow into it."

He was a psychologist. His plan was a Stay Out of the River campaign. He said if people learned to fear the river long before the bacteria became a problem, Lewis Leroy would never come in contact with it to begin with.

I was skeptical. I doubted the Meyersvillians would listen to anything that came from the mouth of predator-eyed Jackson.

"That's what Blake is for," Jackson said. "Blake is a trendsetter. He'll be here next month, after I've had time to do my initial assessments. He's beautiful and people do whatever he says without even knowing why."

So, I waited, with great anticipation, for Blake.

BUT IN THE MEANTIME, I found myself confused. Had Jackson come because the Institute had heard of his predecessors' failures—Brody,

Cody, and Brendan's betrayal of public trust, Preston's crisis of conscience, Todd's achingly slow and nearly invisible progress?

No, Jackson told me. The Institute knew none of that. There was no way for those in 2005 to get information back to their superiors in 2210.

Then why did they keep sending new travelers with new plans?

"We all left on the same day," Jackson told me. "All the plans were already made. We're just arriving at different times. That's part of the plans; that's how they work."

I nodded but I didn't understand. Jackson asked if I wanted to fuck again. I declined. He asked if I wanted to talk about my family or about traumatic memories from my childhood. I declined that too.

Later, when Todd and I were back on speaking terms, I made him explain it because he was always the best at explaining the time travelers to me, no matter how many of them I talked to.

Yes, he told me, every time traveler who had ever come to Meyersville and ever would had gotten into the time machine on the same day, a Monday in June in 2210, one right after another. Though Todd had been the first to arrive, he had actually been the last in the machine. The master plan of the plans was for there to be so many plans that one was bound to work. Many eggs in many baskets, as Preston had suggested on his first day in Meyersville.

But then, if he knew they were all coming, why had Todd yelled at Preston, rolled his eyes at Brody, Cody, and Brendan, dismissed Jackson, and done whatever rude things he'd done to the others since?

"Time is funny," he said. "It makes you forget some things, and it makes your feelings change about others. I spent almost a year here alone and it made me think I was the one who'd get to be the hero, to save us all."

"And now?"

"Now I wish I didn't like everybody in this town so much."

"That's bleak," I said. I suggested maybe he should talk to someone about his feelings of hopelessness and fatalism. Maybe he should talk to Jackson.

He said no, Jackson was a sociopath.

"I'd rather talk to Mrs. Anderson's cows than Jackson. I'd rather talk to a brick wall. I'd rather talk to you."

It was a sad thing for him to say, but I took the compliment nonetheless.

ANYWAY, BLAKE WAS BEAUTIFUL, as promised. He had the face of a Greek statue, puppy dog eyes, and a smile that was just crooked enough to convey the smallest flaw and therefore make him look trustworthy. I had no idea his age. He was, perhaps, ageless.

"I've come from the future where a deadly pathogen that originated in this very town has annihilated ninety percent of human and animal life on earth. If nothing is done to stop it, it will, within eight years' time, kill you and everyone you know. But don't worry; I have a plan to save us all," he said with that crooked smile to everyone he met, and they replied, "Did you, now? Well, isn't that good of you?"

We fucked in Jackson's rented room, where Blake was also staying, but soon thereafter Blake started fucking other girls in Meyersville too. I wasn't jealous. Blake was very popular, and that's what I found off-putting. He was also the first of the time travelers to accomplish his plan with uncompromising success. After a few weeks, I began to hear rumors about the river. Passed from person to person and then in the newspaper and on the radio, there were rumblings about chemical pollution, parasites causing rashes and joint pain, unpredictable currents that could sweep small children to their deaths.

The rumors were varied and many, and nothing seemed to stick, nor could they be corroborated by experts. It didn't matter. The details faded, but the fear remained. And for the rest of the time I lived in Meyersville, people watched their river, once the pride of the region, with side-eyed wariness.

Then came Evan, who specialized in medicinal plants, then Travis the sediment expert, then Dustin, who did something with the mammals that lived at the river's edge, tagging beavers and otters and monitoring their whereabouts. There were three Jonathans, one short, one tall, and one with six fingers on his left hand. They were the goodwill committee, who did nothing to stop the apocalypse, but worked instead to help improve public perceptions of time travelers in general, the Institute having rightly assumed that after several years of *I've come from the future where a deadly pathogen that originated in this very town has annihilated ninety percent of human and animal life on earth. If nothing is done to stop it, it will, within X years' time, kill you and everyone you know. But don't worry; I have a plan to save us all*, Meyersville might be experiencing some time traveler fatigue.

The Jonathans organized canned food drives. They mowed lawns and cleaned out gutters. They helped old people carry groceries. They put on concerts in the park (they were all accomplished musicians, the Jonathans). This worked, at least to some degree, and the anti-time-traveler lawn signs disappeared. There were still those who did not care for the time travelers, who sneered at them and treated them as second-class citizens. Stickers that said, "We reserve the right to refuse service to time travelers," could be found in a few businesses on Main Street. But others began to cater to the time travelers. People had discovered that they had money. At the end of the day, capitalism always wins. Millie, who owned Millie's Diner, asked the Jonathans what foods they missed from back home, and tried to reproduce those dishes. Soy chocolate cake, cricket nuggets, and green pea protein shakes appeared on the menu. I liked the nuggets, though the Jonathans said the consistency wasn't quite right. But they appreciated the effort. The department store stocked black pants and knee-length jackets in all sizes. Some high school kids even lobbied for changing the town motto to "Meyersville: Gateway to the Future." The Jonathans were pleased, though they acknowledged in private that this was a massive misunderstanding of the situation.

There was a Ryan, then a Cooper, then a Topher. Their roles were never clear to me. Regardless, I fucked them all. I had come to think of myself as a collector, of sorts. No time traveler could go unfucked. Some were surprised, and some were unsurprised, some were grateful, and some were remorseful, and some were into weird stuff but most weren't. Some were so sad, I could barely stand it. Like Mitch, a physician who came to Meyersville to establish a mobile outbreak clinic in hopes of quarantining Lewis Leroy as soon as he got sick. Mitch told me that he had three young children back home whom he would never see again. Then he cried, tears running down his bearded cheeks and onto my naked chest.

"That's awful," I said. "Were you forced to come here?"

"No," he said, and cried some more.

By the time Mitch arrived, I was twenty-six. I had never, not even in my angriest teen nightmares, imagined I would still be in Meyersville at twenty-six. My intention had been to leave as soon as possible, to go to a college far away and then on to a big city for an interesting job. None of that ever happened. What did happen was this: During my senior year of high school, my mom got sick. Non-Hodgkin's lymphoma. We drove her back and forth to Sacramento for all of her treatment—chemo, radiation, immunotherapy, a bone marrow transplant. My dad surprised me by suggesting our family leave Meyersville and move someplace where Mom could get the care she needed more easily. But Mom said no. She had come to love Meyersville and our church-adjacent home. She'd learned how to fix all the falling-apart parts of our house. She'd planted a garden. She'd made friends in the church and started new charitable organizations. She was a member of both the school board and the chamber of commerce. Meyersville had her heart and she would not leave. So Dad, surprising me again, left without her. The divorce was swift and amicable.

"He always hated it here," she said when I asked for an explanation.

With Dad gone, there was no way I could go too. I never even asked. I helped Mom around the house and in the garden. I drove her to her appointments. I took classes online, got a certificate in bookkeeping, and took a job with the school district. Mom's cancer went into remission, but then it came back. She died the winter I turned twenty-three. I could have left once she was gone, but I didn't. I stayed in the house and stayed at my job. Todd came to the funeral, and after that we were friends again, but not in a romantic way. And though I knew it hurt him that I continued to sleep with the other time travelers, he never said anything about it.

THE DATE OF LEWIS Leroy's anticipated infection grew closer. The pace with which the time travelers arrived quickened. I had trouble keeping up. I started scheduling them in my day planner. Around town, they clustered in bars and coffee shops, their mood tense. The city offered shuttles between Main Street and the river to accommodate the time travelers who trudged that path each day.

"What's going to happen?" I asked Todd a month before Lewis

Leroy was supposed to get sick. Todd's own research had yielded a fascinating body of information about the Meyersville River. But he had not succeeded in preventing *A. umbrina* from gaining purchase there. Every time he sampled the water, he found more of it.

"I don't know," he said. "There's a lot of balls in the air. It's a complicated situation. I can't say what's going to shake out. But I'm sure Brock will tell us when he gets here."

I asked who Brock was.

"Brock is my boss," Todd said.

BROCK ARRIVED the following week with a loud and confident "I've come from the future where a deadly pathogen that originated in this very town has annihilated ninety percent of human and animal life on earth. If nothing is done to stop it, it will, within thirty days' time, kill you and everyone you know. But don't worry; I have a plan to save us all," and quickly convened a meeting. The time travelers rented the grange hall for the occasion. I asked Todd if I could come to the meeting, and he said he didn't see why not. I wore black in order to fit in. As I entered the hall, I realized fitting in was impossible. The room was packed, wall-to-wall, with time travelers, who waved and whispered hello as I passed. Some I'd been fucking for years. Every single one of them I'd fucked at least once. That wasn't what made me stand out. The reason was much simpler, so simple I was embarrassed at never having considered it before: The time travelers were all men. It was dude after dude after dude. Dude city. Dude-o-rama. This nagged at me.

I made my way to the front of the hall, where Brock was clustered with the other big names in the Meyersville time-travel community—there was miserable Mitch, and sociopathic Jackson, and Preston, who had done nothing for nine years but lament his inability to kill a child. And there was Todd. Brock—who I had met on the day of his arrival, and swiftly initiated into the Mercy Club, as I had heard some of the travelers call it—took my hand with one of his and clasped my elbow with the other.

"So glad you're here, Mercy. So glad. You've done so much for the morale of my troops. Like a one-woman USO."

Though I did not doubt the truth of this remark, I didn't care for the way he said it.

Why were there no female time travelers? I asked. Were there no women left in the future?

Yes, Brock replied with a patronizing chuckle, there were women. But it was unknown what impact time travel might have on their sensitive reproductive organs, and as the tiny remaining human population needed as many breeding members as possible, they were not allowed to use the technology. The female employees of the Institute played supporting roles, all very important, Brock assured me. But they did not time-travel.

"So, no progress gets made in dismantling the patriarchy in the next two hundred years?" I asked. The men shuffled their feet and did not respond.

The meeting was a mess. The time travelers were desperate for direction. Instead, Brock offered platitudes and vagaries. Work had been going well, he said, but now was the time for true action. What action, he did not say. It was time to test their mettle, to fulfill their destinies and their promise: to save us all.

He continued on, but I stopped paying attention. I thought of the women who worked at the Institute. The support team. They probably had just as many degrees as the men who had traveled to Meyersville. They probably had just as many plans. But they were all stuck in 2210, making copies and fetching coffee and maybe even fucking all their male colleagues, not because they wanted to provide morale for the troops, as Brock had put it. But because what the hell else was there to do?

The meeting concluded and everyone left the hall looking despondent. I asked Todd what Brock's title was at the Institute and he said he didn't know. "Honestly, that's all he ever did," Todd said. "Meetings and speeches and bullshit."

The men wished me a good night as they passed by. Some offered to accompany me home. I declined all invitations. I felt I was done with time travelers.

BUT ON THE FEBRILE summer day Lewis Leroy was to seal his own fate and that of Meyersville and all of humanity forever after, I found I could not stay away. I left my house and fell into step with a pair of time travelers walking by. Their names were Chase and Tyler. They were relatively new arrivals, part of a recent cohort who were younger than me. After so many years of fucking older men who acted like they knew something about sex, I'd found this change refreshing. I asked where they were going and they said, "The river. We're all going to the river."

It was a last-ditch effort. A desperate reworking. What would they do now, at the zero hour? The time travelers gathered at the site of the disaster-to-be, sweating in their black clothes. The loudest among them spoke loudly, and the biggest took up as much space as possible. How dumb, I thought, to fall apart here at the end, after everything. How hard was it to make a plan?

While the time travelers stood on the shore, bickering and jostling for space, I walked up the road and then down a dirt driveway to

Chloe and Raymond's house. I had never been close with these Leroys, or any others, but we'd lived in the same town a long time. If nothing else, I was a familiar face. I knocked on the door. Lewis answered and I knew right away his parents weren't home.

"What are you gonna do today, Lew?" I asked.

He said he was going to have a PB&J sandwich, and then go down to the river to cool off because it was so hot inside his house.

I asked if he wanted to come get an ice cream cone with me instead.

"Ice cream's pretty cool too," I said.

He said okay. We walked together toward the soda fountain on Main Street. Lewis sat in a booth and I ordered us both double chocolate cones.

Once we'd eaten our cones, I told him I needed to talk to him about something serious.

"You can't go down to the river anymore because there's a bunch of pedophiles who hang out there now," I said. "Do you know what a pedophile is?"

Lewis nodded. "It's a grown-up who likes to touch kids' parts instead of other gown-ups' parts."

"That's true," I said. "So you'll stay away from the river from now on, right?"

"Sometimes pedophiles get kids to trust them by buying them ice cream," Lewis said.

"That's true," I said again.

"Or candy and toys." He looked up at me. "Do you have candy and toys?"

I said I did not.

"Will you tell the other kids at school not to go to the river either?" I asked.

Lewis nodded. "So they won't get their parts touched."

"Exactly."

I offered to buy him another cone, but he said no, so I walked him back to his house, where I don't know what he did, except that he didn't go to the river because he didn't get sick and die right away, and neither did anyone else.

The time travelers began to drift away from Meyersville after that. Some continued their research projects. Just because *A. umbrina* hadn't infected Lewis Leroy didn't mean it was gone. Other time travelers, I think, just went on to live lives in other places. I never heard anyone talk of building a time machine to get back to 2210. Was it impossible with our primitive technology? Or was the life they had known so terrible, they had no desire to return, not even for the sake of their families and friends? I wondered how many of the time travelers had signed on with the Institute not out of a desire to save the future, but to escape it. Regardless, Meyersville could not hold them, just as I had thought, a decade earlier, it would not hold me. So they left.

Except for Todd, who stayed, and we took up with each other romantically again. He had stopped wearing his black clothes, favoring instead the typical look of Meyersville men—Carhartts, boots, and something flannel, unless it was summer, and then Carhartts, boots, and a plain T-shirt, white or gray. He also stopped referring to the time we were occupying as "the past." He switched over to "the present," and after a few years in the present together, we bought a house just outside town with a view of the mountains and a pasture, though we kept no horses or cows. We worked at our jobs. We made friends. We took pride in our community and our home.

We waited together for the end, however it might come for us.

Appendix: Selected Letters from Grandma Jenna

Dear Marigold,

Lucky, my friends say. So lucky, to be getting a grandchild. Most of their own adult children have said no—no babies. My friends are in various states of grief, denial, acceptance, or encouragement about this. But even the ones who offer full-throated support of their daughters' decisions whisper it to me when we are alone. *Lucky.* And I am. I want you so much, and I want so much for you.

Your mom cannot wait to be a mother. She is counting the days. Thirty-six until your official due date, though really that's up to you. She is worried. The reasons her peers give for not having children of their own weigh heavily. She is so worried, it is enough for two people. Typically, I'm our family's great worrier. I am trying to relinquish that role. A ceremonial passing of the worry torch, if you will.

I have been wondering, what can I do instead?

I wish I had something to give you to express who we are and what we believe. A map for how to live. A talisman for when things are uncertain. I wish we had heirlooms. Good china.

Candleholders. First-edition books. Something, anything, from the old country.

We have some family lore, which I will endeavor to impart through these letters. We have some family secrets. They aren't for you.

Both generously & cryptically yours,
Grandma Jenna

Dear Marigold,

Maybe today you are off from school. It is closed because of smoke, or wind, or the river gone up over its banks again. Depends on the season, or not really. Seasons seem to be going out of fashion. Perhaps there's a tornado warning, which we never, ever used to get, and now we sometimes do. It's possible that you are reading this and thinking, *Tornadoes! Old hat! Those happen all the time.*

Maybe the weather is fine, but it's supposed to turn bad later. Your parents are concerned. They have kept you home.

You are restless. You are in the mood for a story. You have all the time in the world today.

Okay, then. Here we go.

This story begins with a man and his love for radon.

That's what I used to say when your mom and uncles were kids and they wanted to know about our lives before they were born. Where did we live, and what was it like, and what did we do, and were we bored without them around yet? I always started the same way.

This story begins with a man and his love for radon.

Then they would groan because is there anything more dreary than a colorless, odorless gas? They'd wander off before I could say anything else.

It's true, though; your Grandpa Troy loved radon. He loved it because it's dangerous. He loved it because it's old, really as old as the earth itself. He loved it because it's no one's fault. But mostly, he loved it because he thought he could fix it.

Since your mom and uncles never listened to the whole story, they probably think your grandpa took the job at Northwest Suction working with radon because he was an engineer. Actually he became an engineer because of radon.

Before that, he was a home inspector working on contract for a real estate company. We were living in California at the time, and a bill got introduced to the state legislature that, if passed, would require every inspection of homes before sale to include radon testing. The real estate folks were freaking out over this, the cost and the logistics. Your grandpa had never considered radon before. Suddenly, he became infatuated with finding and rooting out this unseen danger. He felt this was a good he could do in the world. He'd been needing something like that. He began testing every house he inspected, and kept doing so even after the bill failed.

Surely, sweet girl, you must know a little about radon already. Your basement has a radon mitigation system, one of several apparatuses in your home that ensure the purest of air for your little lungs.

Radon is the product of decaying uranium. Uranium sounds exotic and foreboding, both because it's radioactive and because humans have learned to make terrible things from it. But really it's old as time—left over from the formation of our galaxy—and as common as dirt. In fact, it's in dirt—mixed up in rocks and soil. So, uranium is decaying and releasing radon all over the world all the time. As it comes up from the ground, radon seeps into buildings through their foundations. It's the number one cause of lung cancer in people who don't smoke.

Ultimately, your grandpa devoted more and more of his professional energy to radon. He began selling and installing mitigation systems himself. But he was frustrated. At the time, the best way to get radon out of a house was with a fan that sucks air from the basement and vents it outside. Not only are these systems large and expensive, depending on the size and configuration of the building, they don't always do the job particularly well. People who rent, or who move frequently, are far more likely to live in radon-saturated environments. He wanted a system that was affordable, portable, and would serve every structure equally well. *Radon justice*, he called it. A radical idea.

He had read an article about one of the first efforts made at carbon capture as a means of combating the excess of CO_2 in the atmosphere. Devices that pulled the gas from the air and transformed it into crystals. He wondered if the same might be done, on a smaller scale, with radon. He envisioned a unit about the size of a milk jug that could be placed in any room to siphon out the hazardous element.

"But if you capture radon, what will you *do* with it?" I remember asking.

Your grandpa waved this question away, assuring me that disposal of radioactive debris is a well-regulated and streamlined process.

Engineer is what your mom and uncles always said their daddy did for work. And I said it too, though he wasn't. He also wasn't a chemist. He was a smart person who learned all he could about one thing, and who changed the way the world interacts with that one thing. I don't know the right word for that, actually.

Northwest Suction is the company that hired your grandpa and paid for us to relocate here, to Spokane, arguably the radon capitol of the American West. The ground beneath the city is heavy with uranium, making it an ideal testing ground for radon innovators. Northwest Suction already held patents for a variety of mitigation devices, but most were just fans in one shape or another. They wanted your grandpa to help make something totally new.

He was always happy there at Northwest Suction, his whole career until the very, very end.

What was I doing all those years? Your mom was three, and I was quite pregnant, when we moved to Spokane. Back in California, I'd been working for a newspaper, but the paper was in bad shape, financially. Print newspapers all across the country were closing and my colleagues were grieving not only our imminent bankruptcy but the death of an industry we had been told was essential to American democracy. Without papers, how could we protect against tyranny, fascism, and free-market capitalism? I was concerned about that too. But I was like a rat on a sinking ship, which is to say I jumped free. In Spokane, I freelanced in advertising, writing copy. Mostly, I stayed at home with your mom and uncles. I was a very anxious parent. The world already seemed so dangerous; I thought if I held my babies close at all times I could keep them safe. Honestly, I've never really let go. Though what safety looks like, in my mind, shifted over time. Once they were all old enough for school, I took a full-time job with a marketing firm and I stayed in that position until I retired.

The apparatus your grandpa and his team ultimately built is called FreeAir. It isn't exactly like what he'd first envisioned—the units are larger, and more costly, than he hoped. But the process they use is referred to as radon capture and, to the best of my knowledge, that's what FreeAir does. He was wrong, however, about the ease of getting rid of the radioactive by-product. Northwest Suction had to contract with the state of Washington to entomb the crystallized radon on the site of the Hanford nuclear facility, buried underground in steel tanks, alongside the materials used in the Manhattan Project for making the atomic bomb.

Why this story, Grandma? Here on your day off, tucked inside with all your clean air machines humming, had you hoped for something more exciting? More adventurous? If so, I'm sorry. I wanted to think about your grandpa, to write him back home for a few minutes. He has been dead two years. I am still always reaching for his hand.

Sentimentally yours,
Grandma Jenna

Dear Marigold,

It is my hope that you know me to be a skilled gardener. I imagine it's something we do together now that you are old enough. Each year, we'll prepare the raised beds in my yard, sow the seeds, and watch as the great mystery unfolds—what will grow?

Your grandpa built those beds shortly after we moved into our house here in Spokane. Though it turned out we never had the time for gardening. The kids used the beds for games and to make little forts. They fell apart over the years. He rebuilt them shortly before he died. Finally, in retirement, we could garden! Then he was gone and I knew I was never going to. It seemed too hard to learn on my own. Too devastating to try something we meant to do together and fail.

A couple months ago my neighbor was lamenting to me about her own garden. She used to be very dedicated to it, and I could count on her for a box of exciting produce once or twice a summer. She said she has no idea what to plant, or when. All the old indicators are gone, or simply meaningless. She isn't even going to bother this year. She seemed so sad, and I was sad for her.

It was also the invitation I was waiting for. If there are no rules anymore, I can't get them wrong. It won't be my fault if nothing grows. I went out that same day and bought seeds without looking at the packages to see what kind of conditions they might need, how or when they should be sowed. I put them in the beds and did not label them. I water when it is my side of the street's day to water things. So far, I have a small melon. I have two tomato plants and one hot pepper. I have a bushy tomatillo plant that has not flowered but still looks nice. I have a spray of wildflowers, brilliant in their oranges, yellows, purples.

Your mom doesn't like that I've given you a name. She doesn't think it's possible to know a person who hasn't been born yet. But you have been born. You are reading these letters, which means not only have you been born, you've been around long enough to learn to read. So it's very much a moot point and all in the past. By now, your mom has surely forgiven me my overreach with regard to baby names.

Besides, she named one of my kids, so it's only fair.

She insisted we call your uncle Nicholas, Nicholas. You've got the book she picked the name from. Although it occurs to me that if you can read this letter, you are too old for *I Am a Bunny*. I hope you've kept it. If you have, we can count it as an heirloom.

Anyway, your mom was so certain that was his name. Your grandpa and I went along. It was sweet, the way she wanted to be involved, the way she thought she knew him. Though Jace chided her once they got older: Why didn't she want to name him as well? Didn't she love him, etc.?

In hindsight, I think it was the only name she could think of. For a long time after, she called everything else Nicholas too. All her stuffed animals, and the characters in her drawings and made-up stories. We got a kitten when the kids were in elementary school and your mom lobbied to name it Nicholas, but we said no because that would be too confusing. We settled on Bing Clawsby instead.

Honestly, I was afraid she'd name you Nicholas if I didn't intervene.

A Marigold is a kind of wildflower. It's native to the Northwest. It grows easily. It thrives in almost any conditions. Plus, think of the cute nicknames. Perhaps you go by Mari, or Goldie.

Helpfully yours,
Grandma Jenna

Dear Marigold,

I have told you a story about your grandpa. Now I feel that I should tell you about your uncles.

Maybe this is unnecessary. Maybe you see them all the time; they are both back in town and they come over for dinner every Sunday, all your birthday parties and soccer games. You know them just as well as you know me.

Or maybe they are ghosts to you. These men you've never met, who, through a turn in any conversation, can fill up a room without warning. We'll never let them go, your mother and I, and so you are stuck with them too.

They were beautiful little boys. Their bright blue eyes and round, happy faces. When we went out for walks, people would stop to stare at them. Everyone is always fascinated by twins. They were never really the same, though, no matter how they looked. Your grandpa and I knew that right from the start. How did we know? It's a secret and I already told you I'm not sharing those.

Your mom's the only one who was ever tricked by their identicalness. Don't give her too hard a time about this—she was just a kid. Kids look at other people but only see themselves.

When he was a teenager, we teased Nicholas for his amazing ability to never take anything seriously. *Nicholas-ing*, we called it when we caught him making a mockery of some task or expectation. It was his joke as well as ours. "Did you write your essay on the War of 1812?" I might ask, and he'd respond, "Nah, I'm Nicholas-ing it, but I'll probably finish tomorrow." He has stopped Nicholas-ing and I am so sad about that.

We have a word about Jace too, though I don't think he knows it.

Jace-ism is the inclination to alter your life's path in the name of a cause or political belief. This is a private joke—something to make the rest of us feel better.

Now Nicholas is preparing to go to California to fight wildfires. All of a sudden he is so serious and driven. I did not see this change in him coming and I am floored by it. Jace is somewhere, maybe India. He is doing something he won't say. He's been gone ten years. A self-proclaimed soldier in the war against climate change. But if it hadn't been climate, it would have been something else. He was always this way.

With worry (even though I said I was trying to do less of that),
Grandma Jenna

Dear Marigold,

I am imagining that the storm outside has intensified. Your mother has hustled you down to the basement. The power is out. The lights went out, and the fans, but only for a few minutes; your home's backup generator has brought them back on for you again. Still, you are starting to feel a little apprehensive. You want a distraction.

Fine, I will tell you *one* secret: Jace-ism is hereditary.

Your Grandpa Troy and I always said we met when we were at Berkeley. Which is true. But more specifically, we met while I was photographing a group of student activists who had chained themselves to an entrance gate outside of the Lawrence Livermore National Laboratory. They were protesting the war in Iraq, demanding that the University of California end both its relationship to the nuclear lab, and its investments in other military weapons manufacturing. The activists stood in a line, your grandpa at the end. I thought him cute with his shaggy curls and his T-shirt that said "VEGAN" with an anarchy symbol in place of the A. The photo I took of him—his face giving away nothing as cops in riot gear cut through the chain at his arm with bolt cutters—ran on the front page of the student newspaper. Later, I won an award for it. By then, we were a couple. I considered myself an activist too. After all, I believed strongly that the United States should not wage an unjust war; that my university should not be in the business of munitions. I hadn't known what to do with those beliefs, aside from photographing others exhibiting them. Once I was with your grandpa, I was at the protests, the teach-ins, the general strikes, not for the paper but for myself. Though really, I was just following him.

It turned out he was also in places I wasn't invited. He and two other students from the Livermore Lab action had made a plan to set a timed explosive device. The target was a luxury car belonging to a member of the University of California's Board of Regents. The bomb was intended to detonate in the middle of the night. To scare but not harm. A how-would-you-like-it-if-the-miseries-you-enable-halfway-across-the-world-were-perpetuated-on-you message. The timer didn't work right. The car exploded six hours after it was supposed to—just as the regent was loading his dog into the passenger seat for a trip to the vet. The man was blown free of the wreckage, unhurt, but the dog immolated. (The accidental murder of dogs may also be hereditary, now that I think of it.)

The student who planted the bomb was arrested but would not give up the names of his coconspirators and so your grandpa went free. He could not bear the guilt—a friend imprisoned, a human being nearly exploded, a dead pet. We graduated two months later and moved to a small town at the edge of the Sierras where I wrote and took pictures for the community newspaper, your grandpa got certified as a home inspector, and no one we met seemed to care about the war at all. We pretended we were just like them.

"Let's work hard and be quiet," I said anytime your grandpa spiraled into despair over how a person who compromises their values might still lead a good life. It's what I thought he needed to hear at the time.

The honest truth is, I miss the young man chained to the gate. I miss myself with him. I wish he had let me help make the bomb.

When Jace was preparing to leave the country, I told your grandpa I thought we should go with him. That's another secret.

With much love & some remorse,
Grandma Jenna

Dear Marigold,

There was a time when there were so many birds in the neighborhood. Extravagant, impossible birds. There were local delights like bald eagles, falcons, and herons. But also birds from elsewhere: cormorants and cranes. Once, a flamingo.

Now there are hardly any birds around here. Even the mundane ones are a treat.

Do we ever go out with binoculars and sketchbooks, looking for birds together, you and I? Is that something fun? Or is it an exercise in futility?

Perhaps by the time you are reading this, something has brought them back.

Your uncle Nicholas came over this evening to help me in the garden. I've run out of space to plant anything else in the raised beds, but I've got a weedy patch of nothing near the back fence I'd like to repurpose. Nicholas offered to till it and I was glad for this. In a week, he will leave for California. We didn't talk about that, though, the topic long since exhausted. We talked instead, as one does when digging in Spokane soil, about radon.

"If we find autunite, we split the profits, right?" he said. His rake had just hit a rock of undeterminable size and he'd gone for the shovel to dig it out.

"How will we know?" I asked.

Autunite is a form of uranium that the US government once mined from Eastern Washington—to the detriment of the natural environment as well as the health of those living and working near the mines. But there's nothing inherently sinister about its presence here. Just a fact of geological history. When your grandpa told people what he did for work, and why he did it in Spokane, they would become suspicious of the ground beneath their feet. He was always so reassuring. Yes, uranium is prevalent, but the dirt is still safe for kids to play with, safe for gardening. Really, really, he insisted, the radon is the most dangerous part.

"Well, it's greenish-yellow and sort of flaky. Named for the city of Autun in France, if that helps." These were the sorts of facts Nicholas used to take pride in not knowing.

"No, that stays in the ground," I said.

Just then, your mom arrived. She'd come straight from her office, still in her work clothes. I hadn't invited her, but I was glad for the visit. Nicholas must have told her he'd be here. There is always a background conversation with those two that I am not privy to.

"Want to dig?" I asked your mom, only because I knew she would laugh.

"I'm here in a supervisory fashion," she said. She pulled a chaise longue near our worksite and reclined, belly full of you tipped toward the bright sky. She'd overheard our conversation and now offered something I hadn't heard her do in a long time—a very excellent impression of your grandpa, speaking on his favorite topic, of course. Nicholas tried his own, less accurate impression and I did mine. It made me glad. How far we must travel on the road of grief before we come to the place where we can again make fun of the deceased.

Finally, Nicholas liberated the rock. It was dark gray, wedge-shaped.

"Are you radioactive?" Nicholas asked, holding it close to his face.

"It's basalt," your mom said.

I proposed she take it home and keep it for you as an heirloom.

"An heirloom in what sense?" she asked.

"A reminder of this splendid day."

"That's not an heirloom, that's a souvenir," Nicholas pointed out.

"Mom, why would you want to give someone a souvenir of a day they weren't even here for?" I could tell she was trying to use her fun voice, but hidden just below it was her worried voice.

And it's true that a souvenir is most valuable for remembering an occasion you suspect you may not get to repeat.

Seeking to balance optimism & pessimism,
Grandma Jenna

Dear Marigold,

I went downtown this morning for the Lahar Remembrance Day memorial. Most counties in Washington host their Remembrance Day events on the actual anniversary of the disaster, but August is pretty fraught for outside gatherings in Spokane, so ours has been moved to June. By the time you are reading this, they might be holding it in April. Or not at all. It was windy at the park, and I was fairly far back in the crowd, which still numbers in the thousands even after all these years, so I couldn't hear the speeches well. The man standing next to me was crying. I put my hand on his shoulder. He thanked me and answered a question I had not asked.

"She would have been eighteen next week," he said. I was struck, as I am each and every year, by the scope of pain all around me all the time.

After the lahar happened, survivors filed into Spokane. Though our city is 250 miles away from Mount Rainier, it became a repository for those she hurt. The city pulsed with loss, a flood unto itself. It seemed like nearly everyone we knew in Spokane was in mourning. Washington is a big state and it is also a small town. But we aren't from here, and lost no one.

Then your uncle Jace left and I thought, *Well, now, here we are; we've lost someone too.* I felt terribly guilty, to equate a son leaving the country with the deaths of other people's loved ones.

For a number of years, your grandpa avoided the memorials. I assumed he felt guilty as well. In hindsight, I think he linked them in his mind with Jace, how his fear for our son swirled into anger, resentment. Then on the fourth anniversary he said he did want to attend.

"It's a lot like radon," he said afterward, and I smiled in spite of the grim occasion. The way he could turn everything back to radon.

Radon's biggest problem is that it's nobody's fault. It's a naturally occurring calamity, and so no one can be made to pay, or assigned to fix it. The lahar, your grandpa said, was exactly the opposite. "We hang out in the park listening to platitudes as if it's something that happened separate from us," he said.

I suggested the memorial was not a place for atonement. That was never its function.

"Exactly. How can we atone for a sin that's everybody's?"

To follow in someone's footsteps, you have to first follow in their line of thought. Your grandpa and Jace—if they hadn't been father and son, they could have been best friends for how similarly they viewed the world.

If Jace really is an internationally wanted criminal, someone would have told me. I'm his mother. The FBI always goes to the mother first, or so I imagine. I don't need to know what he's doing, but it kills me not to know where he is. I hate how he meters himself out to us in agonizingly small doses. Sometimes I am so starved for reassurance, I miss what he is really saying.

One night, four or five year ago, Jace texted your grandpa.

Did you know there are FreeAir units in Khunjerab?

I snatched the phone and wrote back. **You're in the Himalayas?! What are you doing there??**

There was no reply. Your grandpa gently extracted the phone from my hand.

Yes! he wrote. **Pakistan has been purchasing! Permafrost melt is releasing radon fast in high altitudes. Need a quick solution for homes and businesses in the region.**

We stared for some time together at the little dots indicating a response was forthcoming.

Finally, a single line. **I don't think that's what they're being used for.**

Your grandpa called him but he wouldn't answer.

Yours in the quest for knowledge,
Grandma Jenna

Dear Marigold,

The man who set the bomb in the regent's car received a twelve-year sentence but was released after eight. When he got out of prison, he came to stay with us, his own family having distanced themselves following his arrest, and his other friendships fallen away with time. Your grandpa had kept up with him. It was the least he could do, he felt; the only thing he could do.

Derek was his name and he set me on edge right from the start. His face conveyed a kind of aggression at all times, and I assumed prison was to blame. When I went back to my prize-winning photo, I saw the look in him there too. Chained to the opposite end of the gate from your grandpa, he, more than the others, appeared eager for a fight. He said little but would not settle, constantly pacing our kitchen whenever he was in the house. Your mom was a baby at the time. He hardly acknowledged her. That, more than anything else, unnerved me. He was always polite to me, and never said or did anything overtly threatening. But he could not see your mom as a person to be spoken to or smiled at.

"I don't want him near the baby," I told your grandpa.

The next day I overheard them talking. Your grandpa had initiated a conversation about jobs.

"Have you considered something in radon?" he asked. He suggested a factory in Sacramento that made radon fans, where he knew the owner and could put in a good word.

I was aware that prior to Derek's release from prison, your grandpa offered that Derek could join him in his home inspection business. He had even begun taking certification classes online.

Derek took the hint. The next day, while your grandpa was out on a job, Derek asked me to drive him to the bus station. I asked where he was going and he said back to Berkeley. He thought he still knew a few people there. I did not question him on this, though I found his answer to be questionable.

A year later, your grandpa heard that Derek had been arrested again. He robbed a convenience store in Half Moon Bay at gunpoint, but didn't actually shoot anybody. This time he was given fifty years, a function of California's three strikes law, where a third felony triggers an astonishingly long prison term, regardless of the crimes' severity. Apparently, while working construction the summer after high school graduation, Derek got into an altercation with a coworker and hit the man in the face with a wrench. That had been strike one.

What did I even mean when I said he should not be around the baby?

Under the weight of regret,

Grandma Jenna

Dear Marigold,

Nicholas left this morning for California. Your mother and I drove him out to the airport. He seemed excited, confident. But he did not object to our escort or dramatic send-off (there were some tears at the ticketing desk, more at the security line). On the ride home I tried to be of good cheer. Your mother was sullen, her eyes on her phone the whole way. At a stoplight, I let myself read over her shoulder. She was already composing a lengthy text to him. In light of this, I promised myself I would wait twenty-four hours before bothering Nicholas about anything. I could not keep that promise. I called him shortly after he landed to make sure his plane had arrived without incident, as if that were the dangerous part.

When I got home, I saw I had a text from Jace.

If you're worrying about Nicholas, don't. Nicholas is always safe wherever Nicholas is.

I took this for prophecy, even though, as I've said before, Jace and Nicholas aren't the sort of twins to possess such insight.

I texted back, thanking him and saying I thought he was right. Again, I made a promise. I would not ask where he was, what he was up to, or if Jace was keeping Jace safe. Again, I broke it. A mother can't help herself. He hasn't responded. How many months will it be this time?

I've seen Jace four times in the decade since he left the US. The second Christmas he was in Copenhagen, we all went to spend it with him there. It was a lovely trip. A place even colder and darker in winter than Spokane, but lit up bright with lights, like a beacon of something new and better. Jace was so excited to show us everything—his apartment, his friends, the café where he worked. We all left feeling familial and proud—how we'd weathered this storm of his departure and come out the other side. Two years later he'd moved to Paris for a job with an NGO that monitored habitats of freshwater fish in Western European waterways. We went to see him there, just your grandpa and me this time. Again, he was a happy tour guide. We made plans to return the following spring. But on that trip, often Jace left us on our own. He finally admitted he was no longer living in the city—he had relocated to the suburbs. He insisted the metro ride was long and the scenery boring, not worth it for us to make the trek. Was he still working with the fish? He shook this question off and we drew our own conclusions. Ruby went to Europe after she finished law school, backpacking with a friend. They too met up with Jace in Paris, but he spent only a single day with them. The following morning he simply could not be found and they continued on to their next destination without saying goodbye.

He left France shortly thereafter and then there were several years when he claimed different whereabouts—Central Asia, the Arabian Peninsula, Micronesia—but we never felt certain he was really in any of those places. He began his habit of going dark, refusing to acknowledge our calls or texts. His phone number changed frequently.

Finally, he resurfaced for a time. He was in Bolivia, working on a project with solar-powered irrigation pumps. He sent scarves made of llama wool, postcards of the Andes. Heirlooms! After he'd been there a year, Troy and I booked a trip to La Paz. Jace stayed with us at our hotel and seemed not to know the city at all. Just like in Paris, he admitted he was not actually living there, but this time refused to even hint at where. He took us on a two-day excursion into the mountains, to a chain of villages nestled in a valley. It was one of the most beautiful places I have ever seen. It was early spring. Jace told us how in the summer, the villages would have to be evacuated. "There's a glacial lake," he said, and I already knew where the story was going, how when the glacier retreated far enough, the water would spring forth.

"I'm glad they know," I remember saying. "I'm glad there's a plan."

Still, we stood and imagined it. The villages inundated. The survivors forced to move to the other side of the mountains, where their sorrow would become the sorrow of their neighbors by association. Where the neighbors' children would take the burden up as their own.

Back in La Paz, Jace had trouble sitting still. We paid for all his meals and he consumed them ravenously. He looked gaunt, but also somehow taller. He reminded me of Derek, how he'd seemed so trapped in our home and how this had frightened me. But then Nicholas went on his own to see Jace not long after and said he seemed good. That he was living across the border in Peru. Why had he lied to us, made us meet him in another city, another country? Later, I wondered, was it only to draw our eyes to the mountains? Perhaps it was all he'd been doing in Pakistan as well, looking to the peaks, worrying about ice and mud.

At home & away,
Grandma Jenna

Dear Marigold,

Do *you* know how to keep a secret? My mother used to say, "Secrets will fill up your grave before you even get there." She was a very serious mom. Not one for whimsy. I've never believed that secrets were all bad, though, obviously. People mistake them for lies. That's the trouble.

Keeping a secret is not an easy thing, but it is an important thing. Sometimes a secret can hold someone's whole life and they won't even know it, if you can keep it well.

I think you will be a grand secret keeper. You will know danger early, you and your friends, who you will find whenever you can find them. You'll hide this from your mom and dad and probably me too. The desire to make meaning out of chaos will lead you to places you won't want us to know about. It's okay, though. It's not a lie.

Suspiciously yours,
Grandma Jenna

Dear Marigold,

What of your mother? You are wanting a story about her as well. Even though the lights are back on, you have crawled under a blanket to read by flashlight.

Okay, but first: let's hide this letter. A secret between you and me. I'll give it to you later. I know she reads the ones I give her to save for you. That's another secret; they are really for her too. But not this one.

When the kids were small, your mom was always the boldest, but also the most attentive. I mean she had jackrabbit ears. We might have expected that from a quiet child, like Jace. Your mom hardly ever shut up—how were we to know she was listening at the same time? I think she was trying to sort out an order to the world and everyone's place in it.

It's the real reason she won't forgive Jace. When he left the country, he disrupted that invisible order and your mom felt she had to rebuild it. She went to law school full up of ideas for all the good she might do, and the places that work might take her. Instead, she came right back to Spokane, your daddy in tow, and cast her lot with a consortium of personal injury attorneys. When I asked her why, she said, "No matter what happens, people will always want to sue each other." It is a fine job—stable and profitable. She believes if she sticks with it, she'll be able to provide a nice life for you no matter what.

I told you earlier your mom has taken over my place as the family worrier. You might wonder, is this anxiety hereditary too? Yes and no. It is a condition of being charged with someone else's care. The most human of responses. Please remember this when you are older and you are demanding to know from her, *Why is the world the way it is and why didn't you do anything to fix it and in the name of what did you compromise all the things you believed?*

In the name of you.

With generational insight,
Grandma Jenna

Dear Marigold,

This story ends with a man and his love for radon.

One afternoon, three years ago, your grandpa called me at work to tell me the US government was buying the patent for FreeAir.

I think it was because I could not see his face that I did not gather, at first, the nature of what he was telling me.

"Good! Finally, some attention to radon at the federal level!"

"That's not why they want it," he said. I could hear then how choked his voice was. "Their interest is in . . . the by-product of what's captured. Other countries have already been collecting it for some time, apparently."

"Jace knew," I said before I could stop myself. "He tried to tell us, remember?"

I asked if he wanted me to take the rest of the day off. I could be home in twenty minutes, I said. He said yes. He had already left his office.

I loved your grandpa for so many things. The obvious: he was kind and funny and patient and steady and gracious and thoughtful. But I also loved him for his single-mindedness. He never, ever thought FreeAir could be used for anything except making air safer to breathe.

Your grandpa never went back to work. He submitted his resignation the next day, effective immediately, cashed out his stock options. Negotiated a generous severance in exchange for keeping the secrets of FreeAir's workings. It wasn't life-changing money, but it was more than we'd ever had all at once before. I decided to retire early too. Think of all the things we could do: Travel! Garden! It wasn't that I was so desperate to throw off the shackles of my own working life. But without radon, your grandpa needed a new purpose, and I was determined to make it for him. I started planning a flurry of trips. The first was the one where we went to Bolivia and saw Jace and were concerned about him. We never went on any of the others. Your grandpa died three months after we got back. We never learned what the government is actually building with the radon crystals. Before they even bought the patent, they had already seized all the FreeAir by-product from Hanford and moved it to a secret location.

Maybe it isn't a weapon. There are other uses for radioactive substances. "Maybe it's a new form of clean energy," I suggested once to your grandpa, but he did not acknowledge this. There was a lot about FreeAir I never fully understood, though I should have for all he had told me over the years. My attention flittered, the way one's does at the end of a long day when a spouse is talking of their own long day. I didn't think anything was at stake—didn't know how close attention I should have been paying the whole time. In the end, I had nothing to offer.

Or perhaps he just didn't hear me. He was crying when I said it.

He'd spent thirty years working hard and being quiet, thinking he was doing good.

From the depths of grief,
Grandma Jenna

Dear Marigold,

I have changed my mind. I don't think that you are at home, reading letters, on this imaginary day when the weather is bad and the adults are frightened. You have slipped outside to revel in the threat of calamity. You are busy stalking the dirty edges of the flooded river with pant legs rolled. You and your friends wait for thunder peals, goad each other to see who can stay out in the open longest without balking. You press your hands to the asphalt when it is hot enough to burn, for how long? You stand in the middle of the street to feel the wind. It's your birthright and you claim it.

The fires have already started in California. Nicholas called to say his training has been cut short and his unit is being deployed. He does not know when he will be able to call again. I've heard nothing further from Jace. Your mom feels unwell. Your daddy makes her smoothies, brings her cold compresses. Her blood pressure is high and will not come down. Her doctor says it's not safe for her or for you. So, you are coming sooner than we thought. There is a new plan, a better one than any of all of our other plans. Tomorrow, you will be born and I will finally see your face and kiss your feet and press your hot little palm against mine. I will whisper more secrets into your ear.

With the greatest of anticipation,
Grandma Jenna

Dear Marigold,

I want to return once more to the lahar.

For a long time, I blamed the mountain. Not rationally, of course. What happened to her was a man-made disaster. Nearly all disasters are. Still, it is hard not to blame the thing you can see.

She was only doing what a mountain does—holding things. She held them a long time, all that ice and snow and rock and water and dirt. We were complacent, thinking she would hold them forever. She'd let go before. Six thousandish years ago, a volcanic eruption carved a deep groove into her flank. The flood of earth that spilled out covered hundreds of miles. Over time, the groove filled back up with more things for the mountain to hold. And she did hold them. Until the glacier got too hot and came apart, and the water it was cradling rushed back into the groove, loosening all that old material, pulling it down, down, down.

I thought, for a long time, I was a good mountain. I wanted to hold and hold well. Your mom wants it too.

But I am thinking now, we were not meant to hold you. You don't need the heirlooms. You don't need the stories. You don't need the advice. You don't need our anxious hands over yours always saying *Wait*.

Here's what we can do instead—we can be your ancient grooves. Rush down us and past and beyond. Pick up what you need as you go.

Love,
Grandma Jenna

Acknowledgments

Thank you:

Brad Habenicht, Scott Habenicht, Aaron Passman, Marianne Salina, JP Vallières, and Cathie Wigert for reading first (and sometimes second and third) drafts of these stories. You are all so smart and kind, and this book is so much better for your insights.

Sharma Shields, who was also an early reader of many of these stories, and who gave some of them their first homes in *Lilac City Fairytales* and *Moss.* Your advocacy for me and my writing has repeatedly altered the course of my career for the better. I really leaned hard into the "Fiction Science" this time around.

Alex Davis-Lawrence, for setting "Sinkhole" on its strange and lucky path.

Sarah Bedingfield, my fabulous agent, for your unwavering support and encouragement.

Allison Lorentzen, my wonderful editor, whose insights shaped this collection and broadened its scope in such exciting ways.

Drs. Andrew Fountain and Mauri Pelto for taking the time to explain glaciology fieldwork, and the impact of climate change on mountain glaciers. And to Dave Tucker for answering my strange emails about outburst floods, and for your lovely book *Geology*

Underfoot in Western Washington. Please forgive the many, many creative liberties I took with all of that information.

Mount Rainier for being a magnificent, young volcano. Keep holding on.

West Central, Spokane's best neighborhood and my home. I'm sorry for suggesting, even in fiction, that you might someday be turned into high rises and condos.

My parents, Deana Krow and Murray Krow, for always taking me seriously even when I was little and silly, and for always insisting that creativity and humor are essential to a good life. And my mother-in-law, Mary Clare Habenicht, for your enthusiasm, and for your house, where I have done some of my best, and also some of my most panicked, writing.

Walden, my joyful blue-eyed boy, who is not a miracle, but a force.

My brilliant daughter, Bixby. You will surely rush past me and beyond, and I could not be more proud.

Scott, my loudest cheerleader, my best friend, and my greatest love. Provider of many story ideas, good and bad. I am grateful to you for this, and everything else.